Invisible
Wounds

Invisible Wounds

Dustin Beutin

Winchester, UK
Washington, USA

First published by Roundfire Books, 2015
Roundfire Books is an imprint of John Hunt Publishing Ltd., Laurel House, Station Approach,
Alresford, Hants, SO24 9JH, UK
office1@jhpbooks.net
www.johnhuntpublishing.com
www.roundfire-books.com

For distributor details and how to order please visit the 'Ordering' section on our website.

ISBN: 978 1 78535 084 9
Library of Congress Control Number: 2015936228

A CIP catalogue record for this book is available from the British Library.

Design: Stuart Davies

Printed and bound by CPI Group (UK) Ltd, Croydon, CR0 4YY, UK

We operate a distinctive and ethical publishing philosophy in all
areas of our business, from our global network of authors to
production and worldwide distribution.

CONTENTS

To my wife,
To Mom and Dad
To all my other mothers and fathers,
To my friends and family;
Thank you for your support.
And once more, to my wife, who I cannot thank enough.

Acknowledgements

My heartfelt thanks to the many friends and colleagues who toiled on early editions of this book to provide feedback, suggestions and encouragement. Your efforts were invaluable and I cannot express how grateful I am for the help.

And, I would be remiss not to acknowledge the brave men and women in all of America's armed forces, but especially the hard work and dedication of the Army's Military Police and CID Agents who are the basis for this story. Thank you for your sacrifice and service.

"I got a brother in Iraq,
I got no way to get him back.
Like all those people in the sands,
Buried in Afghanistan.

I got a child in crib,
I got a father in a bib,
I got no pills,
I got no skills,
I got no idea what I did.

I just wonder every second,
Of every minute that passes by:
Are we living?
Are we dreaming?
Are we winning?
Will we die?

In a cloud of dust?
In a mushroom burst?
In a series of degradations first?

Or all alone,
In a hospital bed?
Wondering what we
Might have done instead …

With a lifetime.

We paid our dues,
And we did our time,
But, can someone please tell me:
What was our crime?"

The Airborne Toxic Event,
"The Winning Side."

Prologue

Washington D.C.
February, 2010

Special Agent Morgan Huntley passed through the security desk at the Pentagon, headed for the inner ring of the maze-like structure that housed the top commanders of the U.S. military. This was neither the first time that Morgan Huntley had been to the Pentagon, nor was it the first time he had met with Pentagon officials to brief them on a high-profile case. In Morgan's line of work as an investigator for the Army's Criminal Investigation Command, or CID as it was known, every case was high-profile at some level.

It was, however, the first time that Morgan had been summoned for a personal briefing by Colonel Jeremy Franklin, the second most powerful man in the Army's Military Police structure. It was also the first time that an official Department of Defense private jet had been dispatched to fly him direct to Washington D.C. on short notice. These were highly irregular arrangements and they served only to enhance his ever-growing wariness as to why he had been ordered to come here today.

Still, Morgan tried to remind himself that interest in his current inquiry should be expected. After three years investigating major crimes for CID, he had learned that there were two types of cases that always drew immediate attention from the top brass. One was anything involving an officer with the right connections. The other was a violent assault on a woman.

This case had both.

* * *

Morgan had never met the Deputy Provost Marshal before and as he entered the large suite that comprised his office, he immediately disliked the man. Colonel Franklin had the look of a career officer, his smile and his uniform custom-tailored to a fine fit. As they traded salutes, Morgan could sense Franklin's dissatisfaction with Morgan's civilian clothes: appropriate for a Special Agent, but unusual here at the Pentagon.

"Have a seat, Huntley," said Franklin, his eyes glued to Morgan.

"Thank you, Colonel."

As Morgan grabbed a chair, he acknowledged the other officer in the room: Chief Warrant Officer Thompson, Morgan's direct commander within CID. Thompson, who had already arrived at the Pentagon ahead of Morgan, looked tired and pensive.

Franklin gave his best imitation of a human smile, then said, "Huntley, why don't you give me the basic details of your current assignment so I can be sure we're all on the same page."

Morgan knew that Franklin and Thompson were both likely well-informed on all of the relevant details of his case. This being the Army, however, long-standing protocol mattered more than convenience.

"A little over forty-eight hours ago, MPs at Fort Stewart responded to a request for assistance within the base hospital's emergency room. When the MPs arrived, they found 2nd Lt. Kathryn Dover, age twenty-two, undergoing treatment for a broken nose, lacerations to her face, and numerous bruises. Her clothing – civilian – was torn and some articles of jewelry were missing. Lt. Dover was conscious and asserted to the MPs that she had been sexually assaulted by her commander, Captain Isaac Wooster. She claimed that the assault occurred in Wooster's car after he had offered her a ride home from a nightclub just off-base. Following documentation of Lt. Dover's complaint, the MPs on the scene took photos and collected evidence, including her clothing, her smartphone, and samples of semen via a rape kit issued by the hospital."

"I assume you've spoken with people who knew her. What

can you tell me about Lt. Dover?"

"Everyone speaks highly of her. Less than a year out of West Point, she graduated tenth overall in her class, first among female cadets. From what I gather, she's a natural leader, razor-sharp and everything else you would want in an Army officer."

"Any indications that she's been wrapped up in any sort of trouble with fellow officers in the past?"

Morgan looked at Col. Franklin for a moment before answering, weighing where the colonel wanted to take this. Finally, he said, "Nothing I've heard would indicate that she's been involved in anything worth reporting before."

Franklin made another note. "Her alleged attacker?"

"Captain Isaac Wooster, twenty-five years old, on the fast-track since leaving West Point. Graduated middle of his class. Capt. Wooster has been Lt. Dover's commander for a little less than three months. He's well-liked, though several women I've spoken with only went so far as describing him as 'charmingly brash.' He's also the son of the Lt. Governor of Idaho and the grandson of a former U.S. Congressman."

Franklin nodded. "Congressman Wooster sat on the Armed Services Committee for over a decade."

Morgan winced. He now knew exactly where the colonel wanted to take this meeting. He looked towards Chief Thompson, who only met his eyes with a blank stare.

Franklin gave another one of his half-human smiles and asked, "Do you think you've got a case?"

"Yes, Colonel, I do. We found blood and one of Lt. Dover's earrings in Capt. Wooster's car. We've swabbed Wooster for DNA and I have a feeling that it will match with the semen collected from Dover at the hospital. Seven different witnesses saw Dover and Wooster leave the nightclub together two hours before she was admitted to the hospital. There are phone records …"

Franklin held up a hand. "Yes. That is the evidence. But, have you got a case that the Army JAG will prosecute?"

"Yes, Colonel."

"No, Huntley, you don't," said Franklin, his eyes stabbing at Morgan. "You've got ten pounds of shit and a five-pound bag to put it in. Isaac Wooster may be guilty. And he may be an asshole. But, his parents and his grandparents have more friends in the highest reaches of the Army, the Air Force and even the fucking Coast Guard Yacht Safety Club than you or I can count. That adds up to a mess. We aren't going to put Captain Isaac Wooster in front of a Court-Martial and have CNN give wall-to-wall coverage of an officer-on-officer sexual assault. It's bad for the Army, to say nothing of the wrath of a thousand officers who all owe favors to the Wooster clan. Like it or not, this case can only serve to discredit the Army and tarnish everyone who touches it. Given all these issues, from my perspective, we would be best served by leaving this case to rot on the vine."

Franklin looked at Morgan to see if he comprehended. Morgan instead looked at Thompson, who was still giving Morgan that blank stare. "Is this really why I'm here, Chief?" Morgan asked.

Franklin interjected. "I invited Chief Thompson ahead of time to ask if I could trust you to do what was right for the Army."

For the first time, Thompson spoke up. "I told Colonel Franklin that you can be trusted with anything I give you."

"Morgan," said Franklin, leaning back in his chair. "Before you start having pangs of guilt over this, I want to make clear that we aren't just going to leave Lt. Dover hanging in the wind. She was attacked by a fellow officer. We're going to fast-track her career. Anything she wants, she gets. She's just got to play ball."

"What about Wooster? What does he get?"

"Wooster will be dealt with."

"What does that mean?"

Franklin dropped the phony smile. "It means that how we choose to handle Wooster is above your pay grade, Huntley."

Morgan said nothing. He just looked straight ahead at Colonel Franklin.

Franklin took the silence to be an opening, so he continued. "As for you, Chief Thompson has told me that you'd like to be admitted to Warrant Officer School. I have a feeling we can make that happen."

Morgan continued to stare silently at Franklin.

Franklin picked at something on the arm of his chair. "I can tell you're mad. Thompson said you had a pretty good sense of right and wrong. That's alright. Makes you a smart detective. I want you to believe that what we're doing is right for you, for Lt. Dover, for CID and, most importantly, for the Army. Everyone is going to come out of this thing okay on the other side. I assure you that we won't leave Lt. Dover behind."

Franklin and Morgan stared at each other for a long, awkward moment. Franklin cracked first. "Any concerns, Huntley?"

"Do I fly back on the plane? Or do I pay a taxi and then get reimbursed by DOD?"

For a moment, Franklin looked pissed. Then he chuckled. He looked at Thompson. "You're right. Bit of a smart ass." He turned back to Morgan. "You're free to go, Huntley. You and Thompson will be flown back to Fort Stewart."

Morgan and Thompson stood, then turned for the door.

Franklin cleared his throat and both men stopped. "Just so we're crystal clear, Huntley, you are not to make another move on this case without first running it by me. That's a direct order. You do nothing. We'll take it from here. Understood?"

"Yes, sir."

* * *

Several silent hours later, Morgan and Thompson disembarked from the DOD private jet on the tarmac at Fort Stewart, Georgia.

As Morgan set an immediate course for his nearby car, Thompson stepped in front of Morgan.

"Look, Morgan, I know you're upset. I'm sorry…"

"For what?"

"For what happened back there."

"What happened back there?" asked Morgan, looking bewildered.

Thompson squinted and got close to Morgan's face. "What are you doing, Morgan?"

"I'm not sure what you mean, Chief. I'm going to my personal vehicle."

Morgan stepped around Thompson and headed towards his car. As he got inside and closed the door, he heard Thompson yell from behind, "Don't go doing anything stupid, Morgan. You got that?"

* * *

Morgan parked his sedan in front of the Ft. Stewart Officers' Club just after nine at night. He stepped out of the car into the cool evening air and strolled towards the building. It was a Friday, so the place was busy and filled with a wide spectrum of officers.

As Morgan approached, the guard on post at the door said, "Sir, officers only."

Morgan flashed his CID badge. "I'm here on business."

Morgan shouldered past the guard and into the heart of the Officers' Club.

It didn't take long to spot Isaac Wooster. He was in the back of the main hall, playing pool with several friends.

As Isaac Wooster was about to approach the pool table to take his turn, he found that his cue was gripped by a strong hand. He turned to see that the person on the other end of the stick was Morgan Huntley.

Wooster's face turned white and he loosened his grip on the

pool cue.

The other men around the pool table stopped chatting and turned towards their friend. Within moments, it seemed the whole Officers' Club had gone quiet. All eyes were on Morgan, who was holding the cue as if he were about to turn the long, wooden staff into a weapon.

"Captain Isaac Wooster. I'm placing you under arrest on the charge of sexually assaulting a fellow officer and recommending you to the Army's Judge Advocate for General Court-Martial. Please come with me."

I

Chapter One

Kabul, Afghanistan
May, 2010

Special Agent Jason Milner arrived at the small, subterranean bar known as The Brydon a little before 10:00 p.m. local time. As one of the rare businesses in Kabul with a genuine, government-issued liquor license, The Brydon was possibly the most dependable place to find any one of the foreign contractors that lived and worked in the city. Considering that Jason was looking for a man known to be a functional alcoholic, it didn't take a detective to guess that The Brydon would be the best place to start hunting for him.

The subject of Jason's search was a British contractor named Martin Lansley, a man whom most would describe as affable and well-spoken. Yet, despite his excellent reputation as a companion for a night on the town, Jason was not here this evening for the pleasure of Martin's company. That was because Jason had a different description for Martin Lansley: prime suspect in a double-murder investigation.

The bar was nearing full capacity at this hour and no one paid any attention to Jason as he continued to stand just inside the entrance. In fact, The Brydon was one of the few places within this city in which a Westerner didn't attract immediate attention. Afghans were barred by state law from being served alcohol and The Brydon was thus exclusively patronized by foreigners. Tight security in the form of armed guards stood outside to keep any locals from entering and putting the valuable liquor license at risk.

The oddity of being in a bar that existed purely for the benefit of foreigners aside, Jason had to admit that this was the most relaxed he had felt since leaving the United States three months ago. Jason was on a one-year rotation through Afghanistan, responsible for investigating major crimes for Army CID in the Afghan Area of Operations. Jason's experience with Afghanistan had to this point been an endless cross-country journey, highlighted by obscure Forward Operating Bases, hot nights in field tents and unforgiving cold showers. And while his current investigation into the murder of two American soldiers was a tragedy for those involved, the Army's excellent facilities in Kabul had at least offered him a small respite. In fact, if it weren't for the growing complexities of this case, he might have even found himself liking Kabul.

After a few moments of searching, he was relieved to see his time tonight would not be wasted. Martin Lansley was seated on a corner stool of the bar, holding a friendly conversation with the bartender and waving an empty glass. Martin Lansley was hard to miss with a classically handsome face and dark, well-groomed hair that was somehow perfectly manicured at all hours of the day.

Approaching from behind, Jason waited for Martin to finish ordering his next drink, then said to the bartender, "Just a beer for me."

Martin looked up with an easy smile. "Special Agent Milner? I thought American police officers were more partial to whiskey than beer."

Jason sat down next to Martin. "Depends on who we're drinking with."

"Oh?" asked Martin Lansley, turning in his stool.

"Have you got a few minutes? I want to ask you about a rumor."

"Lots of rumors in this country. The place is practically propped up on them five deep."

"I promise it's worth your time."

The bartender brought Jason's beer and Martin's drink. Martin was quick to cover the tab for both, then toasted Jason with his outstretched glass. "A good gin and tonic deserves a moment of silence."

Jason waited as Martin stirred the drink methodically. The men had met several weeks prior as part of Jason's investigation into the execution-style murder of two Kentucky National Guard MPs. The Guardsmen's bodies had been found in a secure cargo area at Kabul International Airport, or KAIA as it was known among the American military. Initially it was presumed that the killer was one of the other soldiers assigned to the jointly shared NATO base at KAIA. Yet, after weeks of interviews with base personnel turned up no links to either the murdered men or the duffel bags of money found in their barrack dorm rooms, Jason's suspicions had fallen on the community of contractors who worked within the confines of the base.

Among the pool of contractors with unfettered access to KAIA, Jason had initially dismissed Martin Lansley. On the surface, Martin was just a well-groomed and harmless socialite who – like most of the contractors working on government contracts – was in and out of the airfield on a regular basis. Yet, as Jason dug deeper into the backgrounds of the civilians who worked at KAIA, the more his attention had turned to Martin and his work for a company called FDC.

FDC was making millions helping the government deal with one of the largest obstacles that faced the U.S. military after a near decade of war in Afghanistan: how to repatriate the mountains of surplus, damaged and oversized equipment the military had shipped into the country since 2002. From inoperable HUMVEEs to excess building materials and every-thing in-between, many of these items could be repurposed if brought back to the United States. Yet, exporting these materials meant dealing with the country's limited infrastructure and a tangled web of civilian powerbrokers whom the military was ill-equipped to handle. The immense costs of paying a private company to deal with these problems on behalf of the military was thus deemed by the Pentagon to be more cost-effective than simply abandoning the materials to the Afghan desert.

Martin Lansley's role in all of this was as a sort of ombudsman for FDC. After several years in his early career spent working for the British Foreign Office, Martin was fluent in both Punjab and Pashto. He married these talents with a seemingly never-ending array of connections to local officials in both countries. Most important to his success, Martin had that rare ability needed to keep material moving in a part of the world where even mundane shipments were known to bog down into never-ending and indecipherable power-struggles.

Martin finished his drink and waved for another. "Now that I'm properly established, tell me about your rumor."

"It's a good one. You remember our conversation a few weeks back?"

"How could I forget? Not very often a British citizen gets to experience a real, live interrogation from an American detective."

"Well, after we talked, I heard a rumor that maybe those two Guardsmen died due to a connection with someone running drugs out of KAIA."

"Do tell?"

"Then I heard another rumor from some contractors there that you're making some money on the side these days."

Martin received another cocktail and worked it once again with a short straw. Jason realized that Martin wasn't going to provide a response, so he asked, "Just a rumor?"

"Everyone here is making a little something on the side. I'm no different."

"Maybe. Maybe not. A few days after I hear this rumor, I get a call from my friends at the DEA back in the U.S. You know who the DEA is, right? They made a drug bust at the Port of Miami a week ago. Two pallets of heroin packed into the back of surplus U.S. Army HUMVEES. Your company, FDC, is listed on the bill of lading. And the whole thing is signed by you, no less. It doesn't take a genius. I've got two dead bodies. Two pallets of heroin. Two duffels of money. And you. I'm wondering if you want to fill in the details for me?"

Martin wiped the corner of his mouth with a napkin. "I'm not sure what you're getting at here."

"I'll cut to the chase. I've got evidence linking you to some pretty damn illegal stuff going on at KAIA and I've also got you on base at the time of the murder of two American soldiers. But, I also figure that the people who pay you to ship their drugs are vastly more important to me. That's what has me interested now. I couldn't give a shit about throwing some low-level operator like yourself into jail, murders or not. I want to talk to the people with the balls to run drugs into the States using the Army's own logistics network. So, I've got two choices. One is to get you to tell me where to find the men who run this little operation. If you do, maybe I'll look the other way on your own indiscretions. Or I can just call it a day, pin these murders on you and walk away from the whole mess."

Martin sipped his drink. "Are we making deals? Is that what's going on here?"

"Depends what you have to offer."

Martin looked across the room and, without turning back towards Jason, said, "I can offer quite a bit, actually. The question is whether you're willing to make it worth my time."

"I don't see what choice you have."

"I don't see what jurisdiction you have."

Jason smiled. "What does your future look like with your face and name splashed all over the front of *The Times*?"

Martin Lansley took a long drink from his cocktail, draining it to the ice. He rattled his empty glass, then set it down on the bar. "I'd be willing to make a business arrangement."

Something about the pompous way that Martin bit off the sentence made Jason want to punch the guy. Instead, Jason took a moment to keep himself calm, then said, "Arrangements, as you put it, are reserved for people with the right information."

"If you assure me that my cooperation will buy me a way out of this, I will give you what you want."

"It will. Tell me what you know."

Martin snorted. "God, you really are quite blunt. Not here. Let's make an appointment for tomorrow."

"No. Now. My office. I've got a bottle of Kentucky bourbon there to keep you topped off."

Martin raised an eyebrow in thought. "Not my usual libation, but if you pay for the cab, I'm willing to give it a nip."

Jason nodded and stood, waiting for Martin to do the same.

* * *

The darkened streets of Kabul were quiet. A cab queued near the curb lurched slowly towards Jason and Martin as they exited the bar.

Nothing about the cab's presence was out of the ordinary. A steady line of taxis were always waiting at The Brydon to take home the crowd of patrons. What did strike Jason as unusual, however, was that the two security men who had greeted him on his way into The Brydon just thirty minutes before were now gone. In their place stood two new guards, their eyes alert and automatic rifles at the ready.

As the cab approached, a sense of uneasiness led Jason to crowd Martin towards the curb, hoping to make a speedy departure. Before they could reach for the door of the cab, however, one of the security men called out behind them, in English.

"Wait."

Jason turned towards the man. Martin immediately put his hands into the air, as if he was expecting trouble.

"What's the problem?" asked Jason.

Rather than provide an answer, the guard just smiled.

Then, in one quick motion, the guard nearest Martin Lansley pulled out a silenced pistol. An instant later, Martin's head exploded in a spray of blood that showered Jason and the taxi in a blur of crimson.

Jason reacted on instinct, pulling his own 9mm Beretta from its holster, but the guard closest to him was already bringing down the butt of a pistol onto Jason's temple. It hit Jason hard on the side of the head. A blinding flash of pain shot through him and he fell to his knees.

Jason shook his head to clear his clouded vision and reached once more for his gun, but the men were on him, pinning his hands. As he opened his mouth to yell for help, he was met with an immediate knee to the gut, knocking the wind from him.

Lungs burning for air, Jason felt the men lift him off his feet and shove him into the cab, face-down in the rear seat. One of the men pinned his knee into Jason's back and shoved the barrel of his gun against Jason's head.

The other assailant wrenched the cab driver from the front seat and took the wheel.

As the taxi started to race away, Jason continued to struggle against the man holding him down. Then a cloth was pressed against Jason's nose, accompanied by the harsh scent of chloroform. Jason tried to hold his breath against the inhalant, then inevitably succumbed.

As Jason faded into darkness, his last thought was that he hoped someone would realize he was gone before it was too late.

Chapter Two

Quantico, Virginia

Morgan Huntley sat in the waiting room reserved for defendants at the offices of the Army's JAG lawyers based at Quantico, eager for an 11:00 a.m. appointment with the capable Lt. Col. Varetzky, his acting defense attorney. Varetzky had phoned last night to say that he would be meeting today with the Army's prosecution attorneys to see if a plea-bargain could be struck on Morgan's behalf prior to the start of his pending Court-Martial.

For his arrest of Captain Isaac Wooster several months prior, Morgan now stood charged with violating Article 92 and Article 80 of the Military Code of Justice. In layman's terms, these were, respectively, the crimes of disobeying a direct order and – Morgan's favorite – *attempting* to disobey a direct order. The max penalty for each of these crimes was exactly the same: six months in jail, a fine and a Dishonorable Discharge. In the Army, even thinking of disobeying an order carried the same punishments as actually disobeying the order itself.

Despite these possibilities, Morgan tried to remind himself that it was unlikely that his case would end in jail time or discharge from the Army. The charges against Morgan were not so much about violating the direct orders of the Deputy Provost Marshal as they were a tool the Army had used to keep Morgan quiet. A dirty move to be sure, but one that Morgan recognized after six years as an Army MP and another three as a CID Agent.

Not that Morgan hadn't tried to insulate himself from this scenario following the arrest of Isaac Wooster. Morgan had personally driven the young officer to Washington D.C and had delivered Wooster in cuffs to the Army's JAG offices at the Pentagon. Of course, Morgan had also made the choice to parade Wooster through the media entrance at the Pentagon just as the journalists were preparing to file their weekend reports in the hopes that some press coverage would strengthen his position.

The media took the bait and used the next week to savor the case with breathless interviews of the entire clan of Wooster politicians. With the Army and Wooster on defense publically, Morgan was certain that the attention would force the Army's hand into supporting his case against Capt. Wooster.

In one sense, the ploy worked: the public spotlight indeed pressured the Army to put Wooster on trial. What Morgan had not foreseen, however, was the depths to which Wooster's connections ran.

Within hours of delivering Wooster to the JAG offices at the Pentagon, Morgan had been remanded to administrative leave by Chief Thompson. Soon after that, he was formally charged with disobeying Franklin's direct orders to leave Wooster alone, as well as the contemplation of the act. The charges were thin, to be sure, but they were enough to get Morgan out of the way.

With Morgan thus incapacitated, Wooster's allies set to getting the young officer out of the mess he had created for himself. Just before the Court-Martial against Wooster was scheduled to begin, the Army's Forensics Lab somehow lost the physical evidence of Dover's clothing and other items collected by Morgan's investigation. Worse, the DNA samples related to the case were found in the open at the Forensics Lab, where they had rotted quickly in non-refrigerated conditions; thus rendering them inadmissible at the Court-Martial. Within a blink of an eye, all that had stood to materially convict Wooster of his crimes had been destroyed.

The Court-Martial against Captain Wooster summarily devolved into a matter of one officer's word against another. Lt. Dover maintained that she had been assaulted and raped, unable to defend herself against a man who weighed eighty pounds more than her. Capt. Wooster admitted that they had engaged in sexual intercourse, but insisted that the act had been consensual. His lawyer argued the well-worn path of how the young officers' state of inebriation had made any interpretation of their choices that night nearly impossible.

By the end, the Generals who composed the Court-Martial all too gladly found Capt. Wooster innocent of the charges brought against him. The Generals even went out of their way during their final comments to make it seem as if the physical abuse sustained by Dover had been over-stated, if not completely fabricated by the young woman.

The Generals did see fit, however, to reprimand both officers for their conduct and judgment on the evening in question. In a letter appended to both Dover and Wooster's files, both officers were admonished for an excess of drinking and fraternization on the evening in question; and for the embarrassment that both officers had brought on the Army.

* * *

During the weeks of the Wooster Court-Martial, Morgan had remained on administrative leave at CID headquarters at Quantico, awaiting his own fate. With his own, pending Court-Martial hanging over his head, the last few months had been a loyalty test. Now, with the Wooster trial over and the young officer safely back in the folds of the Army, Morgan was about to learn his own fate.

Morgan entered the offices of Lt. Col. Varetzky, gave a brief salute and then took a seat in the single chair that sat on the other side of the desk. As he did, Varetzky said, "I have some good news."

"I doubt that it's really what most people would call 'good' news," quipped Morgan.

"The Army is willing to plea bargain. Six months of administrative duty and a delay in your next promotion."

"Is that a good deal?"

"I've seen better for someone with the right connections, but you're not that guy. I'd take it. You'll still have your career afterwards."

"What's left of it."

Varetzky pulled a bottle of Jack Daniels from his desk along with two paper cups. He poured the drinks and pushed one of the cups towards Morgan. "Here. It's better than coffee."

Morgan took the cup and said, "Will it wash the taste of bullshit from my mouth?"

"You know the saying. The right way, the wrong way and the Army way? It would seem that doing things the right way has landed you in purgatory."

"I was under the impression that purgatory offered the possibility of an exit."

"Not the Army's version of it," said Varetzky with a grim look. He took a long drink and sighed. "Your administrative leave has been backdated to the start of your posting to Quantico. You'll be done in a little over two months. You're free once more to take leave if you like. Why not take a few days for yourself before next Monday? A couple drinks and a few days away from this town. You'll be well on your way to forgetting about this whole mess in no time."

"Great."

Varetzky pierced Morgan with a hard look. "Morgan. Have you considered that maybe this whole thing is a sign that you should think about looking at civilian employment? You CID types can always land a job with a local police department."

"My ex-wife said something about that, too."

Varetzky shook his head and chuckled into his cup of whiskey. "You like the fight, don't you?"

"No. I hated fighting with my wife. I just love fighting with the Army."

"Why?"

Morgan took a long drink of the whiskey, draining the cup. "Did you see Captain Isaac Wooster on the news last night?"

"I'm pretty bad about keeping up with TV."

Morgan leaned back in his chair. "Wooster's father is running for Governor of Idaho now. Isaac Wooster joined his dad at a fundraiser last night, talking about his experience with 'false accusations'."

"That's a neat little twist, huh?"

"Oh, it's better than that. You know he was assigned to Fort Irving down in Texas, right?"

"I'd heard. Got a nice little assignment as an Air Force liaison."

"Exactly. A great posting for Wooster. You hear about Lt. Dover's assignment?"

"Afraid not," said Varetzky, leaning back in his chair with his paper cup. "Where did she land?"

"She was shipped off to some tiny Forward Operating Base in the middle of Saudi Arabia. Miles from civilization."

"The Army isn't very subtle when they try to send a message, are they?"

"No, they are not. And, trust me, Lt. Dover got the message loud and clear. She went AWOL right after landing in Saudi Arabia and bought a ticket back to her parents' house in Maine. Army MPs showed up there and arrested her in front of both of her parents."

"Tell me she's not behind bars."

"No. The Army was willing to give her a General Discharge. On one condition: that she sign a permanent Non-Disclosure Agreement relating to the case against Wooster."

"Wooster has powerful friends. I hope she took the deal."

"She did. Three months after she was raped. To the day."

Varetzky gave a pained smile, then turned his eyes to the ground with a shake of his head.

Morgan stood. "I've got to get going. Thanks for the drink, Colonel."

Varetzky gave Morgan a quick salute as he headed out the door.

Chapter Three

Chestertown, Maryland

"The Oriels have a new hitter coming up. Chris Davis. Good-looking kid," said Daniel Huntley.

Morgan sat in his parents' living room with a cold beer in his hand, watching spring-training baseball with his father, Daniel Huntley. At 69, Daniel was just a year away from retiring after three decades working for the same accounting firm in Chestertown. Perhaps in preparation of that milestone in his life, the old man's love of the slowest sport known to man was growing with every day.

Morgan had taken Varetzky's advice and driven out to Chestertown to spend a rare weekend with his parents. Since joining the Army in 2001, his visits with them had been infrequent at best. So far, a few quiet hours of television with his father and a trip to the local Dairy Queen had indeed been just the trick to help him put the Wooster case out of his mind for the first time in months.

Morgan watched the young batter on the television take several pitches. "He's got a good eye."

Daniel nodded. "Natural talent. Never has to work a day in his life."

"Heck, even if he's no good, the signing bonus alone for most of these guys would be enough to live on for a long time."

"They do better than most kids their age, that's for sure. Last week's *Baltimore Sun* said that one in four Americans under age thirty are still living at home. Did you read that?"

"Can you imagine?" chimed in Mrs. Huntley, who had emerged from the kitchen with a bowl of popcorn and a tray of sliced cheeses. "You would put on some weight living here."

Morgan's mother, Shelly Huntley, had already retired last year from a career as a schoolteacher and seemed to enjoy doting on her husband. She grabbed a slice of cheese and sat down on the edge of the couch to watch the game for a moment.

Daniel Huntley was shaking his head as he watched the young batter strike out. "Anyway, my point is, you look at me. I'm sixty-nine and working like a horse. Everything I have, I earned. Worked my way through college and got a job right out of school. No one my age would ever have dreamed of living with their parents."

"The economy's been pretty bad, Dad."

"Ah, don't give me that crap. Don't blame the economy. This is about character. Character is what gets you out of your parents' house. Character defines a generation."

Morgan rolled his eyes and grabbed a handful of popcorn.

Mrs. Huntley took a few pieces of popcorn and held them gingerly over her lap. "Have you heard from Laura recently?"

"Nope," said Morgan, his eyes glued to the television.

"Why don't you call her and see how she's doing?" asked Mrs. Huntley. "Don't you worry about her?"

"I worried about Laura when we were married. That was enough."

Mrs. Huntley leaned back on the couch and picked at a piece of lint. Then, she said, "Maybe she wants to work things out? You never know."

"Mom, she's engaged to another man now."

Mrs. Huntley shrugged. "I wish you two could have worked it out before that."

"She didn't want to work it out. Hence, the divorce."

"Hey, we're trying to watch baseball here," said Daniel Huntley.

Morgan nodded towards his dad, then turned back towards the television. Mrs. Huntley only pretended to watch.

Morgan's cell phone rang. He excused himself and walked out to the front porch.

"You're going miss Arrieta pitching," said his father.

"I'll be right back."

* * *

"Huntley."

"Hi, Morgan. This is Sergeant Ben Ferguson down at the Records Facility in Quantico."

Morgan knew Staff Sergeant Ben Ferguson well. They had attended CID agent training together three years ago. Ben had taken a different path afterwards, though, specializing in research at the CID Records Facility. He was a sort of research gopher, tasked with finding case files, personnel data and other oddities in the Army's arcane record system. Ben's ability to get seemingly impossible-to-find information quickly and efficiently made him an indispensable ally for Morgan in his casework.

"Hey, Ben," said Morgan. "How's life treating you?"

"I'm fine, but we've had an unusual request come through here at Records."

"What's that?"

"Have you heard from Special Agent Milner recently?"

"No, it's been a couple of weeks. He's in Afghanistan. Call his detachment there."

"His detachment is the one that is looking for him. They've asked that we contact friends and family."

Morgan felt his stomach drop. He and Jason Milner were good friends and had been since their days as MPs for the Army. They had both applied to and been accepted in CID around the same time. Their friendship only grew stronger after Morgan's wife left him and they found themselves both assigned to Ft. Stewart. They had even shared an apartment off-base for a period of time.

"I haven't heard anything from him," Morgan said. "They need to send a war party out if they've lost him."

"I think they're trying the quieter routes first."

"Tell them to stop wasting time..."

"I will. If you hear from Milner, do me a solid and call me ASAP."

"Will do."

Morgan ended the call. He looked at his phone for a moment, then dialed Jason's cell phone. The call dropped instantly into voicemail.

"Jason, this is Morgan. Call me right away."

* * *

After dinner, Morgan checked his smartphone again.

He had missed no calls while eating his mother's lasagna, which she had made especially in his honor. Usually he could eat three or four large slices of the heavy, baked dish, but tonight Morgan found himself with little appetite and lost in his own thoughts. His mother noticed, so Morgan blamed it on trying to keep fit.

Slipping into the garage as his mother washed dishes, Morgan texted Jason's girlfriend, Kylie Bower, to ask if Jason had a new phone number. Jason had dated the woman seriously for almost nine months and Morgan knew that he regularly spoke with her from Afghanistan as often as possible.

Within moments, a reply came back: *No. Is something wrong?*

Morgan wrote back: *Can't get in touch with him. You hear from him lately?*

Again, within seconds, the phone buzzed with a message: *He didn't email me this weekend. Worried.*

Morgan took a moment, then wrote: *Let me know if you hear anything.*

Morgan, like Kylie, was growing more and more anxious. Jason had been diligent about keeping regular contact with his girlfriend since he had left for Afghanistan. That he had missed a scheduled check-in with her was certainly a bad sign.

His phone buzzed once more and he reached for it, expecting another text. Then he realized that it was an incoming call. Chief Warrant Officer Thompson's number showed on the Caller ID.

Despite Morgan's assignment to temporary leave, Chief Thompson was technically still his commanding officer. Even so, they had not spoken with each other since Morgan had arrested Wooster.

He pressed the phone to his ear. "Chief Thompson. I thought Warrant Officers were usually in bed by seven at night."

"Funny, Huntley. Where are you?"

"On leave."

"I mean, what's your location?"

"Maryland."

"You going to Quantico tomorrow?"

"That is where I am supposed to be tomorrow, yes. Can't go AWOL after the Army gave me a plea bargain, can I?"

"Don't go to Quantico. I have a change in orders for you. Can you meet me in D.C. for dinner tomorrow?"

"Dinner? Is this a date, Chief?"

"Huntley, I'm not in the mood."

"After a dinner with me, you just might be."

"I'll text you the address of where to meet me."

"Is this about Wooster? I've got bigger things on my mind than him today."

"I'll bring you up to speed tomorrow."

"Is it about Agent Milner?"

There was a pause on the line, then Chief Thompson asked, "What did you hear about Milner?"

"That we can't find him."

"I'll see you tomorrow night, Huntley."

Before Morgan could respond, the call ended. As Morgan put his smartphone away, the door to the garage opened. It was Daniel Huntley. "Quit yappin' on the phone and get in here for some pie your mom baked."

Morgan nodded and followed his father inside, but his mind was far from his parents' kitchen table.

Chapter Four

Morgan arrived just after 8:00 p.m. at the address Chief Thompson had texted to him. It was a small dive of a restaurant that had a sign proclaiming the 'Best Damn Catfish in Virginia'. Morgan doubted the claim was true, but he was willing to admit that he was by no means an expert on the topic.

It was easy to find Thompson inside. Other than a few servers milling around the bar, Thompson was alone in the restaurant.

Morgan sat down in the private, corner booth that Thompson had chosen, from which the two men could see the entire establishment. The waitress came by and Thompson ordered a beer. Morgan followed suit.

Neither man said anything as they waited for the drinks. When the waitress had deposited the beers on the table, Thompson scanned the room one last time to make sure they were indeed alone.

Morgan took a swig from his beer and said, "Kind of an unrefined establishment for a Chief Warrant Officer, isn't it?"

Thompson curled up his mouth in a half smile. "The establishment matches the tone of the conversation we need to have."

"Shitty?"

Thompson nodded. "Special Agent Jason Milner has gone missing in Afghanistan. He will officially be listed as MIA tomorrow."

The words cut right into Morgan's gut. For a moment, he heard ringing in his ears, then his focus snapped back on Thompson as he registered the reality of what was unfolding. "How long has CID known this?"

"The alarm went off about three days ago when his detachment realized no one had seen or heard from him in some time."

"What was the last known location for Jason?"

"He passed through security at ISAF headquarters at Kabul International Airport a week ago."

"Any idea what he was doing there?"

"That was where he had been assigned for the last month. Once word went up the chain, the Brass Hats at CID all set their hair on fire and got to work trying to cover their own asses. Colonel Franklin asked if I would lead the stateside aspect of the investigation into Jason's disappearance."

Thompson stopped to look at Morgan to see how he took that news. Morgan responded with a long drink of his beer to buy time. He had already learned the hard way that if Franklin was involved, there was no hope of coming out of the situation clean on the other side.

Morgan put down the beer and said, "I don't envy you having Franklin breathing down your neck."

"It comes with the territory. Anyway, I want to clear up one housekeeping item out of the gate. Have you personally heard from Special Agent Milner?"

"I got a call from the Records Facility asking if I had heard from him. I called, texted and emailed Milner. Heard nothing back."

"We had the same response."

"What was he working on?"

"I'll bring you up to speed," said Thompson, taking a moment to drink from his beer, "but I want to be clear that this is an official briefing and everything is therefore classified, understand?"

Morgan nodded.

"Just over a month ago, a pair of Military Police officers assigned to security detail at ISAF headquarters at Kabul International Airport were found executed in the NATO cargo staging area. Since Agent Milner was already on rotation to

Afghanistan, CID assigned Milner to the case."

"What information did Jason find out about the deceased?"

"Not much. Other than the men had a large sum of American dollars hidden in their room on base."

"Never a good sign."

"Beyond that, nothing. No weapons, no forensics, no connections. Just the money. And their bodies."

"Nobody around the base knew what they were up to? That seems unlikely."

"No witnesses, no informants. Even their closest friends seemed completely blindsided. That was part of the reason Jason became convinced that the murderer wasn't someone on base. He widened his investigation. Started looking at the list of international contractors – most of them Americans – who had authorization to enter and exit the base to conduct business."

Morgan remembered the contractors he had encountered in his two tours in Iraq. They were thick as flies on most U.S. bases, hired by the American government to perform a variety of tasks that were supposedly better done by private companies than by the Army. Some of the contractors were just people looking to make some extra money through hazard pay for low-skill jobs. Others were old war horses who wanted to get a taste of the action. The dangerous ones were the weekend-mercenaries who craved the excitement of waving a gun in the faces of foreigners without the responsibilities of the Army's Rules of Engagement.

Thompson said, "That's when Jason found a new angle on the case."

"What was that?"

"A rumor."

"What kind of rumor?"

"That a group of retired Army Special Forces had returned to Afghanistan on their own and were running drugs back to the U.S. by posing as independent contractors with authority to ship equipment to the U.S."

"And the thought was that the two MPs, the dead ones, were wrapped up in that?"

"That's right."

"Sounds like a long-shot. I've never heard of Afghan heroin making it to U.S. streets."

"Neither had we. Jason requested that we follow up on it just the same on our end, so we did. Turns out that just in the last month, the DEA had come up with two busts on Afghan heroin. One of them was twelve million dollars of uncut heroin packed into U.S. Army-issued ammo boxes, coming back in a load of returning war material. That one we traced back to a company called FDC, a U.S. company contracting in Afghanistan."

"Did we get a name out of that bust?"

"We did. The man responsible for the consignment was Martin Lansley, a UK citizen employed by FDC. What's more, according to security records, Martin Lansley was at Kabul International on the night the two MPs were killed."

"Did Jason make an arrest?"

"His last report was that he was going to meet with Martin Lansley and interview him before proceeding."

"How long between that and Jason's disappearance?"

"About the same time. We're presuming that Jason was kidnapped."

"Why is that?"

"Because Martin Lansley is dead. Shot in the back of the head. Afghan police found Martin Lansley's body outside of a Kabul nightclub the day following Jason's scheduled meeting with him. Because we only have one corpse, we're assuming – hoping really – that it means Jason was taken alive."

Morgan leaned back in the booth. The waitress appeared with two more beers and offered to bring a plate of catfish for each of them. They both nodded in agreement, then waited in silence as the waitress walked away.

Morgan asked, "Was Jason meeting with Lansley alone?"

"As far as we can tell."

"Nobody has received any ransom notes, videos, letters, anything?"

"Nothing."

"That doesn't sound like a standard kidnapping."

"I agree. The instant that most terrorists get their hands on an American soldier, they usually like to embarrass us. I think that whoever took him wants information that only Jason can provide. Otherwise, why not just kill him?"

"Who have we got on the ground looking for Jason?"

"At this time, we're making the standard inquiries and another agent is quietly doing some grunt work on base."

Morgan's eyes flared with anger. "A CID agent has gone missing and you mean to tell me we're just sniffing around the edges? We should be tearing that entire city up looking for him."

Thompson held up his hand for Morgan to quiet down. "The Provost Marshal himself has put Franklin in command of this full time. I'm sure Franklin is not high on your list these days but everyone is taking this seriously. In fact, the brass already has a plan. One that you have a chance to help us with."

The waitress returned. The men waited as a pair of red plastic baskets was placed in front of them.

"In case you've forgotten, Chief, I'm on Administrative Duty."

"Which, as Franklin has pointed out, means you're unaccounted for. You're a ghost right now. It takes a ghost to catch a ghost."

"What are you saying?"

"We want to send you to Kabul. Undercover. The sooner the better, if we want a chance to find Jason alive."

"What the hell are you talking about?"

"If Jason was on the right trail and our criminals are retired Army Special Forces, then these guys are going to see a CID investigative team coming from a mile away. Someone under-cover as a civilian, though, might have a chance to get close."

"How about we stop messing around and call out the cavalry to look for Jason?"

Thompson smiled and ate a few of the hush puppies that sat in the greasy basket in front of him, washing them down with a swig on his beer.

Finally, Thompson said, "If Jason is still alive and we go charging in on whoever has him, Jason will likely get killed. On that point, let's be frank: there is a good chance that he is already dead. In which case, we want to be sure that his sacrifice isn't in vain. We need to catch these bastards and make an example of them."

"I couldn't care less about putting together a nice show for Congress and CNN, okay?"

Thompson leaned in. "I hear you, but consider the other politics of this. Let's say we call out the whole Army to turn the city upside-down looking for Jason. We tell the Army that we think a group of their former Special Forces golden boys – we don't know who or how many – have abducted him. What if we're wrong? CID would be the laughingstock of the whole military establishment for decades."

Morgan said nothing, but continued to stare at Thompson.

"Besides," continued Thompson, "who else do you trust to find Jason? I know you two were close."

"We are close. But, reality is that the odds of success on something like this are very low. How do I know Franklin's not just trying to find a scapegoat if Jason turns up dead? Someone has to take the blame, right?"

Thompson pushed around some of the fish in his basket, then shoveled several bites of it into his mouth. He pointed his fork at the fish, indicating that it was – indeed – the best damn catfish in Virginia. Morgan ignored his food, waiting.

When he was done, Thompson wiped his mouth and leaned

back in the booth. "To be honest, this is the point in your career where you've got nothing but bad options. Your little stunt with Wooster has left you famous in the wrong way with everyone up and down the line. You need a metaphorical gold star if your career is ever going to make it past 'Go' again. This is a chance, Morgan, to not only find your friend, which I know you must want to do, but also to save your career."

Morgan thought quietly as Thompson picked at the last scraps of his dinner. "If I agree to this, what happens next?"

"I can't tell you that. You've got to decide how far in you want to go. How much you want to risk for a friend. If you go under-cover, you've got to be 'all-in' to make it work and that's not something I can force on you. If you find Jason and you bring this whole mess down, you'll be a hero in CID. You'll clean your slate. But, and I mean it, BUT, if you have a shred of doubt about risking your life for CID or for Jason, then don't let me bother you anymore."

"What's with all the caring about my thoughts? A few months back, you were ordering me to do the wrong thing in the Wooster case. Now you're giving me the chance to choose my own adventure?"

"An agent undercover is as good as dead if they're not completely focused and invested in their mission. We've had our disagreements in the past, sure. A missing CID agent, though? That's an insult to our common bonds. I think you're the right man for this, but I'm not an executioner. If you aren't committed to this idea, then I'd just be sending you to your death and wasting valuable time in the search for Agent Milner."

Morgan looked long and hard at Thompson, trying to get a sense of what he was up to, if anything. He finished his beer in several long gulps and rested the empty bottle back on the table, deep in thought.

Thompson leaned back and grabbed the check off the table. "I know it's a big decision. You can tell me what you want to do tomorrow."

Morgan grabbed Thompson's arm. "I'm going."

Thompson slowly took the check and smiled. "I had a feeling."

Chapter Five

South of Jalalabad, Afghanistan

John Vitters waited quietly inside a hut built of packed earth, seated on a crate that was pushed flush against the wall to form an ad-hoc chair. Outside the hut, the sound of an approaching vehicle signaled the arrival of his business partners.

Dressed in designer cargo pants, a white shirt and a baseball cap, John Vitters looked the part of an international contractor. Just past 30 years old, he was still in excellent shape from his previous service in the U.S. Army. An M4 carbine was leaned within reach and several magazines of ammunition protruded from a cargo pocket on his pants.

A few moments after the car had parked outside, three men walked in to the hut. First was Ethan Griggs, his perpetual plug of chewing tobacco in his mouth and a thin beard that looked more like a five o'clock shadow.

Following him was Alexi Farrat, an American born of Egyptian parents. His dark complexion led many in Afghanistan to mistake him for a local. His ability to speak fluent Arabic and Pashto added to the effect.

The last was David Freer, who was much more easily identified as a Westerner, with pale skin and the symbols for the four band members of Led Zeppelin tattooed on one arm. The tattoos helped to mask a large scar from an ambush attack on a U.S. Army convoy that occurred in a supposedly safe zone of Iraq several years ago.

John Vitters waited for the men to take their own seats in the hut. He then looked at Ethan Griggs and asked, "How were things in Darweh?"

"No problems," said Griggs. "Farrat had a nice chat with the village elders."

"They want more protection at night," said Alexi Farrat on

cue. "They are worried that Kalil's men will return."

"I hope you reminded them that Kalil is rotting somewhere in the mountains?"

"I explained that, but they don't believe me. Plus, their *Arbakai* are very limited," said Farrat, using the local term for armed guards whose function was similar to a local neighborhood watch blended with a state militia.

Vitters thought for a long moment, then said, "See if a few men from our village are willing to spend a week there. Offer a bonus."

"We don't want to spread ourselves thin," said Griggs around his plug of tobacco.

"No, but we also want to keep the elders in Darweh happy. We should show that we respect their concerns."

Griggs nodded in agreement.

"Is that all?" asked Vitters.

"No," said Farrat. "There is more."

Vitters waited for Farrat to continue, who looked at Griggs for confirmation that he should deliver the news. "Martin Lansley is dead."

There was a pause as Vitters considered this, then he turned to Freer. "Last we heard from Martin, CID was sniffing around him, right?"

Freer cleared his throat and said, "When I met with him last week, he said that it appeared the investigation had moved on."

"Knowing CID, I doubt that. I would also assume that if the Army was interested in Martin Lansley before, his death will certainly get CID's attention."

"Any chance the Army did it?" asked Alexi.

"Perhaps," said Vitters. "Or someone interested in forcing our hand, at least."

"Why?"

Vitters smiled. "Because it sets us back. We've lost our logistical partner. With Lansley dead, we have no choice but to seek someone new to help us. Because of that, I have a feeling we're going to meet someone by design."

Freer raised an eyebrow. "Then why play their game? We could just lay low?"

"No. We'll play along. There is opportunity in every setback if you know how to look for it."

Chapter Six

Colonel William "Bill" Kzaltry sat in a small Formica booth inside a small donut shop just outside of Washington D.C., halfway between his offices in Quantico and the heart of the capital. He sipped on an extra-large coffee, watching as Morgan Huntley's car pulled into the parking lot, right on time for the morning meeting that Morgan had requested.

A moment later, the men shook hands as Morgan entered. "Mind if I grab a cup of coffee first?" asked Morgan.

"Sure. And a pair of donuts, if you don't mind. I believe you said it was your treat."

Morgan smiled and nodded, then headed to the counter.

The donuts here were exceptional and Bill had been thinking about them all morning. Yet, he was more eager to find out what it was that Morgan Huntley wanted to tell him. Morgan had called Bill's personal cell phone late last night and asked if they could meet this morning on short notice. While they got together about once a month, this request was out of the ordinary and Bill could tell that something was troubling Morgan.

Then again, Bill mused, everything about their friendship was unusual. It wasn't very often that an Army colonel would socialize on a regular basis with CID Special Agents. Morgan and Bill Kzaltry had met during one of the toughest episodes of Bill's life and become fast friends. Two years ago, Bill's daughter had gone missing. Morgan – at that time a rookie CID agent – had been assigned to the case. Within mere days, Morgan had found Bill's little girl alive and unharmed. Bill's mother, experiencing the onset of Alzheimer's, had mistakenly brought the little girl to her home during an episode of forgetfulness. Too embarrassed to return the child, his mother had hid her granddaughter at her house in a panic.

Through the course of the search, Bill Kzaltry and Morgan had grown close. Since that time, they had kept in touch with regular donut-shop visits and happy-hour meetings. They each had learned to trust the other one as much as any colleague or friend.

The relationship also provided them both with some professional networking that proved invaluable. While Bill was still a colonel in the U.S. Army, he was officially employed by the United States Defense Intelligence Agency, or DIA. The DIA acted as a sort of military equivalent of the CIA. The list of reasons why the military maintained its own ultra-secret spy organization separate from the CIA was long, but could be summed by the fact that none of the service branches trusted the CIA. They instead preferred to create their own intelligence analysis in-house, where they could be insulated from the various intrigues of CIA politics.

Both men relied on the other for valuable information. Bill's work for DIA gave him autonomy and strategic insight into the heart of topics far above Morgan's position as a Special Agent. Morgan, on the other hand, was able to pass along intel gleaned by CID about members of the Army, which DIA found useful in keeping tabs on internal security.

Morgan returned with his own coffee and a quartet of donuts. He set them down on the table and blew the steam from his drink.

"So," said Bill, biting into a donut, "to what do I owe this donut?"

"That donut will hopefully buy me some help."

"I am a cheap date."

Morgan put down his coffee and turned serious. "We've lost one of our own. A close friend of mine."

"Jesus. Sorry to hear that, Morgan. Where was he killed?"

"No, not dead. At least, not yet, officially. He's only MIA at this time. In Afghanistan."

Bill pulled out a notebook and a pen. "Name?"

"Special Agent Jason Milner."

"How can I help?"

"There's a rumor floating around that I want to run past you, but I need this to remain Top Secret. You okay with that?"

"I deal in 'Top Secret' sixty hours a week."

"You guys hear anything at DIA about retired U.S. service personnel returning to Afghanistan and running drugs back into the States?"

"No. Nothing like that."

"Can you do me a favor and check on that quietly?"

"How quiet?"

"Silent would be best."

"Okay, yeah. I can follow up on that. I'm curious as hell now, anyway."

"Right. One other question: you guys have any files on Lieutenant Colonel Jeremy Franklin? He's Army MP Brass, assigned as an aide to General Fowler."

"Haven't you gotten in enough trouble already investing top-ranking Army officers? I feel like some people would learn a lesson by now."

"More like I want to know if I should be investigating."

Bill shook his head and took a long sip from his coffee. "I'll see what I have on him. I'll call you tomorrow after I leave the office."

* * *

The men talked for another thirty minutes and then Bill Kzaltry left for the office. As Morgan watched him pull away from the donut shop, he used his cell phone to make another call.

"Ben Ferguson."

"It's Huntley. Any word on Milner?"

"No. You hear anything?"

"Nothing. Can you tell me who CID has working on his

case?"

"I'm still on my way into the office. Just so you know, there's a chance that with a case this sensitive I'll be unable to view the file without permission from on high. If I am locked out, do you want me to make a stir about getting access to it?"

"Negative. Lay low if that's the case. Any other way we can get that information?"

Morgan heard Ben thinking over the phone. Then Ben said, "We can check with personnel to see if anyone has been transferred to KAIA or ISAF command in the last seven days."

"That would help a lot. Can you have that by tonight?"

"Of course I can. The question will be how many six packs it's going to cost you."

"Send me an invoice on PayPal."

Chapter Seven

The following day, Morgan squared away his things at his short-term rental just outside Quantico, where he had been living since being reassigned to the 501st CID division.

The plan was for Morgan to meet Thompson at a small bar in town, from where Thompson would drive Morgan to Charlotte, North Carolina. In Charlotte, Morgan would spend a week attending a sort of orientation about his cover story. There were a lot of questions yet unanswered on how this operation was to work that would be answered in Charlotte, but first Morgan had to attend to the business of putting his life in the States on hold for an indefinite period of time.

Leaving his place, Morgan parked his car in a long-term storage garage several miles from his apartment. This was so the car would be away from his residence in the off-chance that anyone came snooping around Morgan's apartment. A missing car only indicated that someone wasn't home. A parked car that never moved was a sure sign that someone was far away.

Morgan paid the advance deposit for the long-term parking in cash. He then waited at a bar down the street and ordered a cheeseburger as he waited for Thompson to arrive.

Morgan also used the time to sort through the questions that he had for Thompson. He had decided that he believed the basic premise of Thompson's story. Army Special Forces, or Green Berets as they were commonly known, were trained and elite warriors, to be sure. Yet, the Green Berets spent far less time doing the war-hero act depicted in popular media. Green Beret missions were in fact just as often about training local guerilla forces, performing reconnaissance behind enemy lines or conducting rescue missions. The Green Berets were equal parts diplomat, instructor, spy and combat specialist. At their core, they were tiny factories built to breed, foster, and lead insurgencies.

The result was a tightly bound unit of men who had the skills, language, contacts and training to make a formidable drug cartel. The question was whether a group of former Green Berets really had the intent. That was the part that made Morgan pause. It was one thing to admit that even the most seemingly patriotic of soldiers could be involved in a criminal enterprise. In CID, Morgan had witnessed that on a daily basis. Yet, it was another thing altogether to imagine all or some of a team of Green Berets engaging in a drug-running operation in Afghanistan.

When Thompson finally showed up, Morgan was well into his own lunch.

Thompson sat down at the bar and ordered a beer.

"Drinking lunch, Chief?"

"I had a sandwich in the car," said Thompson, with an air of defiance.

Morgan worked through his fries and pierced Thompson with a hard look. The bar was empty, so Morgan said, "I've been thinking about the Green Beret angle."

"Okay."

"Normally, if we were going to send someone undercover into a gang or some other organization, we would start by making friends with some low-level member and get in from that angle. How does Franklin's plan propose to put me undercover into the midst of a bunch of former Green Berets? This isn't some gang of kids looking for a few friends to put on street corners. They don't want friends. They don't want new blood."

"Correct," said Thompson. "And let me add another complexity. We can't send you in posing as a Green Beret. No undercover CID officer is going to be able to convince a team of Green Berets that he was one of them with enough authenticity to ensure that they believed him. That's a death trap."

"Then, what is the plan?"

"We're going to send you in as a civilian contractor, working with the DEA as part of an initiative to buy opium from the Afghans. The purchased opium is intended for legal distribution to Western morphine manufacturers."

"Is that a real program?"

"It is. DEA just started it. Remember, the DEA is throwing everything it can at the wall to get out of Afghanistan with its reputation intact. They've tried destroying the opium industry. They've tried retraining the Afghans to plant wheat. The problem is, cereal crops bring a fraction of the money that the opium does. Now, the DEA just wants to quietly get the Afghans to sell the opium legally to pharmaceutical companies, rather than letting the Taliban sell it on the street at a premium."

"Okay," Morgan said, pushing around the last crumbs of his lunch, "real program and a reason for a civilian to be in-country. Lots of civilian contractors in Afghanistan. I would be there to make a pilot program work for the DEA. Next problem, though: how does one find unknown persons operating in a country the size of Texas?"

"We've got three bodies and one missing CID agent in Kabul. That's where you'll start."

"I'm going to need some cheese to dangle if we're going to get them to come take a sniff."

"The Martin Lansley angle. I think it is safe to assume based on Jason's reports that Martin Lansley was providing logistics for the drug ring. He's dead now, so presumably, whoever is running this cartel will need someone to move the drugs. With your cover, you'll be perfectly positioned to offer assistance."

"You don't think they'll see through that?"

"It's what we got, Morgan. You'll have a legitimate cover. There's not too many companies that can offer direct service to the U.S. for heroin."

"It ain't much."

"No, it is a hell of a long shot. But, let's say you go there and no one takes the bait? You come home safe. The Army will owe you a debt of gratitude, regardless."

"I still think you might be better off with someone who has more hours undercover."

"We need someone who fits the profile of a contractor. Young. Single. Not afraid of being in Central Asia. With your combat experience from two tours in Iraq, we know you'd be able to hold up in a firefight. Plus, I know it's crass to say, but you've got no wife and no children. If something goes wrong…"

Morgan put up his hand for Thompson to stop. He didn't need to hear him explain the last part.

"I want a deal when I get back," said Morgan.

"I'm not sure I have the authority, but I'll hear you out."

"I want my application to Warrant Officer School given an automatic green light."

"You want a permanent ride?"

"What else am I going to do? I don't think the Canadian army is hiring."

Thompson smiled, then said, "I'll make sure it happens if you can bring this one in."

Chapter Eight

Charlotte, North Carolina

Thompson dropped off Morgan at a hotel designed as a series of corporate suites near downtown Charlotte late that afternoon. Morgan used a new credit card that was attached to a corporate account established in Morgan's name, courtesy of his new cover company, known as GenetiGreen.

According to Thompson, Morgan was to undergo corporate training for the next week at GenetiGreen's headquarters in Charlotte. Since GenetiGreen often provided cover to U.S. agencies, the instructor had a Top Secret clearance with the Department of Defense and was no stranger to the delicacy of the task ahead. The week at GenetiGreen would be a necessary delay and Morgan would use the time to learn how to sound as if he had worked with GenetiGreen for several years: critical to making sure his cover worked well under duress.

After placing his things in the room, Morgan caught a cab to a local mall to buy clothing that befitted his cover as a contractor in Afghanistan.

Morgan bought cargo pants, subdued polo shirts and a field vest of the type journalists might wear, as well as slacks and dress shirts. Thompson had made it clear that Morgan would be reimbursed by GenetiGreen for all of these items, so for the first time in Morgan's life, he bought full price.

When Morgan returned to the hotel, it was just past seven in the evening. He picked up his cell phone and called Ben Ferguson at CID Records.

"What have you got, Ben?"

"Well, the case-file has a security level that I can't access, so I can't view who has been assigned to investigate Jason's disappearance. I could get into the file by asking a friend at CENTCOM to get the approval, but that would bring more people in on this. We still don't want that, right?"

"Correct."

"Right. I also got in touch with personnel. They have no record of any CID agents being transferred to any commands in all of Kabul for the last sixty days."

"Nobody?"

"Nobody. So, either they have given this case to someone who is already in the appropriate command there, which is possible. More likely, though, I would interpret the lack of movement to mean that no one has been assigned the case, yet."

"Alright. Good work. Let me know if anything on that angle shakes loose."

"Are you working the case officially?"

"No comment."

"I'll keep digging here and let you know if I come up with anything."

Morgan ended the call and a minute later, he was once again on another call to Colonel Bill Kzaltry. He heard Bill Kzaltry answer the call just before the voicemail system took over.

"Colonel? This is Morgan. Did I catch you at a good time?"

"Yes. I just dropped Samantha off at soccer practice."

"How is she?"

"Good. Really good."

"Chasing boys, yet?"

"I hope never. I had a chance to look into the questions you had for me. What do you want first?"

"Franklin."

"Turns out DIA has a file on Lt. Colonel Jeremy Franklin, which is mostly filled with RUMINT."

"Right," Morgan said, recognizing the well-worn half-joke in the service branches for a combination of rumor and hard intelligence.

"It seems that he earned himself an investigation from DIA – a quiet one, under the table – when one of our agents came across his name during research into a leak of defense intelligence to the CIA."

"How does an Army MP Officer like Franklin get wrapped up in that?"

"Military Police was responsible for maintaining most of our prisoner facilities in Iraq and Afghanistan, remember? The CIA practically opened their own conference rooms at some of those facilities early in the war. Defense Intelligence got tired of our hard work floating up in CIA reports to the White House, so we started an investigation in 2006. Franklin's DIA file indicates that he was investigated during that time, but nothing concrete could be pinned on him. Lot of suspicions, though. DIA has kept an eye on him ever since."

"Anything that I should know in the file?"

"From the notes, our people thought he was up to no good. One of our guys even called him 'a devious shit' in his official notes. That's about it, though."

"Alright. What about the drug ring? Any rumors there?"

"No one at DIA has heard even a whisper of something like that. I would say that it is pure rumor, unless you've got something else that can convince me to go look again?"

"Franklin is sending me to Central Asia to investigate the drug-ring angle."

"Has Franklin shown you any hard intel?"

"Nothing. Just his word that our missing agent was the source for all of this info."

"You believe it?"

"Not sure."

"That's the whole case file? Just the background investigation from the agent who has gone MIA?"

"That's it."

"Not a lot, if you ask me. You can't even be sure the background came from your missing friend. You think Franklin would lead you astray?"

"I don't trust Franklin at all." Morgan scratched his head and sat on the hard sofa in the room, the phone still pressed to his ear. "I know this is a big favor, Bill, but any chance you can shake the tree a little bit?"

"I had a feeling you were going to ask that."

"How hard do I have to twist your arm?"

"You don't. Truth be told, when I read his file, I immediately got worried about you. I've got calls placed with a few friends in other branches. I'll get back to you when I get something."

"I'm taking Franklin's offer to go to Central Asia, so I'll be out of the regular communication loop. I'll call you when I get some room to breathe."

"Be careful. You read me?"

"Loud and clear, Colonel."

Morgan ended the call and walked over to the mini fridge in the room. It was stocked with several bottles of Jack Daniels. He grabbed one and poured it into a Coke, which was also part of the overpriced minibar within. As long as GenetiGreen was footing the bill, he thought, he might as well make himself comfortable.

Leaning back in the heavy-framed chair in the room, Morgan sipped his drink and tried to figure out Franklin's moves.

It could be that Franklin had just picked Morgan for a bad assignment. Going undercover was always dangerous: what better way to punish him for the Wooster affair?

Morgan's mind came back to the fact that Jason was missing or worse. Maybe Jason had been sent on a wild goose chase that turned bad. Maybe he had simply gotten into something bigger than he could handle. Maybe it was worse than that.

By the time he had finished the drink, Morgan had decided it didn't matter why he or Jason were in this mess.

Jason was missing. Morgan was going to Afghanistan to find him.

If Franklin was playing a game, Morgan would deal with that once he had finished his search for Jason.

Chapter Nine

Charlotte, NC

After an intensive week of non-stop training at GenetiGreen, Morgan was headed back to the corporate suites to pack his things for the flight. As Morgan pulled into the relatively empty parking lot of the facility, he noticed that Thompson's car was already there for their scheduled, final briefing before Morgan departed for Afghanistan. Morgan had hoped to eat something in the small Italian restaurant near the hotel before meeting with Thompson, but since Thompson was probably already inside the hotel making trouble, Morgan headed into the lobby.

Moments later, Morgan opened the door to his corporate suite. Thompson was inside, which is what Morgan had expected. To Morgan's surprise, though, Thompson was not alone. A tall man that Morgan knew all too well was with Thompson, sitting at the small desk in the room: Col. Franklin, the second in command of all Army CID and a man with whom Morgan's only previous encounters had been extremely negative. The colonel still wore the look of bemused cockiness that seemed ever-present on the smug bastard's face.

As Morgan entered, they rose to greet him and shake his hand. Morgan noted that both of them were wearing civilian business suits.

"I didn't realize I would be treated to such a high-ranking visitor, sir."

"Please. Call me Jeremy," cooed Franklin. "Civilians don't have to use titles."

Morgan put down his things and stood apart from the two men.

"I talked to Eldenberg," said Thompson. "Sounds like their travel department has you booked tomorrow to depart for Kabul via London and Dubai. Very luxurious."

"Sure sounds that way."

"Good. Are you clear on how to contact us via the corporate email address and corporate numbers?"

"Yes. Who will be answering those?"

"Thompson will," said Franklin. "Both are linked directly to his personal smartphone. And he'll be in secured communication with me on a regular basis."

"Glad to know it isn't going to post to his Facebook account."

Thompson said, "Do you have any last questions?"

Morgan actually felt as prepared as he had ever been for any case in his entire career after the week at GenetiGreen. It had been hard work and the hours were long. He was led the whole time by GenetiGreen's contracted specialist, Forrest Eldenberg. In reality, Eldenberg was paid by the government to provide these services for GenetiGreen. He had turned out to be possibly the most efficient and effective instructor of Morgan's career and he wished there were more like him.

Most of the orientation led by Eldenberg had focused on learning the intricacies of how to operate as a GenetiGreen employee: from what it was like to deal with HR to placing a sale in the GenetiGreen ordering system. Most importantly, Morgan memorized the names, titles and a few key details about people who were supposed to be his peers, bosses and friends. These details, more than anything, could be the difference between life and death if it came to an uncomfortable quizzing from a curious person in Kabul.

In fact, much of the subject matter they covered had not surprised Morgan, even that his name while in the field would remain unchanged, as a name-change was considered too risky by CID unless absolutely necessary. The changing of agents' names while undercover had recently resulted in blown cover for several agents when they did not respond correctly to their new, false name under pressure. Thus, it was now deemed safer to cover the tracks of an agent's real life than to pretend to be a wholly fake person.

To accommodate this, CID had cleansed Morgan's records from the Army's system, with an assurance that a secured paper copy would be used to reinstate his record upon the end of his cover operation. Eldenberg had assured Morgan that CID was also working with a connection at NSA to wipe all traces of his online persona from existence that might conflict with his cover story. If anyone got suspicious and did some background research on Morgan Huntley, all they would find would be dead air and an online resume that said Morgan had worked as a logistics consultant for the last seven years.

Morgan realized that Thompson was waiting to see if he had any questions, so he replied, "Yes, I have one. Eldenberg mentioned that I will have a contact in the GenetiGreen office who is aware of my background. He said you would give me that information."

"Right," said Franklin, "the GenetiGreen offices are headed by Stan Ingrid. Stan has worked with the government to assist with cover agents in the past. He's a GenetiGreen employee, but he gets a bonus on the side for helping us."

"Is he dependable?"

"I've never heard of any problems."

"Does he know my mission?"

"It's all 'don't ask, don't tell'. He knows only that you're an undercover agent. He'll be able to assist you in making sure that your cover is clean."

"I don't like the idea of another civilian being trusted with my cover."

"It's a necessary risk. He's your boss there. If he wasn't given this information, he might start to ask questions when you weren't actually getting any work done. It's worth the security concerns."

"Yeah, but if it becomes a problem, it's my ass hanging out there. Sir."

Franklin flashed an insincere smile. Thompson interjected and said, "Stan is dependable. He'll have your back."

Morgan nodded. He looked at Franklin for a long moment, trying to decipher what the man might have up his sleeve.

Thompson handed Morgan a packet containing a clean passport, driver's license, IDs and several bank cards that had been created for Morgan's cover. Morgan put the materials in his backpack, then herded the two men towards the door. With that, they prepared to leave.

Thompson turned as the door was about to close and said, "Don't get yourself killed, okay?"

Morgan nodded in agreement, then closed the door.

For the briefest of moments, Morgan reflected on whether it meant anything that Franklin had refrained from also wishing Morgan a safe mission.

* * *

Morgan finished packing, had a light dinner from the small restaurant nearby, and then watched SportsCenter as he tried to doze in the comfort of the corporate suite. He knew he would need rest for the long trip ahead of him, but a tension that seemed to radiate from his brain and straight into the muscles of his shoulders was keeping him from sleep.

Growing frustrated, he turned off the television and picked up a packet of documents provided by the State Department to all Americans departing to Afghanistan on contracts for the U.S. government.

In it were a variety of useful brochures and memos. One document listed the poisonous creatures that made up the Afghan desert, of which the country had more than its fair share. Also provided was a list of friendly consulates, embassies and officials. A long, dry State Department memo provided an in-depth analysis of the various official structures, offices, and customs of the host country.

Perhaps most telling was that the last item in the packet, a State Department memo on handling kidnapping by 'non-state actors', which was a fancy term for 'terrorists'. Most of this summed up to a simple guideline:

"Be patient, as hostage negotiations are often difficult and time consuming. Remember, your chances of survival increase with time. Most episodes of kidnapping or hostage-taking end with no loss of life or physical injury to the captive. Eventually you will probably be released or rescued."

Yes, thought Morgan. You'll 'probably' be released or rescued. 'Most episodes end with no loss of life.' Most, but results were not guaranteed by the State Department. So be patient.

Morgan set down the packet and tried to fall asleep once more. Something in the edges of his mind was still bothering him. Why had Franklin come along with Thompson? This was an important mission to be sure, but people at Franklin's level usually didn't deign to deal with the messy details of a pre-mission briefing.

Morgan sat up and turned on the light. He walked over to his suitcase, which sat on a small table built for the purpose of holding luggage and zipped it open.

Inside, his new and neatly folded clothing was still as he had left it just hours before. He pulled the clothing from the suitcase and moved the suitcase close to the lamp. The lining and zippered pockets all appeared in order.

He ran his hands all over the inside and outside of the bag. Nothing. He put the clothing back inside and closed the case. As he rested the bag back onto the table, though, he noticed that the stitching on the handle had been loosened.

Morgan squeezed the handle, but could discern nothing unusual within. He retrieved a pen from the side table and pushed it into the small opening formed at the edge of the handle: from the other end, a small electronic device encased in flexible nylon emerged.

Holding the device to the light, Morgan immediately recognized it from CID training. A GPS broadcaster used by the Department of Defense; it was meant to provide information on location, speed of travel and elevation. Morgan smiled: so, that was the purpose of Franklin's visit.

A moment later, Morgan opened the mini-fridge and placed the tracking device within the freezer unit. He then took the last bottle of Jack Daniels and mixed himself a final drink.

As he drank it, Morgan reflected on what lay ahead and decided that if he wasn't headed to a dangerous war zone known for its kidnappings and terrorist cells, he might have been tempted to make this contractor business a permanent way of life simply to get away from the annoying, half-assed attempts at cleverness practiced by his bosses in CID.

II

Chapter Ten

Kabul, Afghanistan

As Morgan stepped out of the Kabul International Airport, the first thing that hit him was the smell. The air was heavy with a mixture of automotive exhaust, dust, livestock and a hint of what he was certain was burning feces.

An airport attendant in a dirty, lemon-colored vest approached Morgan. He casually grabbed the yellow cabbie form in Morgan's left hand, which had been issued to him inside the airport at a small kiosk to ensure that Morgan would arrive at his hotel as intended. The man in the vest waved down the next cab in line, which was driven by a young man with a long beard and well-groomed nails.

The cab was an old Fiat and its seats were frayed, but clean. The driver looked at the address and began the laborious process of weaving the Fiat into traffic, supposedly in the direction of the Intercontinental Hotel, where Morgan would be staying during his time in Kabul.

While Morgan had been assured repeatedly that his travel documentation, which included a fresh passport, had been meticulously prepared, he had still worried about how the documents would be received once he arrived in Kabul. His fears had turned to be baseless, however, as he was able to pass through Afghan customs without a hitch and then stopped at the U.S. processing station just past that point. Here, a helpful Air Force sergeant issued Morgan several packets of information that included Morgan's authorization to carry a weapon in Afghanistan. Morgan was given a long series of memos along with the authorization documents reminding U.S. contractors not to kill anyone – especially Afghans – if at all possible.

Morgan looked out from the Fiat as they trundled through the decrepit streets of Kabul. The architecture was a mixture of periodic attempts to build infrastructure in the center of an impoverished country. Some buildings were crumbling mortar-and-clay affairs; others looked like Soviet-era apartment buildings. There was the occasional modern structure, possibly built during the last decade. Structures with reputable businesses inside were guarded by men with automatic weapons and steel doors: vehicle barricades and blast walls usually stood in front to provide additional protection for those inside.

The streets were crammed with dilapidated buses and cabs, as well as the occasional NATO military vehicle. Billboards advertising expensive products and services abounded at every intersection. Butchered lamb and goat hung from ropes in street-market stalls. Twice, they passed livestock on side streets.

Most surprising to Morgan were the women in muddled-blue *burkas* going about their daily lives. The image was surreal, as if all the articles about the women in Afghanistan having to wear such stifling clothing had been something that Morgan had read in a fantasy novel. Here those fictions were given life. Even during his tours in Iraq, Morgan had never seen such a density of the garments.

The totality of the scene passing the windows of the Fiat was like a cross between the common Western renditions of Christ-era Jerusalem and some sort of post-apocalyptic scene in which only the vestiges of the advances of mankind had remained on earth.

As the cab approached the Intercontinental Hotel – not to be confused with the chain of InterContinental hotels, but rather its own, stand-alone operation – they encountered several layers of armed security personnel, who rattled questions at the driver. The driver responded in a calm, business-as-usual way and the Fiat was waved to the next level of security just outside the front door of the hotel. Here the driver got out, opened the door for Morgan and essentially handed him off to the Intercontinental's security staff. Morgan stuffed a handful of afghanis through the window to tip the driver, who already was lurching back into traffic.

It was late afternoon and the lobby was filling with business-people from around the world. Afghan rugs and a stately, 1970s-era decoration scheme made it seem as if the interior of the hotel was a time portal. The clerk at the counter easily found Morgan's reservation. Within minutes, Morgan was in his room. After everything he had been prepared to encounter on arrival in Afghanistan, the normalcy of it all was the most disconcerting aspect.

Sitting on the edge of the bed, Morgan felt alternating waves of hunger, thirst and exhaustion from nearly 24 hours of travel. He wanted to find something to eat, but he felt frozen in place by a certain kind of performance anxiety related to maintaining his cover. In the Dubai International airport, it had almost seemed like a fun game. Now, Morgan was in a country where you couldn't even check in to a hotel without machine-gun toting security at every corner. His Sig Sauer pistol felt insignificant in his holster. He found himself yearning suddenly for the high-caliber weapons that he had carried as an Army MP during security patrols in Iraq.

Finally, Morgan found his feet and worked his way into the bathroom to clean up before heading down for dinner, where he hoped to put the creeping sense of isolation out of his mind.

Chapter Eleven

Morgan scanned the dining room of the formal restaurant that was part of the Intercontinental's lobby. The dining room was nearly empty, save for a handful of diners picking at plates of hummus.

The host appeared, wearing a dated, but clean tuxedo. "Table for one, sir?" he asked in British-tinged English.

Morgan smiled. "Is there somewhere I might feel a little more comfortable dining alone?"

The host nodded politely. "If you would like, sir, we offer grilled kebabs of various kinds on the pool deck for guests. Take the elevator to the top floor."

Morgan followed the host's outstretched hand and walked back to the bank of elevators. Several moments later, he was let out onto the top floor.

He exited to a well-lit, outdoor deck that featured an eight-foot deep, filtered swimming pool lit from below by gleaming lights. Surrounding it were deck chairs, planters, flowers and – as the host had mentioned – a large, flaming grill manned by three chefs who tended long kabob skewers. Fifty people filled the surrounding pool deck, eating and conversing with one another. It could have been a scene from a swank hotel in the United States or Europe. It was hard for Morgan to remind himself that just outside, there were barefoot children playing soccer with a deflated ball in the remains of a crumbling building.

Morgan approached the grill and found himself unable to remember the phrase for "please" in Pashto. He pointed at one of the huge kebabs. The man at the grill nodded, then used a large knife to run the meat off the skewer onto a plate. Grapes and fresh pieces of the local flatbread rounded out the meal.

Morgan found a seat next to a tall American in black slacks who had graying hair and gleaming black shoes. Morgan took a bite of the meat, which he recognized was lamb, then slowly worked his way through a handful of grapes. The next piece of lamb that Morgan tried gave him pause, as it was almost stomach-churning in its richness.

The man next to him noticed the look on Morgan's face.

"That's the tail fat," the man said with a southern accent.

Morgan tried to wipe the intense, greasy taste from his mouth with the flatbread. "I'm sorry, can you say that again?" Morgan asked.

"It's fat from the tail of the sheep. They weave it on the skewers to keep the meat moist. Ya'll get used to it," he said. "Hell, ya'll start to crave it in your sleep."

Stuffing more bread into his mouth, Morgan said, "I'm not sure about that, but I'll take your word for it."

The man smiled and stuck out his hand. "John Davis."

"Morgan Huntley."

John pulled out a business card and handed it to Morgan. It read:

John Davis / Structural Engineer

Morgan felt in his pocket and realized that his GenetiGreen business cards were still in the plastic wrapper within his carry-on.

"Sorry, I left mine in the room."

John waved his hand. "No worries. It's a small country. We'll run into each other again." John surveyed Morgan for a moment. "First time here?"

"That obvious?"

John smiled. "Not too bad. Ya'll have that jet-lagged look, that's all."

Morgan pushed the remaining pieces of fat to one side of his plate. "Is it always this crowded?"

"Yeah, but ya'll should see the places that serve liquor. They do a real business at night." John politely waited for Morgan to finish a mouthful of food, then said, "Speaking of business, what's your line of work, if I may ask?"

"I'm contracting for GenetiGreen here in Kabul."

"Pay well?"

John was obviously not the shy type. Morgan realized he had no clue what he should be paid in the open market. He figured that if GenetiGreen was flying him Business Class or better around the world, the job must pay well by most people's standards, so he said, "Yeah, it's good money."

John smiled a big, crooked smile and leaned back in his chair. "Yup, me too. Best damn business decision I ever made was coming here. I worked in Iraq few years back and that was good money. The Afghan contracts are better, though."

Morgan was trying to think of small talk, but the jet lag was slowing his brain tremendously. All he could think to ask was, "You been out here long?"

"Yeah, few years now. This'll probably be my last contract."

John gulped down a big mouthful of air to hold down a belch. As he did, the scent of alcohol on his breath made it obvious that he had been drinking whiskey prior to coming down to the pool. "I've saved enough working in these two warzones to retire before I turn fifty-five. Ain't that something? And I got a social-security check coming ten years after that. Uncle Sam sure took care of us, didn't he?"

John leaned back and produced a set of toothpicks. He offered one to Morgan, who declined. John stuck one in his mouth.

"You know the British came here twice in the 1800s to conquer the Afghans?" asked John rhetorically. "The Brits didn't even really want to conquer it so much as they wanted to use it as a big firewall against the Russians to protect the real money down in India. The Brits, they pretty much got their asses handed to them the first time by the Afghans. But, being boring bastards, the Brits came back for seconds a few decades later. The second go-round wasn't much to write home about either. British didn't get much out of either one of those wars. Just a lot of dead soldiers and some crumbling old forts to prove they came through."

John paused to control another belch, then continued. "The Russians, they didn't really want it, you see? But, they figured that if the British wanted it so damn bad, it must be worth something. A century later, the Soviets finally got around to coming down here. Then they got their own asses handed to them for a decade by the Afghans. What do they get out of the deal? Just dead bodies. Not much else."

John looked at Morgan to see if Morgan was still following.

"Next come the Americans and NATO a few decades later. We grab it out of principle. We build a government from scratch and wet-nurse it for a decade. But, just like the Russians and the Brits, the U.S. is going to have nothing to show for it. I suppose maybe the people in charge knew that going in, but that wouldn't have been a very good marketing strategy for the invasion, would it?"

John took a moment to switch his toothpick to the other side of this mouth, then asked, "Only one group has ever been able to conquer this place. You know who that was?"

John waited to see if Morgan knew the answer.

Seeing that Morgan didn't know, John said, "We did. You and I. We came here and made a shit pot of money. British didn't. Russians didn't. Hell, America's just spent a freighter full of money in this country and is going to take a bath on the whole thing. You and me, though? We've got some fat bank accounts, ain't that right?"

Morgan gave a polite smile. "I guess we do."

John was literally getting tears in the corners of his eyes as he laughed at his own accounting. "Cut a big, fat hog in the ass, that's what we did."

Morgan's plate of food was empty now, so he stood to take his leave.

"Hey, bunch of us going out to the bar to spend some money, tell some war stories later if you'd like to come, Morgan."

"Thanks, but I think I'm going to try to get over my jet lag first, if you don't mind."

John nodded in understanding, shook Morgan's hand and, as Morgan left, said, "See you around, Morgan."

Chapter Twelve

The next morning, Morgan stepped out into the lobby of the Intercontinental, where several dozen Western contractors were reading papers, drinking coffee or waiting for others to meet them before leaving the safety of the hotel for the day. Morgan's choice in clothing allowed him to fit in with the other Westerners: cargo khakis, a polo shirt and a blazer, which provided room for his pistol in a shoulder-holster.

The bellman arranged a cab for Morgan. Several minutes later, Morgan was on his way to GenetiGreen's Kabul offices for his first day of work.

The morning scene in Kabul was a flurry of activity. They passed a market wherein a group of women and children were spreading vegetables on mats to be sorted. Men in cafes were drinking tea from glassware. The occasional guard stood outside of heavily armored building entrances.

Fifteen minutes later, the cab arrived at a small, recently built office building. Outside of the building, several layers of security were posted to prevent any cars from approaching within the range necessary for a car bomb to do real damage.

Once in the lobby to GenetiGreen's suite, Morgan showed his badge and paperwork to the polite female secretary, Shruti. She was of Indian descent and spoke British-styled English. Shruti took Morgan's paperwork, then disappeared into the office behind her.

The office was a bare place, filled with few creature comforts: even so, it was like traveling through a time-warp after coming out of the streets of Kabul. Morgan could hear several American voices coming from within and could see an empty conference room that was wired with the latest communications equipment. The scent of coffee hung heavy in the air.

As Morgan was looking through the outdated American magazines on a side table, he heard someone clear his throat.

Standing near the receptionist's desk was a man in his early forties with sandy-blond hair, freshly pressed grey slacks and a smile that was capable of capturing a woman's heart in an instant.

"Morgan? I'm James Poole, Senior Consultant to GenetiGreen's Kabul operation."

"Morgan Huntley."

"Come with me and I'll show you to your desk."

Morgan followed James around the corner into the main office. Most of the floor space was devoted to large cubicles, though some private offices lined the walls. James brought Morgan to a group of three men, who stood together inside a cubicle.

"Hey guys, this is Morgan Huntley. He's here from the Charlotte office and will be helping me set up logistics contracts with some of the villages in the area."

Morgan shook hands all around and got a pair of business cards before James moved them along.

They then stopped at a large office, where a muscular man in his late forties was working feverishly at a laptop. James knocked on the door, then entered.

"Stan, this is Morgan Huntley, our new consultant from Charlotte."

Stan smiled and stood to shake hands with Morgan. "Glad to meet you. I'm Stanley, though everyone just calls me Stan."

"Stan is the director of our office."

Stan smiled broadly. "Thanks, James. I've got a few documents I need to cover with Morgan in private, so I'll take it from here."

James nodded and then closed the door behind him.

Once Stan was sure that James was indeed out of earshot, he said, "I'm aware that your real employer is our Uncle back in D.C. I hope someone told you I would know that before you left."

"I was informed."

"Good. I've had a few situations where my 'guests' were surprised that I was in the loop."

"I can imagine that was uncomfortable for both of you."

"It led to some temporary discomfort, yes. As far as anyone in the office knows, you report to me. Once a week, we'll get together and talk business. If you actually conduct any real business, just bring it past my desk and I'll make sure all the paperwork gets done right so that it looks like you really know what the hell you're doing."

"Okay, Stan. I know you've done this before, but I want to remind you that my life very much could depend on you keeping quiet."

"Of course. Like I said, you're not the first person we've had come through here on a day pass, so to speak."

Morgan tried his best to smile.

"Anyway," Stan continued, "this afternoon, you'll need to head down to the U.S. Embassy and meet with the people in the Economic Section. They have been drafting a list of proposed villages in the area that we think might be willing to partner on this opium purchase project. We called yesterday and made an appointment for you with the embassy."

"Okay. Anything else?"

"Nah, that's it. James will get you all settled. You two are going to be sharing an office."

Stan pointed towards a door a dozen feet from his own office and said, "I apologize for the arrangements, but we're limited on space here. Let me know as soon as you need anything, okay?"

* * *

Two desks filled the windowless office that Morgan was to share with James Poole, one of which was already crowded with James's materials and computer. The second desk had been prepared for Morgan's arrival with a computer and monitor.

Morgan set his things down on the empty chair and noticed that James was eyeing Morgan's Sig Sauer pistol, which was protruding from his open jacket.

"How did you get permission to carry one of those?" asked James. "I've been trying for three months to get GenetiGreen to authorize me to pack a little self-defense."

Morgan looked down at the gun, then at James, crafting his thoughts before he said, "Oh? My boss insisted that I carry it when I'm in the field."

"I'm in the field all the time. Not that GenetiGreen cares, right? You have any experience with it?"

"Had to go to a mandatory training, but that's all." Morgan wanted to change the topic, so he asked, "What is it you're working on, by the way?"

"I coordinate the DEA's efforts to assist the Afghans in planting new food crops instead of opium. We provide the seeds, the equipment, the educators and the know-how to get the stuff to market."

"You know I'm working on buying opium from the Afghans, right?"

"Yeah, the DEA is super excited about that program."

"Doesn't it sound a little bit like we're working at cross purposes?"

"Different packages for a wide market, is what I say."

Morgan nodded. James looked at him with a critical eye, then asked, "Who is your boss back in Charlotte? I should ask him for a little help with the weapon authorization."

Morgan's mind drew a blank, so he said, "Um, well, they're not my boss anymore, you know? Now Stan is."

"Yeah, but what was their name? I would love to send them an email."

Morgan finally remembered a name and said, "Uh, Karen Holt."

"Karen Holt? That was your boss?"

"Yeah."

"You were reporting to the Senior Vice President of US Operations?"

Morgan nodded, but he felt less sure that he had given James the right name. His mind was still drawing a blank as to whether this was the right person in his cover story.

James smiled and turned on his computer. "No wonder they think you're special enough to carry a weapon in this country. I'll send her a quick line and see if she can help me out."

"Wait," said Morgan, his mind finally clicking on the name that was his supposed boss. "Karen was the one who approved the sidearm. My boss was Walter Yinnell, Director of Government Relations."

James turned and said, "No, you said Karen was your boss."

"Did I? Jet lag, you know. Walter Yinnell was the one who helped make sure I got it approved. Email him."

James raised an eyebrow, then said, "Okay, sure thing. Oh, one other thing. What are you up to for lunch today?"

"I've got to head to the embassy this afternoon for a meeting."

"Great. There's a market near there with outstanding food. How about we head over together, grab lunch and I'll hang out while you do your embassy thing?"

Morgan was glad to be off the topic of his pistol, so he said, "Okay, James. Sounds like a plan."

* * *

Morgan and James arrived just after 1:00 p.m. at the U.S. Embassy, which was located in the center of the city near Massoud Square. It then took the next hour to pass through embassy security. As they waited, James made a pair of calls to schedule an appointment for himself with his contacts in the DEA office at the embassy.

"No sense wasting all this time in line to get in," said James, as he hung up on the secretary at the DEA. "Might as well go see someone and get some business done."

"I'm sure."

"They love to see me. I bring them nothing but bad news on the failures to turn this country into the breadbasket of Central Asia."

"Maybe you should tell them they're also paying me to convince the locals to sell more drugs."

James smiled. "Good point. You never know when the left hand is oblivious to what the right hand is doing."

They inched forward in line, nearing the security desk.

"How soon are you intending to get out in the field?" asked James.

"Tomorrow, if I can make it happen. I have an appointment with someone named Gurman to act as my guide."

"Gurman's a good guy. Former Pakistani intelligence."

"Sounds shady."

"As far as I know, he's always brought his guests home safely."

Morgan nodded. Moments later, they were finally passing through security. As they went their separate ways to go to their respective appointments, Morgan and James agreed to meet in the lobby when they were done.

An embassy staffer escorted Morgan down a long corridor of offices and showed him to the Economic Section. Moments later, a tall, thin American man in a business suit came to the front with a folder in his hand.

"Are you Morgan Huntley?"

Morgan showed him his Visitor's ID badge.

The man handed the folder towards Morgan. "Here's the list. Good luck out there."

Morgan flipped through the folder, which was merely a list of villages, geo-coordinates and names of local leaders.

"Is that all I get?"

The man nodded, then walked away before Morgan could say another word.

Just five minutes after leaving the lobby, Morgan was back there, waiting on a bench for James. He felt a wave of jet lag rush through his body and leaned back to try to rest.

Chapter Thirteen

Victoria Solano washed her hands resolutely with the dedication and process of someone who had been taught the very meaning of medical cleanliness. The attention to detail came as routine after seven years as a nurse: first with the U.S. Army, then with the State Department as a Health Practitioner to three embassies. She had always loved the fastidious nature of the act, but like many had warned her, the sense of imprisonment that came with being assigned to the U.S. Embassy in Kabul had taken much of the joy from even the most beloved aspects of daily life.

Victoria dried her hands and walked into the hallway of the embassy's medical wing, trying to remind herself that her career goals required her to be in this place. Assignments weren't always this much of a drudgery either, she thought. She had loved her first two assignments prior to coming to Kabul.

The first stop had been the U.S. Embassy in Kenya. A dangerous place, to be sure, but the small size of the embassy there meant that she was responsible for much more than the usual nurse's work. Adding to her happiness in Kenya had been the ability to work with a doctor who had treated her as an equal and a professional: a rarity in her line of work.

Following Kenya, she was transferred to the U.S. Embassy in Kuwait. One didn't get to pick and choose very much at Victoria's level within the State Department and she had expected to be sent to the Middle East eventually. Kuwait, though, was actually a preferred destination of many State Department employees. In addition to being a relatively safe country, the medical needs of the embassy employees there tended to be low due to the country's modernized standards for medicine, infrastructure and food.

Still, the stop in Kuwait hadn't been a reprieve from a rotation to an unpleasant assignment if she wanted to grow in the State Department. Among a variety of undesirable postings, Iraq and

Afghanistan were considered the worst for obvious reasons. In the current career environment at the State Department, however, she knew it was unlikely that she could escape a posting to one of these destinations if she wanted to advance.

Thus, five months ago, when she had learned she would be assigned to Afghanistan, Victoria did so with the hope that taking a rotation here would at least burnish her career credentials. After two rotations in Iraq as an Army nurse, where she had gotten a close-up look at the constant stress of deployment in a war zone, she was more annoyed than afraid of taking a turn in such an undesired location.

Of the many small outposts within Afghanistan and Iraq she could have been sent to, the U.S. Embassy in Kabul was at least considered something of a blessing. Even with what amounted to a premier assignment, she chafed against the feeling of detention that came with essentially being detained inside the embassy and Camp Eggerts, the Army base attached to the U.S. Embassy for protection. She couldn't imagine what hell it would have been to spend a year at the U.S. consulates in Herat or Mazar-e Sharif.

With just another seven months to go before the possibility of reassignment came available, she was glad that at the very least she was busy enough to fill most days. Today she had already seen several staff members for cases of food-borne illness, which they had collectively encountered eating outside of the embassy the night before. As usual after her morning schedule, Victoria had an hour before her next set of appointments, so she headed towards the cafeteria for lunch.

As she passed through the lobby of the embassy, she saw the usual cadre of American and foreign citizens waiting to do business. Out of the corner of her eye, though, someone in the crowd grabbed her attention. Victoria stopped and took a long, hard look.

Then Victoria realized that she was looking at her best friend's ex-husband, Morgan Huntley, sitting on a bench in the lobby of the U.S. Embassy. Even more odd, was that he was there in civilian clothing. After Morgan and Laura's marriage had dissolved over his refusal to leave the Army, here was Morgan at the U.S. Embassy, wearing cargo pants and a business shirt.

Victoria walked towards Morgan, still dumbfounded. He didn't appear to notice her approach.

"Hello, Morgan."

Morgan looked up and, within an instant, turned white as a sheet. "What the hell are you doing here?" he asked.

"I work here. What are you doing here?"

Morgan ran a hand through his hair and scanned the room in a near panic. "I left the Army."

Victoria looked at him with a questioning stare. "So, what are you doing here?"

"I'm working for a company called GenetiGreen."

"What, like corporate security?"

"No, more like an advisor. A consultant."

"On what?"

Morgan smiled and said, "Just have to leave it at that. How have you been?"

Victoria felt like Morgan wasn't saying something, but she decided to drop it, so she replied, "Good. Career is going good."

"You liking it here in Afghanistan?"

"Can't wait to get out of here, actually."

The color had returned to Morgan's face and he smiled casually, the way he always did just before making a joke. "I just got here and I'm already excited to leave."

Victoria smiled back. "Well," she said, "I better be going. It was really nice seeing you."

"You, too. Take care."

They shook hands and Victoria headed towards the embassy cafeteria. As she walked, she tried to collect her racing thoughts. Two separate worlds had just collided in jarring fashion and she wasn't quite sure yet how to process the encounter.

* * *

Morgan turned back into the lobby and saw that James was looking for him.

"Ready to go?" asked James.

"Yeah. Let's get out of here."

James nodded slowly, then walked towards the front door. "Come on," he said, "I'll give you the Kabul highlight tour on our way back."

* * *

As Victoria reached the door to the cafeteria, she looked back through the lobby for Morgan once more.

She saw him headed towards the exit, but he was walking with another man. The man was handsome and dressed similar to Morgan.

As Morgan reached the security desk, the man who was with him turned to say something.

Victoria saw the man's face clearly. It was familiar to her, though she couldn't place how she knew him or his name. She was only certain that she had seen the man in the U.S. Embassy before.

An instant later, both Morgan and the man had disappeared.

Chapter Fourteen

Returning to the Intercontinental, Morgan used his Blackberry to type out a status update to Thompson's false GenetiGreen email account. With the message sent, Morgan went to the small café in the lobby and bought an international calling card.

In the back of the Intercontinental's lobby stood a bank of wooden payphone booths of the type that at one time could be found in every major hotel throughout the world before the advent of the cell phone. While many Afghans had cell phones, there were still enough people without such devices that payphones remained a common sight throughout much of the city. The advantage of a payphone to an undercover agent couldn't be measured: it was rare that someone could anticipate the need to tap a payphone before a person used it to make a call. This made a payphone an imperfect but effective means of communication for someone in Morgan's position.

Morgan used the calling card to dial Col. Bill Kzaltry's personal cell phone. There were a series of clicks as the line went through the international routing to connect the call and then Morgan heard the calm voice of Kzaltry on the other end.

"Kzaltry."

"Hey, Bill. It's Morgan."

"I didn't recognize the number. Came up as 'Restricted'."

"Technology is amazing these days."

"Sure is. How is your trip?"

"Fine. I wanted to know if you've gotten any information in the past few days?"

"Actually, I have. You got a few minutes?"

"I do." Morgan pulled out his notebook and a pen.

"Okay, I met with several contacts in Naval and Air Force intelligence. All had the same information as we did at DIA: no word of American personnel shipping drugs out of Afghanistan."

"That's what I was afraid of."

"Don't worry, it gets better. I had lunch with an old pal of mine who works at the German Embassy. He's an aide or some crap, but in reality, he's in the German intelligence network. The Germans have troops stationed throughout Afghanistan as part of their NATO commitment, so I figured this guy might have some information for me."

"What was your contact's name?"

"Dieder. That's all I can give you. You know how it goes."

"Right. What did Dieder have to say?"

"He said an inquiry had come through the German Embassy addressed to the U.S. Joint Chiefs of Staff on something of this nature. Apparently, some German troops assigned to the NATO mission in Afghanistan had come across a rumor of a drug operation in Afghanistan being run by Americans, which they had reported up through their command structure. The Germans thought it important enough to pass it along through the embassy."

"What happened with that?"

"According to Dieder, the Joint Chiefs forwarded the inquiry to the office of the Provost Marshal. They cc'd the Germans on the memo."

"When was that?"

"In January of this year."

"Who received it?"

"Dieder didn't remember while we were at lunch, but when he got back to the German Embassy, he looked it up for me."

Morgan waited, then asked, "Who, Bill?"

"Col. Franklin's office."

"Why am I not surprised? That places Franklin with knowledge of this long before my case started. And a really long time before my colleague disappeared. Any word from Dieder on a response from the Army?"

"Yes. Franklin sent back a memo a month later indicating that the Army had looked into the matter and found nothing to indicate that retired U.S. personnel were returning to Afghanistan."

Morgan scribbled these details in his notebook, then said, "Bill, I know this is a lot to ask, but do you think there is any way you could find out more?"

"Well, you might be in luck. Turns out that Franklin's file is due for an update."

"What kind of update?"

"DIA likes to pay return visits on some people that are of concern to us. Part of making sure we don't get caught with our pants around our ankles if someone we cleared in the past has turned rotten again."

"You going to follow him?"

"To start. I'll see where that gets me. I'm authorized to even conduct a discreet interview with him, so I might go there if I think I can pull it off without creating any problems for you."

"That would be quite a feat if you can pull it off, Bill."

"Tell me about it."

"Alright, let's do it. I'll check back in with you in a few days and see where you're at."

"Sure thing. And, Morgan, keep your ears to the ground. The Germans didn't think too much of Franklin, either."

"Right. You too."

Chapter Fifteen

South of Kabul, Afghanistan

The next morning, Morgan was riding inside an aging Land Rover over a dirt road in the countryside, three hours outside of Kabul. To call the pathway that they were on a 'road' was a misnomer: really, it was of a pair of ruts that traversed the desert.

As the SUV careened steadily onwards, the landscape bounced past like visions of a moonscape. Afghanistan's countryside was eerily foreign, unlike the romanticized deserts of the Arabian Peninsula or the rugged beauty of the American west. The Afghan desert was more aptly described as a wasteland with flashes of momentary beauty.

Driving the SUV was GenetiGreen's interpreter for the Kabul office, Gurman Khatwa, a former Pakistani army intelligence officer who spoke both Pashto and Punjab, as well as English. He was a well-dressed man who smelled of cigars and carried a pot belly with dignity. Gurman was one of the most important men in GenetiGreen's operation in Kabul, since Gurman could navigate the incessant checkpoints and other complexities of traveling within this country. Morgan quickly learned the reason for Gurman's success, other than his ability to speak the language: Gurman carried a seemingly never-ending supply of cash in various currencies that he applied liberally to grease the wheels at each stoppage on their journey.

Today's trip was more important for Morgan than possibly even Gurman realized. Morgan's first operational move was to build a local buzz about himself within the community of contractors in Kabul. This was needed to make his sudden appearance within the contractor community in Kabul seem organic. It was theorized during planning that if Morgan could naturally get the rumor mill in Kabul going about his business work, his suspects might be willing to float out of the woodwork to contact him.

"Getting close now," Gurman said. "You can smell the *Arbakai*."

"What are *Arbakai*?" asked Morgan, struggling with the pronunciation.

"Each tribe has men who are assigned to guard the villages and fields. They take turns, ten days at a time."

"Paramilitary?"

"I am not sure what that is. Most of these men are not trained in a militaristic sense. They are fierce and passionate about protecting their village and families."

"Do they know we're coming?"

"They know our car. Our company has been here before."

"Do you know who we'll be meeting with? All I got from the State Department was the geo-coordinates for this village."

"I've met the tribal elders, though not the elders from this specific village."

"What's the difference?"

"Every tribe is part of a bigger tribe and every tribe is divided into smaller tribes and down into villages. How all of these relationships come together forms the basis of alliances, grievances, marriages and wars."

"Who is the head of this tribe?"

Gurman shook his head. "It's more complex than that."

Morgan shrugged and let the conversation drop. He had read the State Department's write-up on the social structure of Afghanistan. Neither that document nor Gurman's explanation was making sense of the matter.

As Gurman bounced the SUV across a particularly rough patch of road, Morgan saw in the distance several young men in drab, loose-fitting clothing. They held Russian-made AK-47s at the ready. Gurman slowed down, then stopped as he reached them.

Gurman rolled down his window and spoke in the lilting

language of Pashto for several minutes with the young men. Eventually, the three men allowed Gurman to move forward.

Five minutes later, Gurman parked the SUV in the center of a small village composed of mud huts. Several small children were outside the Land Rover before the doors were open. Gurman handed out pieces of candy to the children, who then disappeared into thin air, presumably to devour their prizes.

Morgan scanned the village for any signs of welcome, but saw none. Gurman waited near the SUV.

"What do we do now?" asked Morgan.

"We wait."

Several minutes later, a flap to a hut opened and an Afghan man in his mid-thirties waved the men inside.

Gurman and Morgan entered the cool hut and took a moment to adjust their eyesight. Inside was a threadbare rug on which was placed a tea-service set. Around the rug sat three older Afghan men, each wearing a headscarf and a vest, their eyes fixed on Morgan. The eldest man in the room waved his arm and Gurman sat. Morgan followed Gurman's lead.

The eldest man asked a question. Gurman interpreted. "He wants to know if you would like tea."

Morgan could tell from the way Gurman posed the question that he was supposed to accept the tea, so he nodded in agreement. The tea was poured and each man took his cup, drinking it slow and methodically. Morgan didn't drink much tea and, as usual, it just tasted to him like warmed-over dishwater.

The men sat quietly, all eyes on Morgan. He cleared his throat and said to the eldest man in the room, "We want to help your village."

Gurman interpreted and the elder signaled for Morgan to continue on.

"We are looking to buy opium."

After Gurman had relayed the statement, the elders remained impassive.

Morgan continued. "We want to establish a contract with your village to buy any opium you grow and sell it as morphine in Europe or America. Legally."

Morgan watched as Gurman translated, then the youngest of the three elders spoke back.

"I thought the Americans had told us growing poppy flowers was bad?" Gurman interpreted.

Morgan took some time to consider the question. "We have realized that it might be better to pay you for what you can grow, rather than forcing you to fail with other crops."

The three men leaned together and spoke in hushed whispers. Then the oldest man said, "First your country wants to destroy our poppy fields. Then it wishes to buy opium from us. How do we know you won't change your mind again?"

"We are learning."

The elders talked again in hushed tones. The youngest of the three offered more tea. Everyone accepted.

The eldest man then asked Gurman something. The two talked in rapid-fire syllables that Morgan couldn't comprehend. The elders then rose.

Morgan also stood, a step behind Gurman.

"It's time for us to go," said Gurman.

Morgan looked at Gurman. His eyes indicated that there was no argument to be had, so Morgan shook hands with each of the elders, then found his way back to the entrance of the hut.

As they exited the hut, Morgan turned to Gurman. "What happened there at the end?'

"The elders wanted to know how the Kabul cricket team did last weekend."

Morgan stopped. "That was it?"

"And they talked about a local boy who was very ill. He is doing much better after some German aid workers came to the village. They didn't trust the pills they had given the boy, since they were pink. They thought it was a trick. The boy is recovering and they are excited for the aid workers to return tomorrow. They asked if I thought the aid workers would be offended by a small gift of thanks."

"Do we wait for an answer?" Morgan asked.

"No," said Gurman. "They will consider your offer in private. We will return some other time and see what they think of it."

"Any sense as to what they are going to say?"

"They will tell us when we return."

"When should we return?"

"Not too soon. And not too late."

"What the hell does that mean?"

Gurman shrugged.

Morgan watched in frustration as Gurman entered the SUV and started the engine.

Chapter Sixteen

The drive back to Kabul was just as efficient with Gurman at the wheel as it had been on their way out to the village. By the time they returned to the GenetiGreen offices, Morgan calculated that Gurman had spent in the neighborhood of three hundred dollars in bribes.

"You get reimbursed for that, I hope," Morgan said as Gurman accelerated away from yet another checkpoint.

Gurman shrugged. "It goes into the expense report under a variety of titles, but one cannot simply list 'bribes' as a line item."

"It's usually frowned upon in our country."

"Stan marks it down as 'Lobbying'. I don't see much difference, really. Truthfully, tell me, what is the difference?"

"The only difference is that lobbying isn't illegal."

Gurman shrugged.

A few minutes later, Gurman dropped Morgan off at the office. It was late afternoon and when Morgan got upstairs, he found that neither Stan nor James were still in the office. His coworkers, however, were just in the process of shutting down their computers for the day.

One of them, a tall man of Nordic stock named Eric, walked over to Morgan.

"How was the first trip into the badlands?" asked Eric.

"Not bad. Not good, either."

"It's a success when you come back with no war stories."

Morgan nodded. "Where's Stan? I figure I should report in."

"Stan has a conference call with the bosses back in the States tonight, so he's home taking a nap. He won't care if you check in with him tomorrow morning. We're heading out for drinks, if you would like to join us."

"I've got about twenty pounds of Afghan road dust in my

clothing."

"So does everyone else."

"Alright, sure. Where do you want to go?"

"Your pick, since you're the new guy."

Morgan thought for a moment, then said, "I've heard The Brydon is good."

"The best."

* * *

Several hours later, Morgan was draining beers with Eric and the rest of the guys from work. They had carved out an entire section of the bar to themselves at The Brydon, an underground restaurant in central Kabul that was packed to the gills with foreigners. The cacophony of the establishment was a mixture of English, German, Slavic, French, Italian and several other languages that Morgan couldn't quite place in the cloud of noise.

Morgan had used the last few hours to press his coworkers subtly for knowledge and information about his case. Unfortunately, while his coworkers were nice, they proved to be of little use. In fact, his coworkers spent most of their evening casting long eyes at the handful of women in the bar. The female patrons, for their part, appeared to be regularly scanning The Brydon to determine their safety from the hordes of sex-starved men.

The best Morgan was going to salvage from the night, he realized, was to at least get some local information from his coworkers. He had returned to pressing Eric for information about the other people in The Brydon, since Eric had admitted to being there on a near daily basis. Given the opportunity to speak his mind after six beers, Eric was at the moment engaged in a long verbal essay on his opinion of the worst types of Westerners in Kabul.

"And God help you if you run across some international aid

worker. Once they find out that you're getting paid to be here, they go into a holier-than-thou act about how everyone is making money in this country. It's capitalism, darling. Maybe you don't care about having a roof over your head, but I do."

Morgan drank slowly from his beer and sensed the conversation drifting to a stop. Hoping that Eric wanted to keep going, he asked, "You ever see any military types in here?"

"All the time. More than half these people are former military. I guess it comes with the territory. Something in their blood. They like the danger."

"You ex-military, too?"

"No, I went to Georgetown straight out of high school and got a job with a boutique consultant. I got a lot of exposure in international agriculture there and GenetiGreen snapped me up. I figure my time out here in Afghanistan counts as my service."

Morgan looked around and smiled. "I don't see too many uniforms in here."

Eric didn't pick up on the joke and said, "Too many rules about getting on and off base."

"Oh," said Morgan. "You don't think they come in here posing as civilians?"

Eric shrugged. "Why would they want to?"

"I don't know. Maybe the government wants to spy on us?"

"Eh, they can just tap our phones and read our emails. We don't do anything these days without leaving an electronic trail of breadcrumbs. What's the point in sending people to spy on us?"

"But, what if these guys were looking out for themselves?"

"What do you mean?"

"Like, what if they finished their tour with the Army or the Marines and decided to come back to Afghanistan to run a business?"

"Nothing illegal about that. Like I said, half the guys in here are retired from one service or another. Once they get it in their blood, they can't let it go."

"Sure." Morgan once again felt the conversation stalling, so he said, "Hey, you're looking dry. Let me get another round."

Morgan fought for the attention of the bartender and ultimately succeeded in getting a quartet of British pint-sized cans for his fellow GenetiGreen employees.

Once Morgan returned, Eric was talking with a pair of men that Morgan had not yet met. As Morgan approached, Eric waved at him.

"This is Morgan Huntley, our new consultant. He's fresh in from the States."

The first man, who was handsome and in his early thirties, stuck out his hand. "Greg Baker. Nice to meet you, Morgan." Morgan shook, then turned to the second man.

"Andrew Carlisle."

"Nice to meet you, too, Andrew."

Eric took a hard swig from his beer. "Don't bother asking them what they do."

"Why is that?"

"They're on defense contracts. Secret projects. Like building new outhouses for the Army or an extra KFC at Bagram," said Eric, smiling over his beer.

"It's not that bad, really," said Greg, coolly. "It's just that if anyone found out that we're charging the same for an outhouse in Kabul as a small home in D.C., somebody up top might get their wrist slapped."

Morgan couldn't help but chuckle.

"When did you get out here?" asked Andrew.

"He's fresh meat," said Eric with a grin.

Greg and Andrew each chuckled knowingly.

"What's funny about that?" asked Morgan.

"Nothing funny. You've got a long way to go, that's all. How long you planning on enjoying the city of Kabul?"

"Six months."

"Six months is not too bad when you're working for Uncle Sam."

"I'm not working for the government."

"Ah, but aren't we all, in a way?" asked Greg.

"Hell yeah to that," said Eric.

Andrew took another sip from his cocktail glass and then asked, "What is it specifically that you'll be doing out here for the next six months?"

"It's classified," said Morgan.

Eric took another pull from his beer, then shook his head. "Shit, you can tell them. We're part of the grand scheme to turn Afghanistan into Iowa. I spend most of my day behind a computer managing seed stock from the States. Morgan gets to go out in the field and talk to actual people. He's working on the export side of things."

"Exports?" asked Greg with a certain deal of curiosity. "Hardly much more than dirt is worth exporting around here."

"As I'm learning."

The man named Andrew cut in. "What have the Afghans got to export that's of any use?"

"Oh, you'd be surprised." Morgan took a drink of beer and let the conversation fall on an awkward silence. It was better to seem loyal to the concept of secrecy than to openly describe his cover story in front of his coworkers.

Finally, Morgan grabbed his beer and said to the men, "Know which way the bathroom is in this place?"

Eric pointed to a curtain in the back corner.

Morgan nodded to the men and walked away.

* * *

After crossing the room, Morgan looked back.

Eric had returned to his GenetiGreen coworkers, leaving Andrew and Greg at the bar. Andrew was already on to other things, as well, keeping an eye on a woman with brown hair and doe eyes.

Greg, however, was still watching Morgan. They made eye contact for a long moment, then Greg raised his glass in a mock salute. Morgan raised his own beer in return, then disappeared into the men's room.

* * *

John Vitters finished his beer and waited patiently as David Freer continued to hit on the woman at the bar. Their cover story as defense contractors had worked well on numerous occasions, the inherent secrecy of the work preventing either of them from having to answer any background questions that could lead to their cover stories being blown.

Freer worked under the name 'Andrew Carlisle', a name that he found especially funny for reasons that John didn't quite understand. Vitters went by 'Greg Baker', a simple name that had the benefit of being neither memorable nor interesting.

After a few more minutes, Vitters nodded at Freer that it was time to leave. To appear as simple faces in the crowd, they had to be sure to come and leave with the nightly swell. Plus, tonight, Vitters wanted to be well on his way out before Morgan Huntley returned from the restroom.

As hoped, they were on their way out the door long before the crowd had thinned enough to make them memorable.

* * *

Thirty minutes later, they had returned to their lodging: a small unit in a building that had been converted recently to corporate apartments.

Freer grabbed a beer from the fridge and flopped onto the industrial-grade couch that adorned the room.

"What did you think of that last guy," asked Vitters.

"The guy from GenetiGreen?"

"Yeah, Morgan Huntley."

"Seemed interesting. I don't know, what did you think?"

Vitters leaned on the wall, lost in thought. "Perfect timing, that's what I think. Too perfect."

Freer took a long pull from his beer. "It was quite a coincidence that he arrived in the last few days, huh?"

"Yeah, quite coincidental. Works in exports. Arrived right when we needed a new logistical network. And working for GenetiGreen. Doesn't that name ring a bell to you?"

"It did. Why is that?"

"CIA has been working that cover for the last few years, that's why."

"Shit. It's a front company?"

"I'm sure they have some legitimate employees. I'd like to find out if Morgan Huntley is one of them."

Chapter Seventeen

Washington D.C.

Bill Kzaltry sat on a rooftop across from a four-story apartment building in a premier area of Washington D.C., a high-powered Nikon camera in hand. He had been here since just after five o'clock in the morning, watching the glass lobby doors to the apartment for Colonel Franklin of the U.S. Army to leave. From that point on, Kzaltry's day was about to get very interesting.

Bill Kzaltry had spent the entirety of the previous week following Colonel Franklin with the blessings of his superiors to conduct a standard review of the man. Securing authorization for an update to Franklin's file had been easy enough. His superiors agreed that the suspicions mentioned in the file warranted an update to their knowledge of his comings and goings. Plus, Bill had offered them one other tidbit: Franklin – a married man of twenty years – had a mistress and an apartment in D.C.

According to copies of the documents that Franklin had submitted as part of his security check when he was promoted to lieutenant colonel, the apartment was supposedly for late nights at the Pentagon. Instead, it was his all-too-obvious bachelor pad to the casual observer, where Franklin spent frequent nights with a series of girlfriends over the last three years.

The problem created a sticky situation for Franklin, since extra-marital affairs were seen as a security hazard by all of the military branches for anyone working in the highest echelons of the service, to say nothing of the moral implications of cheating on his wife. Girlfriends and marriages were a volatile mix to be sure, but they also opened the possibility of blackmail by foreign agents or betrayal of bedroom whispers to an unfriendly government by a jilted lover.

Within hours of contacting his friend at the FBI, Kzaltry knew the full name, address, occupation and public history of

Franklin's girlfriend. Keandra Jordan was a graduate of American University with a degree in art and had worked as a waitress at a small café called Le Jardin for several years. She lived in her own apartment in D.C., which she shared with another woman.

With that information in hand, Bill Kzaltry had trailed Col. Franklin diligently over the last few days, noting the patterns of the career Army officer's life. Using his position on the rooftop where he now sat through the week, Kzaltry had taken a series of photos of their various arrivals and departures. He had also gotten a few, good clear shots of Col. Franklin and Keandra separately going through their normal, daily routines within the apartment, including a stunning shot of Keandra exiting the shower in her full, naked glory. Col. Franklin was much more demure about his showering habits and always remembered to keep the shades drawn when he bathed.

To Kzaltry's disappointment, though, the lovers were quite good about keeping the windows covered when they entered the more amorous stages of their evenings. These were the photos that Kzaltry wanted the most. Even with permission from on high to pursue the matter of Franklin's comings-and-goings, Kzaltry was limited in the amount of time he could continue to invest in this pursuit. Thus, it was time to give fate a little nudge.

Which is why Kzaltry was happy to see Col. Franklin make his usual departure from the lobby of the apartment at 6:00 a.m. sharp. Kzaltry then spent the rest of a long morning waiting for Keandra Jordan to depart as well. She finally left the place around 11:00 a.m., leaving the apartment deserted.

Ten minutes after Keandra Jordan's departure, Kzaltry followed a friendly neighbor into the apartment building, who was kind enough to hold the secure, interior lobby door open for him, giving him access to the stairwell.

* * *

Kzaltry quietly took the stairs to Franklin's fourth-floor place. Once outside the front door to the unit, Kzaltry waited to make sure the shared hallway was deserted.

Satisfied that he was alone, Kzaltry opened a small, electronic lock-pick tool provided by the DIA from his pocket. It was a simple-looking device, about the size of a small flashlight. The user simply inserted the tip into the lock and pressed a button on the end while turning the device until the small teeth in the lock-pick connected with a sequence that allowed the tumbler to give. Kzaltry always found it amusing that the government was much more efficient at picking locks than the typical house thief.

Franklin's locks were a simple, matched handle and deadbolt set. Kzaltry had the handle unlocked in just under sixty seconds. The deadbolt took him longer, leaving him sweating with nervousness by the end as he worried about a neighbor appearing in the hallway.

Lucky for Kzaltry, neither happened. He entered the apartment and closed the door behind him, testing the locks. Both worked flawlessly, showing no wear or damage from his lock picking.

He made his way directly to the bedroom, which was in the corner of the apartment with windows facing two directions. Kzaltry chose the window facing his favorite rooftop and set to work on the blinds.

The blinds were the roller type that came down from a simple reel, operated by a cord and covered by a valence. Kzaltry took his time disassembling these items. He found the point at which the spool spun within the housing, then carefully pushed a flathead screwdriver into the spool and dislodged it from its contact point. This effectively disabled the roller shade and made it impossible to raise or lower.

He then set to putting the valence back together over the roller shade.

A knock at the door stopped Kzaltry dead in his tracks. It was a pounding, angry knock.

Quietly, Kzaltry padded towards the front door. He heard no keys in the lock. Cautious, he quietly looked through the peephole to see who had come to visit.

On the other side of the door was a man in civilian clothing that Kzaltry recognized as another tenant within the apartment. The man waited for a moment longer, then knocked on the next neighbor's door.

This neighbor, an older woman in a tan dress, opened the door and greeted the man. "Hello, Paul."

"Hi, Mrs. Vantz. Is your cable out?"

"Yes, actually. I was just about to call the cable company."

Kzaltry heard the third neighbor's door open. It was a young mother with a toddler by her side. She, too, had no cable and the three got to talking about the repeated problems of the cable company.

Satisfied that no one was going to come into the apartment over the cable company's failings, Kzaltry set back to replacing the valence over the roller shade.

Five minutes later, he returned to the door and saw the hallway was now clear again. He quietly opened the door, locking the handle behind him. Kzaltry had wanted to lock the deadbolt from the outside as well using his lock-pick kit, but didn't want to risk running into the neighbors. He quickly worked his way to the stairwell and disappeared out of the building, hoping that whoever returned home first would assume that Keandra had simply forgotten to lock the deadbolt.

* * *

Kzaltry spent the rest of the day in a coffee shop near the apartment.

As evening approached, he made his way back to the rooftop of the neighboring building. By this time, Keandra was already home, apparently not having a shift at the restaurant. She was reading a book in the living room. Thirty minutes later, Franklin arrived and came up through the lobby. The lovers spent the next hour eating from cartons of take-out food that Franklin had brought home, along with a bottle of wine.

Kzaltry worried that perhaps the two would pass on lovemaking this evening. There was also the risk that Franklin was the kind of person to immediately call the apartment's supervisor when his blinds were broken. Maybe, Kzaltry realized, it would just make more sense for the DIA's photo lab to just Photoshop a few shots to make it look like they were making love rather than go to this level of effort to get the real thing.

Then Kzaltry watched with bemusement as Keandra left Franklin as he did the dishes, pulling a pink Victoria's Secret bag from hiding. She waved it in front of Franklin and then disappeared into the master bathroom.

A short time later, the two were in the bedroom. As Keandra disassembled his shirt, Franklin pulled on the shade to lower it. He soon realized that it was inoperable.

Like any red-blooded man, though, Franklin summarily ignored this mechanical inconvenience and turned his attention to the scantily clad woman in front of him, who was far more interesting than a simple roller shade.

Kzaltry took advantage of this impassioned disregard to snap a series of stunningly provocative photos of Col. Franklin being a rather poor husband.

Chapter Eighteen

Morgan walked through the GenetiGreen offices, looking for Stan.

It had been a week since Gurman had escorted Morgan to the village outside of Kabul and, since then, Morgan had been stuck in the city. Every attempt to have Gurman provide escort and translation services had been blocked by Gurman's unavailability.

To fill the time, Morgan had been sure to visit each of the various establishments frequented by Western contractors throughout Kabul on the premise that he wanted to get a feel for the city. At each of these bars and restaurants, he had pressed for rumors or information on U.S. military personnel – retired or otherwise – posing as contractors, or running drugs out of Afghanistan. Other than a few drunken laughs and some interesting stories of life in Afghanistan, Morgan had gotten no further with his discussions. It was hard to stress these angles further while maintaining his cover as an interested rumormonger and Morgan yearned to be in his normal role of being able to ask hard questions until he got an answer.

Morgan had also returned to The Brydon several times in an attempt to find anyone that had been there on the night that Martin Lansley had been killed. Foremost on his mind was whether Jason had been with Martin before the British contractor had been found dead in the street outside of The Brydon.

Morgan knew from his briefings in the States that Jason was supposed to meet Martin the night that both men had gotten into trouble. To this point, though, he had been unable to confirm whether they had actually met, or even if they were together when Martin had been slain, or when Jason had been abducted. While he had been able to talk with several people who claimed to have been in the bar that night, no one remembered seeing Martin before he had been shot. The one remaining potential witness that Morgan wanted to speak with was the bartender who had been working that evening: a Frenchman by the name of Louis.

Still, the lack of progress was also making Morgan's daily email updates with Thompson at CID increasingly terse. Morgan had little to report and Thompson was demanding to know why Morgan had not taken more ventures into the countryside. Morgan knew Thompson was right, which was what annoyed him the most. Morgan needed to get out to the villages, where he could generate buzz about his cover and perhaps attract some attention, if there was any attention to be had.

He hoped Stan could help him.

Morgan found Stan in the small kitchen that was attached to the office suite, where he was microwaving a cold cup of coffee.

"Stan, I'm wondering if you can help me with a problem."

"Shoot."

"I need to get into the field with Gurman. He hasn't been available once in the last week."

"Resources are tight around here. Have you tried making an appointment?"

"The two appointments I've had were cancelled when the car became unavailable."

"One of those was my fault."

"What about the other one?"

"Take it up with James."

"What's the point of making a schedule for using the car if someone can just claim they have an urgent matter and take it?"

"These things happen."

"So, what you're saying is, I should just claim my matter is urgent and take the car?"

Stan stuck his finger in his coffee, testing the temperature. "There's nothing stopping you from hiring a private translator and car."

"I can't afford that."

"You can submit the expense report." Stan looked around conspiratorially, then said, "Your expenses aren't going to be quibbled over by anyone back in Charlotte. Just send it in. I'm sure it will be approved."

"Cute."

"Just remember: nothing pays the bills like success."

Morgan nodded. "Where do I find these outside resources?"

"Oh, ask around. You'll find that it can come together pretty easily."

Just then, Morgan's Blackberry buzzed with the receipt of a new email. He looked at it: an email from Chief Thompson's GenetiGreen email account that read, *Call me as soon as you can.*

Chapter Nineteen

Twenty minutes later, Morgan was in the lobby of the Intercontinental. The payphones were deserted, so Morgan chose the booth on the far end, near the wall. He didn't expect anyone to come along: most of the guests of the hotel were outfitted with the latest smartphones and had no interest in the payphones.

Pulling the information from his Blackberry, Morgan used his international calling card to dial an established relay number. The telephone number was for a local area code in North Carolina. Once dialed, it connected with a secure scrambler in the Pentagon and then on to Thompson's office. Thus, with Morgan's public payphone likely untapped and Thompson's end scrambled, they were able to establish a relatively secure means of talking when the necessity arose.

After a series of buzzing and pops, he heard Thompson pick up, sounding as if he were on the end of a vast tunnel. Morgan had forgotten the impressions of distance that an old-fashioned phone could provide.

"Hello," said Thompson.

Morgan replied with the secure phrase they had agreed upon. "This is your old friend."

"Old friends bore me."

"I got your message," said Morgan, "what's the problem?"

"I have bad news. We've found Special Agent Jason Milner."

Morgan felt his stomach drop.

Thompson continued. "His body was found in an abandoned building outside of Kabul last night by the Afghan police. He was delivered to the State Department today, where he was identified by their medical personnel."

"How did the police come across the body?"

"Kids playing in the building found him."

"Any indication that the body was meant to be found?"

"No. No notes, no videos or other messages. Appeared to have been dumped there, not placed."

"I need to see the body," said Morgan.

"We can't risk your cover."

"What is there to hide anymore? We need a full-court press."

"I told you that there are too many politics. Besides, the primary objective is still the big picture. If we're going to catch these guys, you need to remain in place."

"You've read my reports. I think we're snatching at shadows."

"These things move in ebbs and flows. You're probably closer than you think. Keep working the angles you have."

Morgan let out a long breath. "Alright. I still need to see the body, though. The forensics might help me get going down the right path."

"We have assets in-country who will attend the autopsy and report back on the forensics. I'll make sure you get a copy."

"I don't want a copy. I want to see the body."

"Corporate consultants don't have that kind of access, remember?"

Morgan was quiet for a moment, then said, "As soon as that report is hot off the press, I want it in my inbox."

"You got it. Stay safe out there."

"Thanks."

As Morgan was about to hang up, he heard Thompson on the other line say, "And I'm sorry about Jason. He was a good man."

Morgan hung up, then said to himself, "I know. That's why I have to see him."

Chapter Twenty

Morgan waited in line at the U.S. Embassy's security desk as the personnel processed each visitor's request to enter the embassy. After what seemed an eternity, Morgan was next to speak with one of the men who were checking in visitors.

The man gave Morgan a tired look. "How can I help you, sir?"

"I'm here to see Victoria Solano."

"Do you have an appointment?"

"No."

"Is she expecting you?"

"She knows me."

"You'll have to fill out this request."

He took the form and within a few moments, had completed it. Since Morgan was already sure to be taped by the numerous security cameras in the building, he figured leaving a small paper trail was the least of his sins. He even included a small cover story about a rash on the back of his leg.

The man handed the request to a clerk, who disappeared into the building.

Ten minutes later, the clerk returned with a handful of documents. The man behind the desk flipped through the stack of documents diligently. After a moment, he called out, "Morgan Huntley."

Morgan approached the desk. The man handed Morgan a badge and a document. "Head straight back to the reception area. Then wait for Miss Solano to meet you in reception."

* * *

Victoria closed the door and said, "I only have authorization to treat employees of the U.S. government."

"I need your help with something," Morgan said, his eyes searching for any sign that she couldn't be trusted with what he was about to tell her.

"Okay, what is it?"

"First, I do need you to swear to secrecy. Can you at least do that?"

Victoria gave him a puzzled look, but when she could see that he would go no further without an answer, she said, "I promise."

"I'm not really here as a civilian. I'm working undercover for CID."

Victoria shook her head in disbelief, which turned to soft laughter. "It's a good thing you told me. I almost emailed Laura to tell her I ran into you."

"Did you?"

"No. Something stopped me. Must have been woman's intuition."

"Thanks. So, now you know my secret. Can you keep it?"

"Sure. What do you need help with?"

Morgan licked his lips, which had suddenly gone dry. "Do you remember Jason Milner?"

"Handsome guy that was always hanging around when you and Laura were still married, right?"

"That's right. A good friend. Friend of Laura's, too. He was assigned at KAIA and was investigating a double homicide. He went missing just over a month ago. That's why I'm here in Kabul."

Victoria held her hands to her mouth in shock.

Morgan continued. "I just got the bad news that we all feared."

Victoria looked at Morgan for a long second, comprehension washing over her face. Her eyes watering with tears. "Oh no. How?"

"They found him somewhere on the outskirts of Kabul. I don't know the cause of death. The body is supposed to be here. I need to see him."

"You're going to need a letter or some other chain of custody to investigate the body in an official capacity."

"That's what I need you for. My cover story is that I'm a civilian contractor. I would have no access to the right permissions without blowing my cover. I need your help to get in there and do my job."

Victoria shook her head. "If I got caught letting a civilian tamper with a deceased person, it would probably mean my career."

"Please," said Morgan, "I'm flying blind here and need information. You probably know better than me that what can be learned from a dead body is pure gold to an investigation. I owe it to Jason to get in there."

Victoria nodded. "I understand, but …"

"If you understand, then you know why I need your help."

Victoria shook her head, but went to her computer station. After a few moments, she turned back to Morgan. "Jason's body is here." Victoria looked at her monitor for a while longer, then said, "Come back at nine tonight. Certain professions like mine are allowed to host evening visitors. It will be quiet then. I'll put you in the log as needing a follow-up for emergency medication."

"I listed my medical concern as a rash near my ass."

Victoria rolled her eyes, then said, "Allergic reaction to a scorpion sting. Need to have you in for a follow up to make sure you don't swell up and die."

Morgan smiled. "Thanks. It means a lot to me."

* * *

In another section of the city, John Vitters waited as his computer worked its way through a sophisticated VPN system to establish a secure, untraceable connection to the internet from within the corporate apartment.

Freer was just returning from a day of tailing Morgan Huntley.

"What'd you find out about GenetiGreen's employee of the

month?" asked Vitters.

"Strange day. Went to work. Left there early, went back to his hotel. Then he left the hotel thirty minutes later and headed straight to the embassy. He was there for another hour, then went back to the hotel and stayed there the rest of the afternoon."

"Doesn't sound like the schedule of a man who is hard at work for a major U.S. corporation, does it?"

"Not at all, in my opinion. More like the lazy, self-indulgent schedule of someone who works for the government, if you ask me."

Vitters nodded in agreement. "There's not much background on him online."

"I've convinced myself that he is bad news, David. I vote we put an end to all this right now."

"Too rash. I think Huntley might be of use to us," said Vitters, his hands pressed to his lips in thought.

"We're not looking for people to spend quality time with, Vitters. We're trying to run a business here."

Vitters looked at Freer and smiled. "Funny you should mention that. I was just thinking about how to spend some quality time with Morgan Huntley."

Chapter Twenty-One

Just before nine at night, Morgan prepared to leave the Intercontinental for the U.S. Embassy.

As Morgan departed the lobby, he casually swept his eyes through the late-evening crowd, looking for familiar faces. Morgan didn't see anyone who appeared to be watching him and, thus satisfied, he hailed a cab from the security men outside. Within moments, Morgan was whisked away into the night.

In fact, there was indeed a man watching Morgan closely from within the lobby: a middle-aged Afghan in a Western-styled business suit named Jelal Entim. As Morgan's cab departed into the night, Jelal took a cell phone from his pocket and dialed the number for his employer.

He heard the American voice on the other end and Jelal said, in English, "He has left for the evening."

The man on the other end of the line thanked Jelal, then ended the call. Jelal put the phone back in his pocket and quietly strode out of the lobby and into a small café, where he ordered a coffee to pass the time until Morgan returned.

* * *

Morgan arrived at the U.S. Embassy and presented his identification to the security desk. The embassy's security staff checked their register of evening visitors and verified Morgan's appointment with Victoria Solano. Within moments, he was allowed to pass into the reception hall.

Victoria was waiting in the lobby, wearing her scrubs.

"They let you wear anything else around here?"

Victoria looked at her scrubs. "I don't really remember the last time I wore something other than this during the day."

As they passed into the medical wing, Morgan noticed that the other offices were empty as Victoria had promised. They continued quickly past her own office and towards the end of the corridor. Further into the medical wing, the rooms changed in tone from medical offices to surgical theatres.

"The benefit to being one of the most important embassies in the State Department is that we have all of the latest and greatest toys."

Morgan nodded. They reached a large, secure door marked 'Morgue'.

Victoria said, "Wait here."

Victoria entered a code and headed through the door. After about ten seconds, she returned and waved Morgan into the room.

The morgue was divided into two sections. The front area was an antechamber with several desks and a couch. Its use was to manage the comings and goings of the various administrative functions of the morgue.

Beyond this was a second security door. Victoria keyed in her code and the door opened with a loud series of clicks. The room within was painted in the harsh, plain lighting that seemed to be the preferred ambience of coroners throughout the world. Rows of refrigerated drawers sized for human bodies lined the walls, and exam stations were placed so that several people could work at once at each table.

"Jesus. This is bigger than the morgue at Fort Benning," said Morgan.

"They've expanded it twice since 2001."

Victoria checked a chart on the wall, then worked her way over to a storage drawer near the middle of the room. She snapped on a pair of gloves and opened the drawer, revealing a set of body-bagged remains. She handed Morgan a set of rubber gloves, a hairnet and Vick's Vaporub, which he placed under his nose.

"You ready?" she asked.

Morgan nodded.

Victoria opened the body bag. At first, Morgan wasn't entirely sure who was inside the bag. It was a man who appeared to be Jason's age. The body had clearly been left to decompose for days on end, leaving the skin slacked, ripped and misplaced. Identification of the face was difficult.

Morgan looked at Victoria.

Despite her years of medical training, she was doing her best to keep her emotions in check. Examining a total stranger was one thing: handling rotted corpses that had once chatted with you at a friend's backyard barbeque was another.

Morgan walked around to the left side of the corpse and inspected the arm.

"It's him," said Morgan. "Tattoo of an eagle on his left bicep."

Victoria looked at the tattoo, which was barely recognizable in the body's current state.

"Has anyone else seen the body?"

Victoria looked through the paperwork and said, "Just the head medical examiner. He performed a preliminary investigation to establish identity. The preliminary report indicates no known cause of death, though this will be investigated in the autopsy. That won't be performed until the Army's assigned investigator is here to attend it."

"Then we better tread carefully and not leave any evidence of our own investigation. Did the coroner list a preliminary time of death?"

"Yes. Around three weeks. He based it on the deterioration of the skin"

Morgan looked at Victoria, then back down at the body. "Then he was killed shortly after he went missing."

Morgan reviewed each of Jason's hands for signs of bruising. There were blue marks surrounding the flesh around Jason's wrists and several deep cuts.

He pointed to these and said, "He was alive and restrained for some time. Dead bodies don't fight against their bindings."

Victoria examined the wounds. Morgan said, "Check his ankles and see if he has similar marks there."

Morgan examined each of Jason's arms looking for other injuries, burns or signs of assault, but found nothing.

"He's got the same marks on both of his ankles," said Victoria.

Morgan nodded and handed his notebook to Victoria. "Can you measure the depth of the wounds?"

Victoria went to a drawer of tools and brought forth a measuring tape. She worked it into each of the wounds and wrote down the measurements.

Morgan continued reviewing the chest, the neck and the genitalia for injury. He saw nothing that would indicate a cause of death. No knife wounds, no bruising to suggest that he had been beaten.

Finally, he inspected Jason's head. He started with the back of the head and reviewed the entire scalp, then moved to the face. As Jason's skin swam over the loose-fitting flesh and various fluids leaked from the body's facial cavities, Morgan felt a mixture of vomit and adrenaline pool within his own throat.

"No signs of a bullet wound or injury to the throat. Lot of facial bruising. Some missing teeth that I am pretty sure he had when he left for Afghanistan."

Morgan gently put Jason's head back on the gurney and wrote in his notebook. He took the measurements from Victoria and added them to his notes.

He turned to Victoria and asked, "Do you see anything that I'm missing?"

"Let's check one more time."

Morgan nodded and they re-inspected the body once more.

After several minutes, Victoria waved Morgan over to the Jason's right side. She was looking at his arm and rubbing the skin gently.

"What is it?" he asked.

She pushed the skin against the flesh and it showed a ruddy, subdued hint of red. "You see that?"

"What?"

"The coagulation of blood under the skin?"

"Okay, yeah, I guess. The red, you mean?"

"Right. I'm not a coroner, but I am surprised how much blood is still in the corpse considering the condition of decomposition. There should have been much more blood loss in three weeks"

"Okay. So what does that mean?"

Victoria thought for a moment. "Usually it's a sign of an overdose. Something related to a coagulant."

"I'll check that against the autopsy when I get it." Morgan stepped back for a moment. "Sadly, we're going to have to leave the search for fibers and hairs to the coroner tomorrow. That type of review will be too intrusive."

"Dr. Kopcheck will conduct the autopsy. He's a very thorough man, despite the heavy workload. He'll do a good job."

"Where are Jason's belongings?"

Victoria pointed to a bag that was stowed under the sliding shelf in a rack built for the purpose. Morgan handled the bag carefully and emptied its contents onto an examination table.

"Check his pants for his wallet."

Victoria eased her way through the pockets as Morgan looked through the other items, including Jason's socks, shoes, underwear and shirt. As far as interesting details or evidence, Morgan came up empty: even the shoes had been cleaned of the normal dirt and sediment that might indicate where a person had been just before they died.

Morgan was about to inspect the inside of Jason's shoes when they heard a voice in the hallway, which caused them to freeze. The voice grew steadily louder. Morgan put the shoes down and slowly kneeled to the ground. Victoria stopped him with a gentle hand on his arm.

"It's just one of the doctors using an international cell phone in their office. They like to come down here. Better signal and more privacy."

Morgan nodded. They heard the door of an office snap shut in the hallway and the voice fade away.

After counting through the items once more, Morgan said, "His notebook is missing. Jason always carried a small notebook with his case notes."

Victoria fished through the pile of small belongings, but no notebook was hidden among the other materials.

"They must have destroyed that or taken it. Any luck finding the wallet?" Morgan asked.

Victoria shook her head.

Morgan carefully stuffed the clothing back into the bag. Then they turned back to what remained of Jason.

Victoria stared at the body. "Why would someone kidnap a man off the street just to do this to him?"

"Information. They probably wanted to find out what he knew first."

"You think he told them?"

Morgan looked at Jason for a long time, then said, "I think the men who took him were professionals or working for professionals. We'll have to wait for toxicology, but I won't be surprised if they say he had barbiturates pumped into his system to get him to talk."

"Why not hide the body better so we wouldn't find it?"

"I think this was a mistake."

"Why?"

"If they meant to send a message, they wouldn't have let the body decompose like this. You don't take a chance that your message will be ruined before someone gets it."

Victoria nodded in understanding.

In the harsh light of the morgue, Jason looked like a worn movie prop from a horror film. Not a man who had shared long nights of beer and laughter with Morgan. Not a person who had held their own dreams of advancement, a family and an easy retirement. Certainly not like the little boy in the photos that Jason kept in their apartment of him on his father's knee, laughing at one of his father's silly faces.

Just a lump of rotting flesh left abandoned in a decrepit building in a country that most Americans couldn't spell prior to 2002.

Morgan reached over and closed the body bag and then quietly whispered to Jason's corpse, "Don't worry, man. We'll get them."

Chapter Twenty-Two

Morgan left the embassy and headed straight for The Brydon. Seeing Jason's body in the morgue left him with a need to do something – anything – to lift the feeling of helplessness. He had yet to speak with Louis, the bartender who was working the night of Martin's death. Although Morgan would have preferred a conversation to occur at a time when they might have some privacy, he reasoned the risk of people overhearing his questioning of the bartender was growing less important with every wasted minute.

When Morgan arrived at The Brydon just past 10:30 at night, it was half-full with its average, weeknight crowd. Most of the drinkers were well into their fourth and fifth rounds of the evening.

Morgan found a spot at the bar and waved for the bartender.

As he approached, Morgan asked, "Louis, right?"

The man nodded. "What can I get for you tonight?" asked Louis.

"Just a beer."

Louis worked through a small refrigerator behind the bar and pulled out a beer, handing it to Morgan. As Morgan pulled out the cash, he asked, "You ever hear of Martin Lansley?"

Louis fixed Morgan with a questioning look. "Why?"

"Were you here the night he died?"

"Yes."

"Just a normal night for you?"

Louis shrugged.

"Was Martin Lansley alone when it happened?"

"I don't know. I was here inside."

"I mean, did he walk out of here alone or with friends?"

"Those kinds of questions are not good in Kabul, you know that?"

"Just tell me. Did Martin walk out of here alone?"

"I don't involve myself in such things. Neither should you."

"Did you know the other guy's name?"

"I have other customers."

Louis walked away and served a few drinks. As he did, Morgan pulled out a pair of one hundred dollar bills and put them under a coaster.

A moment later, Louis was back to clear the bar and grabbed the tip. He looked at it, then at Morgan, who was still drinking his beer. Louis grabbed a second beer from the fridge.

As Louis deposited it on the counter, he leaned close with a subtle nod. "Martin Lansley left with another man that night."

Morgan scrolled through his Blackberry and then held up a photo of Jason on the screen for Louis to see.

Louis looked at it and nodded. "That was him."

Morgan nodded and said, "Thanks."

Louis nodded and walked away again to the far end of the bar, as far as he could get from Morgan.

Morgan finished the first beer, grabbed the second and turned around on his stool.

Beer in hand, Morgan scanned the room, his thoughts far away. Then something caught his eye that brought him back to reality. In the back corner, seated at a small table were Greg Baker and Andrew Carlisle, sharing a bottle of red wine from small, squat glasses.

Greg saw Morgan looking at them, raised a glass and waved Morgan over to their table.

Morgan walked over, carrying his beer.

"Have a seat, Mr. Huntley," said Greg Baker.

Morgan sat down next to Andrew, who shook Morgan's hand.

"We saw you come in a little while ago, but it looked like you were having an intense conversation with Louis," said Greg. "Can I offer you a glass of wine?"

"I'm in more of a beer mood."

"Fair enough. How is business?"

Morgan almost didn't remember what business Greg was referring to, but then cleared his throat in order to collect his thoughts. "Plenty of problems."

"Oh? Louis helping you out with them?"

"Just getting advice on where to get a new pair of socks. Well-cared-for feet are the key to happiness, I always say."

"That's a good philosophy in life," said Greg. "How about your work problems? Louis providing you consulting services?"

Morgan cracked a small grin. "Just trying to find a way to get around in this country. We're damned short on interpreters, drivers and vehicles back at the office. It's proving quite an obstacle."

"It can be a hell of a problem in this country."

Morgan took a sip of beer, then asked, "You guys know anyone who might be able to help me with that?"

"We're out in the countryside visiting the local villages most days, actually. We have a full-time interpreter. Though, I also speak a little of the local language, as does Andrew."

"A little is all you really need in this country," said Andrew. "Money does most of the interpreting here."

Morgan nodded.

"Then again, I don't know much about your work," said Greg, with a coy smile. "So, I'm not sure we can really help you."

Morgan didn't say anything.

Greg said, "How about quid pro quo? We'll tell you what we do. Then you can tell us what you do."

"Okay. You first."

Greg poured himself another glass of wine, then said, "We're building schools out in the countryside. We coordinate the various work sites, making sure the raw materials get to where they need to be. You know, make sure we have labor on site and the blessing of the local powers. You name a local big shot and we've probably met them."

"Doesn't sound like a defense contract."

"It's a different kind of war." Vitters took a drink from his glass of wine. "Your turn. What is your business in Afghanistan?"

"I'm working on establishing contracts for the U.S. government with local farmers."

"Contracts for what?"

"You might not believe it, but the U.S. government wants to buy opium from the locals."

Andrew laughed. Greg shook his head and said, "You've got to be kidding?"

"I'm not. We're trying to get the local villages to sell opium to the Europeans with the U.S. government as the middleman. From there, it will be turned into pharmaceuticals. My company handles the negotiations and the logistics."

"You've got a legal license to buy drugs and sell them in the open market?" asked Vitters. "How in the hell did you get that gig?"

Morgan shrugged. "It's proving a lot harder than you would think."

Greg and Andrew looked at each other in seeming disbelief, then Greg said, "Well, that being the case, I think we can help you. We know plenty of villages that have little patches of poppy plants growing out back who would probably be willing to listen."

"I'm here to do big deals."

"Don't worry. These guys grow plenty. If you're willing to go tomorrow, we can give you a ride and some assistance with the locals."

Morgan looked at both men, then asked, "What's the catch?"

"No catch. We need a few of these villages to open their arms and let us build schools. We've been looking for a way to get our foot in the door. If we can deliver them a fat U.S. government contract, I'm sure they would be more than willing to listen. It's synergy at its finest. We bring you in, you bring us in. Sound good?"

"Too good to be true."

"The best things in life often are."

Greg pushed a business card onto the table for Morgan. Morgan reached into his own pocket and pulled a pair of cards for Greg and Andrew. They took these and then the men shook hands.

"We'll pick you up outside this place tomorrow morning," said Greg.

Morgan said, "Great. My cell is on the card. Just give me a call when you're here."

Chapter Twenty-Three

Despite a career that involved daily encounters with the emotional strains of grief, angry patients and overbearing doctors, Victoria usually had no trouble getting a sound night of sleep.

Seeing Jason Milner's body, however, had given her an evening filled with fitful dreams. Through the long night, a series of unexpected emotions worked through her subconscious as she tried to rest: anguish over the thought of Jason Milner's death and, to her surprise, fears for Morgan Huntley's safety.

It was this last emotion that bothered her the most. Before Morgan and Laura had gotten a divorce, she would have counted Morgan as a good friend. The divorce had happened quickly, though it had not come as a shock to her. She had counseled Laura through much of her decision-making leading up to the divorce.

Laura was, at that time, just ending her own career as a nurse with the U.S. Army and struggling with a diagnosis of Post-Traumatic Stress Disorder, or PTSD, from several years of treating soldiers in Iraq during both the invasion and the occupation. The stress of what Laura had seen coupled with her need to resolve the emotional and mental crises that were crushing her life was the reason behind her departure from the Army. It was also why she needed her husband, Morgan, to also leave the Army. The constant contact with the Army was making her existence a daily struggle from which she needed a clean break. Morgan, however, was reluctant to leave his own career.

For some reason, Morgan refused to acknowledge how his own, continuing career in CID was causing as much stress to Laura as had her own time in the Army. After much soul-searching, Morgan and Laura's marriage had come to a final head when Laura threw down the gauntlet: it was either time for Morgan to leave the Army or she was leaving him.

Morgan refused. Within a month, Laura had filed the divorce papers.

Once the divorce was finalized, Victoria ended all communication with Morgan, which at the time seemed to be the best way to support her friend to build a new life. Really, it had been an easy choice. Victoria was already a million miles away at the U.S. Embassy in Kuwait when the divorce came through. The feelings of worry and care that had welled-up within her overnight for Morgan had therefore left her confused. She had never disliked Morgan or thought he was a bad person. She had also never understood why he refused to leave CID when his marriage was falling down around him. Yet, he had never done anything mean or harsh towards Laura.

Which wasn't even to say that Victoria necessarily would have made a different choice than Morgan under similar circumstances. Victoria had always prioritized her own career, twice breaking off meaningful, long-term relationships. While a nurse in the Army, she had ended a two-year relationship with a fellow soldier when her service ended and she was headed for the State Department. During her move from Nigeria to Kuwait, she had also ended a six-month relationship with a British doctor who swept her off her feet at a goodwill dinner between the embassies. He had made it obvious that she would have to follow his career around the world if they wanted to stay together. She might have done that, but he had also made it clear that he had no interest in a real marriage, which had been the deal breaker. Why should she give up her own career for a man who never intended to marry her?

Just after five in the morning, Victoria surrendered to the frustrations of a bad night of sleep and headed to the embassy's gym for a quick workout. Following a shower, she was in her office just after six and digging into a pile of paperwork. Her early start was a rarity among the medical employees in the embassy, which was still largely deserted at this hour.

As Victoria worked on files in the nearly silent medical wing, she heard the distinctive squelch of a security keypad in the hallway as it replied that an entry code was invalid. Victoria paused and listened again. She wondered if her mind was playing tricks on her or if someone was short on their morning coffee.

Then, she heard the subtle tapping on a security keypad and once more the jarring error tone of an invalid code. Once more, the tapping of the keypad. This time, the sound of the door opening echoed through the hall.

Perhaps it had been the night of worrying over Morgan or the knowledge that Jason Milner had been murdered. For whatever reason, Victoria felt a chill race across her spine and a feeling of insecurity at being alone in the medical wing.

She tried to put it out of her mind and return to her work. Her thoughts, though, wandered back to the sound of the keypad minutes before. The various personnel who worked in the medical wing knew their entry codes without fail. They pounded the numbers into the numerous security doors dozens of times a day as they headed in and out on their daily duties. If someone had made a mistake on the keypad that was one thing: but two errors in a row seemed unlikely to her.

Victoria walked into the hallway, which was empty. She heard nothing other than her own footsteps as she walked along the hall. As she passed each door, she checked to see if a fellow doctor or nurse was within who might have heard the same thing as her. Each door was still locked or the room empty.

Finally, the only door remaining was that for the morgue, the keypad glowing and awaiting a code for entry. She entered the security code for the door and pulled it open slowly.

Inside the morgue, the lights were on. Victoria heard someone working within the examiners room. She let the door to the administrative room slam behind her, announcing her presence.

A familiar man appeared in the doorway to the examiner's

room. Then she realized it was the same man she had seen talking to Morgan on the first day they had met in the embassy lobby. She still couldn't remember his name, but she was certain that he was not medical personnel.

What bothered her more, though, was that beyond him, she could see that Jason Milner's body had been moved out of the chilled storage drawer and onto a rolling gurney.

"Only medical personnel are allowed within this room," she said to him.

The man smiled and reached into his pocket, pulling out an ID. "It's okay, ma'am. I'm with the Army."

Victoria hesitated. She didn't want to go closer to the man. "What's your name?"

"Special Agent James Poole, U.S. Army Criminal Investigative Command. It's on the ID card, if you would like to check."

Victoria picked up a handset phone that was on a desk, pushing zero to connect with security.

A man picked up the line. "Security."

"There is an unauthorized person in the morgue. Please send someone down immediately."

"Yes, ma'am. We're on our way."

James shook his head as he overheard the conversation. He walked back to Jason's body and slowly wheeled it towards the door. Victoria felt her skin tingle with fear as he came closer, trying to decide if she would block his passage or step out of the way.

James seemed to sense this and he held his ID out at arm's length again, close enough for Victoria to see. It showed a picture of James, along with his full name, along with the letters 'CID' emblazoned at the top.

"See," he said. "Army CID. You know who that is, don't you?"

"Sure. And I know that Army CID would have the necessary paperwork to transport a body. You got the right forms?"

James shrugged helplessly and put his ID back into his

pocket.

"I thought so," said Victoria.

At that moment, the door opened and in stepped a pair of U.S. Marines, along with a man in a suit who Victoria recognized as a top security officer for the embassy, Edwin Fitzgerald.

Fitzgerald looked over the situation and then turned to Victoria.

"Ma'am, is this the man you referred to on the phone?"

"Yes. It appears that he intends to transport this body from the embassy without authorization. Plus, I know for a fact that this body is scheduled for an autopsy here later today."

Fitzgerald clearly recognized James and smiled politely as he walked over to greet him. James wore a crooked half-smile. Fitzgerald gently took him by the arm and led him into the morgue. The two men spoke in hushed tones.

A few moments later, they came back. Fitzgerald opened the door to the hallway for James. James smiled at Victoria, then pushed the gurney with Jason's body towards the door and took his leave into the hallway.

The two Marines followed, but Fitzgerald stayed behind. He let the door close, leaving him alone with Victoria.

"What the hell is this?" asked Victoria.

"I'm sorry, Mrs. ...?"

"Miss Solano."

"Miss Solano. Thank you for contacting us. You did the right thing. Fortunately, we know who he is and he has permission to remand that corpse into his own custody. I've asked him to submit the appropriate paperwork as soon as he gets back to his office."

"Bullshit. That's not how this works."

"I'm sorry you feel that way, but that's all we can do at this time."

"You really expect me to believe you would let a CID agent walk out of here with a body without the appropriate paperwork?"

"I have no comment on that. Have a good day."

Fitzgerald gave the sort of smile a D.C. lobbyist would be proud of and opened the door for himself, exiting into the hallway.

Victoria waited a moment, then quickly walked to her office.

She had Morgan's cell-phone information written on his appointment request form. She called the number, but was sent directly to voicemail.

"Morgan," she said into the voicemail system, "call me as soon as you can. It's urgent."

Chapter Twenty-Four

Outside Kabul, Afghanistan

Morgan kept his eyes focused on the dirt road ahead as Greg bounced a well-worn Ford Suburban across the uneven terrain. The Suburban had been modified with heavy bumpers, fortified front grills, a large communication antenna and bullet-proof glass. In the back seat was Greg's interpreter, an Afghan named Joseph. According to Greg, Andrew Carlisle had stayed behind in Kabul to attend to a meeting he had in the city.

"Joseph? That's not a very Afghan-sounding name," said Morgan, glancing into the back seat and looking at Joseph's long form. "What part of the country are you from?"

"North of Jalalabad."

"And the name?"

"My father was Russian."

Morgan nodded. "Is he still here in Afghanistan?"

"I do not wish to talk about it."

Greg said, "There aren't too many Russians still hanging around in this country."

Morgan nodded. "Not exactly fond memories."

"No," said Greg, "not that our country has too many fond memories here, either. I've been meaning to ask: did you serve? You seem to have the bearing of a military man."

"Army."

"Me too," said Greg. He gave a mock salute and said, "Sergeant Greg Baker, U.S. Army, Retired. You?"

Morgan had practiced this part of his cover, so he said, "I was Army Reserve, communications."

"You do a rotation out here?"

"Iraq in 2004 and 2005. You?"

"I was in Afghanistan twice, Iraq once."

"That's quite a service record."

"Wrong time, wrong place, I guess. When did you head back to Fort Living Room?"

"2007. You?"

"In some ways, never. I left the Army, but then joined on with this new venture about six months later."

"Why is that?"

"NCO, that's why."

"Right," said Morgan, recognizing the commonly used acronym for "No Civilian Opportunities."

They banged along the rutted road for a little more and Greg asked, "You married?"

"I was."

"She leave you while you were overseas or did she wait for you to finish?"

"I was back in the States."

Greg looked at Morgan, waiting to see if he would go on.

When Morgan kept silent, Greg said, "Yeah, I'm part of the divorcee club, too. My wife left me before I got back. She started banging a civilian in Georgia before the end of my last tour. Broke my heart."

"Sorry to hear that."

"Ah, I don't blame her, I guess. What kind of life was it for her? We got married and she had dreams of a suburban house; couple kids; weekend cocktail parties. Instead, she got women's support-club meetings and military-base apartments. While the rest of the country was debating whether to shop at Costco or Target, she was trying to figure out how to plan a life around a husband who was never home."

Morgan nodded. "It's tough on the spouses."

"Why did your wife leave you? She get the civilian blues?"

"She was Army, also."

"A Desert Fox, huh?"

"A nurse. We got married while still in the Army. We were different people when we got on the other side. Went our separate ways."

Greg nodded. "No shame in it. Lot of guys couldn't keep their marriages together when they came back. Out here, things make sense: you have a job and everyone thinks you're normal. Back there, you beg for a job, clean the house and hope you don't have PTSD."

They rode along for a while longer in silence as the road kicked up a heavy cloud of dust.

"We called that 'moon dust' when we were on tour out here," said Greg. "Afghan dirt is like something I've never seen. Sticks to everything. Super fine."

"I've noticed. I can taste it in my mouth at night."

They stopped at a checkpoint of *Arbakai* on the outskirts of a village. Greg rolled down his window and said a few words in Pashto.

Morgan noticed that the men obviously recognized Greg.

He also noted that Greg did not offer a bribe.

The men quickly waved Greg through the checkpoint. Greg smiled at Morgan and maneuvered the SUV towards the village.

"That's the first time I've seen that," said Morgan.

"What?"

"No bribe necessary."

"We've been here before."

* * *

Greg brought the Suburban to a halt within the center of the village. No children ran out to greet them as had happened when he had traveled with Gurman.

After they had exited the SUV, an Afghan man in his mid-thirties waved for them to enter a hut.

As their group walked towards the hut, Morgan could see a series of expansive poppy fields in the distance, easily identified by the unique, neck-like stalk that bore a heavy flower-pod at the top. Greg pointed to them and said, "I told you I had a bearing on the good stuff."

Morgan said nothing as they headed inside the hut.

The interior of the hut was very similar to the experience Morgan had encountered with Gurman. Tea was presented and accepted. No words were exchanged. The village elders were a group of three men, though this time the man who was eldest was not at the center, but instead seated off to the side. Clearly, he was not in charge.

Greg spoke to Morgan, gestured towards the man in the center and said, "This is Iqbal, the village leader."

Morgan nodded in respect. Greg then said something to Iqbal in Pashto, during which Morgan heard his own name.

The man said something in rapid-fire Pashto and Joseph transferred the statement into English. "I welcome you to our village."

Morgan nodded in return.

Greg then said to Morgan, "Okay. It's your show."

Morgan cleared his throat. "I would like to make a business deal with your village on behalf of the U.S. government."

Joseph translated and Iqbal nodded in a manner that indicated that he had heard this before.

"I was wondering if your village grows opium?"

After Joseph had translated the question, Iqbal gave a short laugh. Joseph translated. "Is that your question?"

Greg leaned to Morgan and said, "You saw the field outside, right?"

"Just trying to establish a rapport, that's all."

"Maybe just get into the offer."

Morgan looked at Iqbal and described the offer from the U.S. government. Iqbal listened patiently to the translation from Joseph.

Morgan noticed that as Iqbal listened, he repeatedly glanced towards Greg as if he were awaiting direction.

Finally, Joseph said, "He wants to know how much you will pay per kilo?"

Morgan sat there, dumbfounded. He hadn't expected to be asked for a rate and it took him a moment to remember what the starting point rate was for GenetiGreen's price sheet. Morgan wrote a number on a piece of paper as he had been instructed to do by the corporate training specialists in order to prevent confusion. The elder looked at it and said through Joseph, "Too low."

Morgan looked around the room. All eyes were on him. This was his chance to deliver on his cover, an opportunity to prove that he could develop a signed contract for selling opium to the U.S. government. He took the paper back and wrote a new number. One that was astronomical compared to his previous offer.

He handed it to the elder, who reviewed it impassively. He waited, expecting that the tribal elders would council. Instead, Iqbal said something short and Joseph translated.

"I accept."

Morgan stared straight ahead, unsure of what he was supposed to do next, not wanting anyone in the room to notice. He thought back to his training in North Carolina, but his mind was drawing a blank.

Greg said, "Well, there you go. What do we do now?"

Morgan finally remembered that in his backpack was the standard GenetiGreen contract. "Well, we need to draft some paperwork."

Over the next twenty minutes, Morgan and Iqbal – with Joseph's assistance – went through the paperwork, establishing the agreement.

When they had finished, the two men shook hands. Morgan began to rise, but Iqbal asked a question. Greg jumped in before Joseph could translate.

"He wants to know when they will be paid."

Morgan said, "I'm not sure."

The answer was translated and Iqbal gave a displeased scowl.

Greg said, "Do you know the answer or …"

"I have to check with my company, that's all."

"They're going to need a firm date."

Morgan thought and then said, "I'll have a check for you next week."

This was translated and Iqbal smiled. They then shook hands again.

* * *

As the three men drove out of the village in the SUV, Greg turned to Morgan and said, "Nice work back there."

"Thanks. You think you got anything out of it for you and Andrew, as well?"

Greg smiled. "They'll be thrilled to see us again once they get that nice check from you. That's a big win for us."

Morgan nodded, then said, "You seem to have a good grip on the local language."

"Yeah, it helps."

"Where did you learn that?" asked Morgan.

"Corporate training. A little practice."

Morgan smiled politely. For the rest of the ride back to Kabul, his mind was only half on the small talk with Greg.

The rest of his focus was elsewhere: on how he was going to convince Stan at the office to cut a large check for Iqbal, for one thing.

And about mandatory language-training for U.S. Green Berets.

Chapter Twenty-Five

Kabul, Afghanistan

It took most of the afternoon to get back to Kabul, as the main highway had slowed to a crawl due to a tipped-over truck. By the time Morgan arrived via cab from The Brydon to the GenetiGreen offices, the place was already emptying with Happy-Hour caravans to the city.

As he walked in, Morgan remembered to power on his Blackberry, which had been shut-off on the trip to the village to save battery. He felt his Blackberry vibrate to indicate new messages that had been unable to deliver during the day. He made a mental note to check those messages after he found Stan.

He located Stan in the conference room, where he was preparing for an evening phone conference with the U.S.

"Stan? I need a few minutes of your time," Morgan said as he entered the conference room, closing the door behind him.

"Hey, Morgan. What can I do for you?"

Morgan sat down and Stan pulled off a pair of reading glasses.

"I've made a deal with one of the villages. A contract to purchase one hundred kilos of opium."

Stan's eyebrows raised. "Well, I guess I should say 'congratulations'. You got the paperwork?"

Morgan handed over the contract to Stan, who flipped through it. He stopped on the page that outlined the contracted rate.

"Morgan, this is a very high price per kilo. I'm not sure this will pass muster."

"I needed to get something on the books for my cover. Maybe get some nearby villages interested."

"Here's the problem. I have to report back to North Carolina for approval. This deal is so far in the red, I can't possibly justify it."

Morgan nodded. "I can't go back out there and cancel it. That would cause complications."

Stan exhaled and stared at the contract as if the numbers might change if he glared long enough. "Alright. I'll stick up for this one. No more sweet deals, you got it?"

Morgan nodded. "There's one other thing."

"What's that?"

"They need a check next week."

Stan laughed and leaned back in his chair. "That's not how this is done."

"I gave my word."

"No way GenetiGreen can do that."

"I need to deliver, Stan."

"Look, that's not something I'm going to go to bat on."

"Just tell the folks back in Charlotte to bill the Army. It will work out in the wash."

Stan glowered at Morgan, then shook his head. "I'm sorry I ever gave you that piece of advice. Alright. I've got to figure out how to drop this bomb when I call North Carolina in an hour, so get out of here."

"Thanks, Stan. I owe you one."

"You bet your ass."

As Morgan left, Stan said, "And no more of this shit. You want to do something special next time, you got to ask me first, got it?"

"No problem."

Morgan left and walked into the hallway.

* * *

As Morgan returned to his office, he found James Poole inside. James was surfing the internet, but turned to face Morgan as he entered.

"Where you been all day?" asked James, innocently playing with a pencil.

"Out and about. You?"

"Worrying about you."

"Why is that?"

"People have a bad habit of disappearing in this country."

Morgan stopped and looked at James. "That's an interesting thing to worry about."

"Just worried, that's all." James stood and said, "Well, I guess better go check out the happy-hour scene. It's been awhile since I had a drink with the boys."

Morgan watched as James left. For a long time, he stared at James's empty chair.

Morgan remembered the message on his Blackberry. He called his voicemail inbox, then listened to Victoria's message.

One minute later, he was on his way to the U.S. Embassy.

Chapter Twenty-Six

Vitters and Freer parked their SUV in front of a small home nestled amid a series of similar structures in a residential area of Kabul not frequented by many Westerners. At one time, this neighborhood had been a favored stronghold of Taliban party members and their families. Though the Taliban were no longer in control, many of the people in this area were still sympathetic.

The man they were coming to see was simply known as Rajudi, who was a middle-aged Pakistani and an agent for Pakistan's version of the CIA, known by its Western acronym, the ISI. Whenever Vitters had a research problem that he couldn't solve from his own connections, he would outsource the project to Rajudi. The price of Rajudi's work was high, but so was the quality that he delivered.

While both men trusted Rajudi, they did not feel so safe as to come to this meeting unarmed. In addition to a backpack filled with American dollars, Vitters also had a pistol in a shoulder holster under a light jacket, as well as another in the back of his jeans. Freer was armed in a similar manner.

As Freer kept a cautious hand near his own sidearm, Vitters knocked on the front door in a casual manner.

A woman in a veil answered the door, then silently waved them inside.

She led them into a living room, which was lit dimly by several lamps and filled with threadbare furniture. Rajudi sat on a couch, smoking a cigarette and dressed in plain business clothes. He waved for Vitters and Freer to sit across from him.

"Gentlemen," he said, "it is a pleasure to see you again." His voice had a distinctive British accent.

"I'm glad you are willing to meet with us on short notice," said Vitters.

"I am always willing to do business. Able, though, is a different problem."

Vitters and Freer smiled.

"Now," said Rajudi, "let us get to the meat of it. Did you bring the payment?"

Vitters shook the backpack.

"May I have it?"

Vitters slowly handed the bag to Rajudi, who kept his eyes focused on every move that his guests were making. Vitters stopped midway.

"No tricks," said Vitters.

Rajudi raised an eyebrow, then took the bag with an easy smile on his face.

"I'll count it later," he said, as he placed the bag on the floor. He then clapped his hands together in the style of a magician. "This man you've been asking about, Morgan Huntley. I want to be sure I have the right name."

"That's him. What can you tell us about him?" asked Freer.

"It seems our friends in the Taliban are also very interested in this man."

"Is that a good thing?"

Rajudi smiled. "It could be for you."

Rajudi held out a small file folder dramatically, then pushed it onto the table between them. Vitters took the folder and looked through it.

There was silence in the room for a short time as Vitters reviewed the contents of the file. Finally, Freer asked, "What is it?"

"Bunch of things. Morgan Huntley's passport. And his credit report," said Vitters.

"Isn't your credit report supposed to be super private?" quipped David Freer.

"The best source of intelligence ever created," said Rajudi. "The American credit bureau system provides everything one needs to know about a person's life. Where they live, where they bank, whether they're broke or rich, their debts. We have administrative logins for all three major U.S. credit bureaus." Rajudi smiled and leaned forward. "You'll notice where Morgan Huntley's paychecks come from, of course."

Vitters looked up. "The Department of Defense."

Freer rolled his eyes. "Shit. He's a fucking spook."

"No. CIA guys don't draw pay from DOD."

"That is right," said Rajudi. "There is more. The Taliban has become very adept at investigating these matters. I think you will find that what is in that file will be well worth what you have paid."

* * *

Twenty minutes later, Vitters and Freer were in their vehicle, headed back to the corporate apartment.

"You think CID wants to make a move on us?" asked Freer.

"I'm not sure. Whatever it is they are planning, I think we have time."

"So, what's the next move?"

Vitters fell quiet as he drove. It was several blocks before he said, "I propose to invite Morgan Huntley for an honest conversation."

"That's not what I had in mind."

"I think he might like to hear what we have to say."

"What are you going to say to him? You're looking for us. Here we are."

"Maybe."

"You better ask Farrat and Griggs what they think."

Vitters nodded. "We'll get them on the SATPHONE tomorrow morning."

Chapter Twenty-Seven

Victoria led Morgan into her office at the embassy. She closed the door behind him.

"What's wrong?" asked Morgan. "Your message sounded like there was an emergency."

"Who is the man that came with you to the embassy the first day we saw each other?"

"James Poole."

"How do you know him?"

"Why?"

"Tell me."

"He works with me at GenetiGreen."

"Is that all?"

"What's going on?"

Victoria said, "I saw him leaving with you the day that we first ran into each other here at the embassy. Is he a CID agent?"

Morgan tried to wrap his head around Victoria's question. "Is James Poole a CID agent?"

"Is he undercover for CID?"

"He's just a GenetiGreen employee as far as I know. Why?"

"Yesterday morning, he used a security code to access this wing and to enter the morgue. I caught him taking Jason's body."

Morgan put his hand to his head and rubbed his scalp as he tried to digest the information from Victoria. "Was anyone with him?"

"He was alone. When I came in, he already had Jason's body on a rolling gurney."

"What happened next?"

"I called security. James talked in private with one of our chiefs of security. Then the chief of security ordered the Marine guards to help James wheel the body out of the building. No questions beyond that. No paperwork was left behind."

Morgan thought about this for a long moment. "Did security

tell you why they let him go?"

"No."

"There is no way he is CID. The State Department and the Marines hate it when the Army is sniffing around in the embassies. If he was Army CID, the security chief would have blown his top. Did anyone else show up looking for the body later?"

"Yes. The coroner came through an hour later and was incredibly pissed."

"Did James have any documentation from the Army?"

"None. The coroner also called CID in Quantico and got stonewalled." Victoria reached into her desk and pulled out a small file folder. She handed it to Morgan. "But, I did get this," she said.

Morgan opened the file folder. Inside was a copy of the State Department's file on James Poole. On it was a variety of information, almost every line of which was meaninglessly marked out with 'N/A'.

Victoria said, "You notice anything odd in there?"

"I'm not sure. You've had longer to look at it, so you tell me."

Victoria pointed turned the file to the third page, which was the State Department's record of James's travels. It had no entries.

"It's blank?" asked Morgan.

Victoria nodded. "No one gets a blank travel page in State Department travel records. Well, nobody, that is, except a certain intelligence agency in the United States government."

Morgan closed his eyes in frustration. "James Poole is a CIA agent. I'll be damned."

"Why would the CIA want Jason's body?"

"I don't know," said Morgan, "but there are few, if any, good reasons. But, it does add to my theory that we were never meant to find the body."

"Why is that?"

"The night that Jason disappeared, he was supposed to be meeting with a man named Martin Lansley. That man turned up dead in an alley outside of a bar here in town that same night. According to the bartender, Martin left with Jason."

"Why kill Jason someplace else, then?"

"You would make a hell of a Special Agent."

Victoria shrugged and Morgan continued. "That's exactly the right question. Could be a lot of answers. Maybe they wanted to find out what he knew before they killed him. Maybe Martin fought back and got himself killed in public when the men had planned to kill them both somewhere quiet. Both possible. But, right now – and perhaps I'm being a bit self-centered – but right now, my leading thought is they took him away simply so that we wouldn't know they killed him. A dead CID agent would provoke a much different response from CID than a missing agent."

"If that's true, why would the CIA want the body?"

"There's only one person who can tell me that."

As Morgan put the file folder back in her hands, she grabbed his arm. A ripple of electricity pulsed through Morgan's body.

"Be careful," she said.

For a long moment, they stood there, her hand still on his arm. Then Morgan ripped open the door into the hallway.

Chapter Twenty-Eight

The next morning, James Poole entered his office at GenetiGreen to find Morgan Huntley sitting in the center of the room, a series of empty coffee cups strewn about.

James stared at Morgan for a long time, then said, "Since you're in my chair, I'm going to assume you haven't had enough coffee yet."

Morgan said, "We need to talk."

"About what?"

"Where were you yesterday morning?"

"You wouldn't like that question any more than I do."

"Where were you?"

James leaned on the door and flashed a cat-like smile. "I feel like you already know. The question is how?"

"You were at the embassy."

James looked for a long moment at Morgan, then said, "I was."

"What interest did you have in Jason Milner's body?"

"So, let me guess. You're with the Army? That makes you CID, right? Investigating the dead CID agent. You shouldn't have let me know that."

"Might as well. I know you're CIA."

"What makes you think that?"

"I have my sources."

James picked at something on his shirt, then looked at Morgan and said, "Okay. You got me. Now, what are you going to do with that information?"

"You've taken the body of a slain CID agent, which is evidence in an ongoing investigation. Where has the CIA gone with it and what do they want with this case?"

"We were asked by CID to claim it for them."

"Bullshit."

"It's the truth."

"We would have used our own people for that."

"CID didn't want State sticking their nose in the Army's business. The only way to get Jason's remains out of the embassy without an official State Department autopsy was with a little help from the CIA. Jason's body is currently on its way to Dover Air Base, where it will be met by CID Forensics for an autopsy."

"I'm going to call CID and verify your story, so is that your final answer?"

James smiled. "It is."

"Who at CID ordered this move?"

"Classified information."

Morgan sat up straight and glared at James. "I'm worried that we're working at cross-purposes here."

"Don't worry. We're on the same team."

"Are we?"

"We are."

"If that's so, then tell me what you know about Jason Milner and Martin Lansley."

James looked at the ceiling in exasperation. "I'm not a detective."

"Certainly the CIA knows something."

"Not much. Just errand boys doing a favor for the Green Machine."

Morgan and James stared at each other for a few seconds. Finally, James said, "Is that all? Are we done?"

"Sure. For now."

"Well, I've got some work to get done here."

Morgan stood. "Just so we're clear, if I find that you're interfering with my case, I'm going to be a very pissed-off person."

James smiled. "I'll keep it in mind."

* * *

An hour later, Morgan arrived back at the Intercontinental Hotel. He found the payphone booths to be empty and he used his calling card to call Thompson.

"Thompson."

"This is your old friend."

"Old friends bore me."

"I've got some real bad news here."

"What's that?"

"According to a contact I have in the embassy …"

"What the hell are you doing talking to people at State? You're supposed to be undercover."

"Hold on, Chief. That is not the problem right now. According to my source, Agent Milner's body has been taken from the embassy."

"What?"

"That's what I said. CIA came in to the embassy and claimed the body, which they claim they're taking back to the U.S."

"On whose orders?"

"My contact says that the CIA did it on Army CID's behalf."

"Where the hell are you getting all this?"

"Sources."

"Don't give me that shit, Morgan. Who?"

"I can't burn them, Chief. But, I need you to follow up on this immediately. Who authorized Milner's body to be removed from the morgue and where is the body?"

"Are you sure about this?"

"I would not raise this kind of a stink over just a rumor."

Thompson was quiet for a long moment, then said, "Alright, I'll look into this right now."

"Good. I'll get back with you shortly and see what you turn up."

Morgan ended the call and walked over to the elevator from the lobby. As he waited, he again scanned the room in an attempt to find faces that looked familiar. He still had yet to catch anyone spending too much attention on him or being in the lobby just a little too often. It was either a sign that no one was watching him or that the people who were watching him were highly skilled.

The elevator arrived and Morgan headed into the open doors. As he did, though, he thought that for the briefest of moments, a local businessman in a simple grey suit was watching him just a little too closely. As the doors closed, Morgan made a mental note to remember the man and see if he was there tomorrow.

Chapter Twenty-Nine

Washington D.C.

Col. Kzaltry stalked through the Pentagon towards the inner ring of offices, known as the 'E' ring. These offices, located deep within the massive building, represented the highest levels of power within the military. Kzaltry could feel the atmosphere shift as he entered the rows of doors in this section, headed towards an appointment with Col. Franklin.

As a member of Defense Intelligence, Kzaltry could command a meeting with almost anyone throughout the Army, even someone as highly placed as Franklin. Thus, it had been easy for him to schedule the meeting with Franklin, though he had been forced to lie to Franklin's secretary that the meeting was about coordinating surveillance efforts in high-profile cases.

Kzaltry arrived at the offices of the Provost General. The office secretary greeted Kzaltry with military formality and then escorted Kzaltry into Col. Franklin's office.

Franklin was drinking coffee and working on a government-issued desktop computer. Franklin turned to face Kzaltry as he entered the room, then returned the crisp salute of his fellow officer. "Take a seat, Colonel. Coffee, tea?"

"No. Thank you, Colonel."

Franklin waved his secretary out of the room, who closed the door behind him.

"So," said Franklin, "what can I do to help DIA?"

"A complicated matter."

"Aren't they all?"

"Yes. I apologize, but I think I'm going to catch you off-guard. I'm not here to talk about coordination of evidence collection in high-profile cases."

Franklin said nothing, but a grimace covered his lips.

"I've heard through channels," said Kzaltry, trying to keep

momentum, "that CID is investigating a rather strange situation in Afghanistan."

"I'm afraid I wouldn't be able to confirm or deny any details about ongoing investigations, Colonel."

"I was afraid of that."

The two men sat quietly for a few moments, eyeing each other.

Finally, Franklin asked, "Is that all, Colonel?"

Kzaltry leaned forward in his chair. "Let me paint a picture. If there was a rumor that retired Army Special Forces were moving drugs out of Afghanistan and CID was aware of it, what would CID do with that information?"

Franklin looked at Colonel Kzaltry for a long time, then said, "Well, if that was true, we would start an investigation, to be sure. Do you know anything about such a crime being committed?"

"In the case I just described, what would CID's jurisdiction be?"

"CID has the authority to investigate any matter that impacts the Army. In the scenario you just described, the crime is being committed in an Army theatre of operations, likely involving Army resources."

"Why not hand the matter over to the locals?"

"Have you ever met the Afghan police? 'Rag Tag' would be a compliment."

"Yes, I can see your point there. But, I wonder, though, would CID handle the matter quietly or risk embarrassment to the Special Forces if such a rumor turned out to be true?"

"Nothing is quiet in D.C."

"CID keeps things quiet all the time. I've seen many investigations ..."

"Every case is unique. We would handle it in the manner we deemed best."

Kzaltry nodded. "I'm worried that you're not telling me the truth, Colonel. I have it on good authority that just such a case exists. I doubt you've been left out of the loop."

Franklin stood and said, "I think that ends our meeting, Colonel."

"Sit down, Franklin."

Franklin glared at Kzaltry. "You have no authority and I will also point out that you lack the rank to …"

"I'm DIA, Colonel, so we both know that none of that crap applies." Kzaltry waited a moment to be sure that he had Franklin's attention, then said, "I have a friend at the German Embassy who mentioned that you were directly informed of American troops running drugs out of Afghanistan. What did you do after receiving that information? Oh, and please keep in mind that you can answer my questions now or reap a shit storm in public. Colonel."

Franklin continued to stand, his hand gripping the back of the chair, eyes burning red with anger. "We deemed it to be bad intelligence."

"That doesn't sound right. I have it on good authority that not only have you sent a CID Special Agent named Morgan Huntley out to look for Americans running drugs back to the U.S. from Afghanistan, but that you've lost another agent already in the process. How am I doing?"

"How did you get that information?"

"I want to know what you're up to in Afghanistan."

Franklin cracked a devious smile. "You're grasping at straws, Colonel. Now, if that is all, I have a lot to do."

Colonel Kzaltry didn't move. Instead, he pulled an iPad from his briefcase and opened it, then turned it around for Franklin to see.

"Recognize that man?" asked Kzaltry.

Franklin leaned over to inspect the iPad, which displayed a picture of Franklin in a passionate embrace of his mistress. Kzaltry scrolled through the pictures, each one more graphic than the last.

"That is not your wife, I might point out," said Kzaltry.

"Shit."

"Yes. Shit, indeed. It seems you have compromised your security clearance. Among other problems."

Franklin shook his head and stared hard at Kzaltry. "You guys in DIA are dirty bastards."

"The way I see it, I've got a blank check to ask whatever questions I need answered. Agreed?"

Franklin's face was bright red with fury, but he nodded slightly.

Kzaltry put the iPad back in his briefcase. "I'm not here to make your life difficult, you understand? DIA has been worried about you ever since you got a little too close to the CIA in Iraq. We heard from the Germans that you responded to an inquiry: that there was nothing to a rumor of American personnel sending back drugs to the U.S. Yet, now you've got agents in the Afghan AO investigating that very matter. I need you to come clean with me so I can report back to DIA on your intentions."

Franklin managed to keep his voice under control. "What do you want?"

"Colonel, I want answers to my questions. Nothing more."

"What are the questions?"

"Is CID investigating a drug ring in Afghanistan?"

"Yes."

"Do you suspect retired Army Special Forces?"

"We don't suspect. We know."

"The investigation is that far progressed?"

"No. Our investigation is still ongoing, but other assets in the region have confirmed it."

"What are you planning on doing with this information? Are arrests forthcoming?"

"No. We're going to shut down these bastards."

"How?"

"Using our friends in the CIA, I'm sorry to say. The matter is too delicate for us to handle through the Army."

"What about your agents?"

"What agents?"

"Morgan Huntley. Why a risky undercover operation on the ground there after you already lost Jason Milner?"

"I want to know how you got those names."

"Answer the question."

Franklin leaned on the back of the chair. "We have our own dirty laundry to attend to. Huntley's mission is to not come back. Understand?"

Chapter Thirty

It was just after seven at night in Kabul and the crowd in the lobby of the Intercontinental was at its peak. Morgan coasted through towards the secluded payphones. Once certain that he was alone, he used his calling card to call Ben Ferguson's cell phone.

"Ferguson."

"This is Huntley. You got a minute?"

"I'm just about to eat a cheeseburger, but, yeah, go ahead."

Just hearing the word 'cheeseburger' made Morgan's stomach growl with hope. "What have you got on your end?"

"No progress, that's for damn sure. If there is an agent assigned to that case, I can't find it. But, I have found one interesting thing. Someone tried pulling your records."

"Oh? Who?"

"A Freedom of Information Act request. It was denied."

"Who signed it?"

"Someone with an 'All-American' name that claimed to work for University of Wisconsin. It was a bullshit name. We don't really know who it was."

"That's not good news. Any clues on who it might have been?"

"None."

"Right. Any way we can follow-up more on that angle?"

"Government and military are barred from investigating citizens for a FOIA request."

"Alright. Thanks for the heads-up. Anything else on your end?"

"Nothing here. What about you?"

"I need background on someone's service record."

"Alright, who we got?"

Morgan gave him the names of Greg Baker and Andrew

Carlisle, as well as what he suspected would have been their years of service based on their age.

After a few minutes of searching, Ferguson said, "I got nothing here that matches. You sure you got that information right?"

"I do. Anything in the other services?"

"Just checked. Nothing. What's this about, Morgan?"

"Sorry, Top Secret."

"You sure you don't need to get it off your chest? My girlfriend says I'm a good listener."

"Thanks, Ferguson. I'll check back with you soon."

"No problem."

Morgan ended the call and then once more picked up the receiver.

On the other side of the world, Bill Kzaltry's phone rang, but the voicemail system picked up. "Bill, this is Huntley. I wanted to know if you've made any progress regarding the matter we discussed. I will call back in 48 hours."

Morgan pressed the cradle and then dialed a third time.

"Thompson."

"This is your old friend."

"Old friends bore me. You especially."

"What have you got on Jason?"

"Nothing to worry about."

"I doubt that, but go on."

"Turns out you've got a bad source there on your end. Jason's body is still at the U.S. Embassy in Kabul and will be undergoing an autopsy later today."

"Who told you that?"

"I went all the way to the top on this, Morgan."

"Who at the top told you that?"

"Franklin himself checked on this. I have it direct from his office that they are certain that Jason's body is still at the U.S. Embassy."

"That's bullshit. Who gave him that information?"

"I'm not going to dignify that with a response, Morgan. I'm not sure where you got this rumor that Jason had been taken from Kabul, but rest assured that he is in the embassy."

"I need to know who the source is so I can verify."

"You're not getting that information, Morgan. We need to keep our assets in silos. Unless, that is, you want to tell me who YOUR source is there at the U.S. Embassy?"

"Listen, Chief, this thing is already bad enough. I don't need you playing games with me on the other end."

"This isn't a game, Morgan. We have to keep you under tight wraps. That means no information is to be shared that could allow you to compromise your cover."

Morgan had the phone in a death grip and took a deep breath before continuing. Thompson was smart, but he wasn't devious or crafty. He wouldn't make up a lie about Jason's body. That meant Thompson was at least willing to peddle lies on behalf of someone with ties to the CIA.

Morgan said, "Okay, Chief. When can you get me a copy of the autopsy?"

"I won't be able to do that."

"Why not? Did the CIA throw the body into the Atlantic on the way to Dover?"

"The body is at the U.S. Embassy in Kabul. You can't have a copy of the autopsy, because you're undercover and U.S. civilians wouldn't have a copy of a CID autopsy report in their possession, that's why."

"Procedure says …"

"I don't give a fuck about procedure, Huntley."

Morgan kept his cool and gave Thompson a moment to breathe. "So," Morgan said, trying to act casual, "how am I supposed to get the key findings from the autopsy into my hands?"

"I'll let you know what you need to know."

"If you get a copy of the autopsy."

"Once I get a copy."

"You're not going to get a copy, Chief."

"Why is that?"

Morgan could hear Thompson's anger rising again, so Morgan decided that the conversation had gone on long enough. "I've got to go. I'll check in again later."

He could hear Thompson starting to say something, but Morgan hung up the receiver before the words came through the phone.

For a long time, Morgan stood in the phone booth, his mind running through the various possible meanings of Thompson's lies. Then, Morgan decided to make one more call. But for this call, he only needed his smartphone.

Within a few moments, Morgan heard Greg Baker answer, "Morgan. How the hell are you?"

"How did you know it was me?"

"I've already got you saved in my contacts. Actually, I was just about to call you."

"Sure you were."

"No, really. I wanted to know if you wanted to get together to talk some shop."

"Funny, I was going to call you for the same thing."

"Great. What are you up to tomorrow?"

"I'm free most of the day."

"Good. Have you ever been to Babur's Gardens?"

"Can't say that I have?"

"There's a pavilion in the center of the garden. Tomorrow at ten?"

"Sure, no problem. I'll see you there."

Chapter Thirty-One

Morgan arrived at Babur's Gardens just after 9:30 a.m. and followed a simple sign towards the center pavilion. The gardens had been restored recently and were possibly the cleanest place that Morgan had seen in the city. There were terraced pathways and well-manicured spaces that weaved through four square segments of gardens that made up the park.

Morgan was early to the pavilion. He found that Greg Baker and Andrew Carlisle were already waiting for him.

"I see that you were eager to get here, huh?" asked Greg.

"You too."

"Why not? It's the best place in the city."

"I was wondering why you wanted to meet here instead of your office?"

"Isn't it nice to be out in a clean, open space filled with grass?"

Morgan nodded.

"Any news on the payment for our friends at the village?" asked Greg.

"I have approval to deliver a check to them this week."

"Need help delivering it?"

Morgan looked at both men. "Depends on your schedule, I guess."

Greg shrugged, then looked at Andrew, who raised his eyebrows in anticipation. "The problem with this country is that there are no secrets here. That's the other reason we wanted to meet here, outside of the office and with a little privacy."

"Privacy?"

"Indeed. Word gets around. And word about the deals that YOU can make has already gotten around. Other people in town want to jump in bed with you."

"Why is that?"

"Morgan, people in this country would kill to have your calling card: money for drugs. It's a good loss-leader, as they say.

We don't want to lose the edge on your services."

"What do you propose we do about that?"

"We want to be your exclusive partner."

"I thought you were in the business of building schools."

"We think there is a great opportunity for us to provide ongoing assistance with transportation, security and translation. What we get from being there alongside of you is access. That is all."

"Seems odd to me, Greg. Why are you so interested in escorting me around to make deals on opium? It's not a very scholarly practice."

Greg gave Morgan a coy smile. "You have to make strange friends in Afghanistan to get ahead."

Morgan waited for Greg to continue.

Greg smiled again and then said, sheepishly, "We may have told you a white lie about we do."

"You don't have a contract to build schools?"

Andrew chuckled. "Not exactly," he said.

Greg nodded at Andrew's comment, then said, "We are actually in a more neutral position, you might say. We handle a very delicate operation in the countryside. The kind of business that would benefit from a better logistics supplier. One with access to the kind of deals you're making."

Morgan sensed his heart beating rapidly in his chest. What had once been the hypothetically extreme had materialized in front of his face. Trying to remain calm, he said, "I'm not sure a contract with your company would meet the stringent requirements of my employer. There are strict rules about who we buy our products from."

"There are ways around such complications."

Morgan pretended to review the detailing on the sides of the pavilion, buying time. Then he said, "What's in it for me?"

"Doesn't doing business feel nice?"

Morgan shrugged.

"Maybe this conversation would be better served at our operations out in the field," said Greg. "That way, we can give you a more accurate sense of the scope of our business."

Morgan eyed Greg warily. "That sounds fine."

"How does tomorrow work for you?"

"I'm relatively free."

"Good. No need to pack anything. We'll be returning by evening. As long as it works for you, we'll pick you up at The Brydon tomorrow morning."

Morgan nodded. "I'll see you there."

Morgan strode off towards the entrance to catch a cab, hoping to move as quickly as possible before the swirling cloud of adrenalin in his body caused him to make an unfocused mistake.

* * *

Morgan returned to the GenetiGreen offices and spent the rest of the day searching the internet for information on Greg Baker and Andrew Carlisle. His efforts came up empty, which in many ways confirmed his suspicions that he was indeed being approached by the drug cartel itself. Whether they knew who he really was or that he was really here to meet with them he could only hope was still a secret.

Morgan had also come back to the office in the hope that he would encounter James Poole to ask him a few subtle questions about the final destination of Jason's body. Unfortunately, Morgan learned that James had scheduled himself to be out for the rest of the day, so Morgan would have to wait until he returned from his visit with Greg and Andrew to follow on that line of inquiry.

Somewhere towards the end of the day, Morgan found his mind wandering. And his hand reached for his smartphone. Within a moment, he had dialed the number for Victoria Solano's office.

"This is Miss Solano."

"It's Morgan."

"Hi. I'm glad you called."

"Why is that?"

"Oh, just worried."

"Thanks. You free for dinner tonight? I owe you after your help."

"Shoot. No, I have appointments all evening."

"Too bad. Maybe day after tomorrow?"

"That sounds good. I'm still a little shaken up by what's been going on."

"Why is that?"

"It's a little unusual by my daily standards to have spies and dead friends rolling through my office."

"It will be okay."

Morgan wasn't entirely sure where the conversation was headed and was trying to think of a way to say goodbye, but his mind kept drawing a blank. Victoria asked, "What are you up to tomorrow?"

"Depends who is asking."

"Don't play games."

Morgan was quiet as his mind began to click through a thousand thoughts, all of them too big to process while still on the phone. He realized the silence was becoming awkward, so he said, "I have business out in the countryside during the day. I should be back by evening."

"Will you call when you get back?"

Morgan's brain was two steps behind his mouth as he said, "Yes, I'll call."

He could hear Victoria smile through the phone as she said, "Great. I won't keep you anymore. Call me tomorrow."

"Okay," said Morgan. The call ended moments later on a series of polite goodbyes, but Morgan continued to stare at his phone for a long time after the call was over.

As he headed out of the office to catch a cab, his mind was busy. Not with tomorrow's meeting with Greg Baker. Instead, he was trying to figure out what the hell had just happened on the phone with Victoria Solano.

Chapter Thirty-Two

South of Jalalabad, Afghanistan

Greg Baker turned the up-armored Suburban off the highway from Kabul to Jalalabad onto a dirt road that seemed well-traveled. Alone in the back seat, Morgan casually felt inside his jacket for his sidearm and spare ammunition clips. The sensation of their heavy weight against his hand calmed his nerves, as he watched the on-rushing expanse of the Afghan desert.

Greg Baker turned around in his seat for a moment and said, "I apologize, but the local paving leaves something to be desired by American standards."

"I've noticed."

"When you think about it," continued Greg, "it's just a different perspective on the matter of pavement. What have roads ever brought to the Afghans other than invaders? Why build a pathway by which a foreign army might more quickly control your country?"

"We've done alright in America with the best road system money can buy."

"True, but our roads also allow the government to control us effectively. There is no portion of the country that is out of reach of the long arm of the U.S. government."

Morgan said nothing.

"I don't want to sound anti-government. It's just that, roads are a double-edged sword. They take you where you want to go. They also allow quick access to those who wish to control you. I respect the Afghans for seeing that roads are just a means to their own destruction. They're a proud and strong people. Unconquerable, if you ask me."

"Someone should have told our government that bit of advice a lot sooner."

"The U.S. could have won here if they had focused less on

bases and more on roads. Bases are the tools of conquerors, not liberators."

"All that aside, I'm sure most Afghans weren't fans of the Taliban."

Greg shrugged. "Once the U.S. leaves, the Taliban will be back in charge of this country within a year. They might not be what every Afghan wants as a ruling party, but the Taliban also represents something of Afghanistan. They did not rise up in a vacuum. They are not aliens from another planet who descended on Afghanistan. Whether we want to accept it or not, there are enough Afghans who agree with the Taliban in this country that they will probably have a clear path back to power when the U.S. leaves. The only way to have changed that would have been genocide, which – thankfully – I don't believe the U.S. has the stomach for pursuing."

Morgan let the conversation drop as he looked out the front window. In the distance ahead, he saw a checkpoint approaching. Greg didn't slow down. In fact, as he approached the checkpoint, the men manning it, who looked better armed than the usual *Arbakai*, stood to the side and allowed Greg's SUV to roar past without stopping.

"They must know you pretty well," said Morgan. "Or are you trailing a crate of one hundred dollar bills?"

Andrew said, "We're the boss."

"They work for you?"

"You are now on company property," said Greg.

"Company? What's the name of your company?"

"Oh, it's a little less formal than that."

"What does your business do, exactly? I still don't seem clear on that."

Greg said, "I'll explain in due time. For now, just enjoy our corporate holdings, which are passing outside of your window."

Morgan looked out of his window. In the distance he could see fields filled with the distinctive forms of poppy plants. He said,

"I take it those aren't wheat fields?"

Andrew smiled and said, "No, sir, they are not. The U.S. DEA was through here just a few years ago, trying to get the locals to plant wheat, as well as some modified corn and barley. A whole parade of agricultural contractors, advisors and scientists have been all over this area trying to get the locals to plant food crops."

"Let me guess. No big successes, right?"

Greg said, "People forget that it took the Europeans a couple hundred years to figure out how to grow tomatoes and corn effectively when the seeds were brought back from the New World. We're asking the Afghans to learn how to cultivate unfamiliar crops in less than a decade. Meanwhile, they are starving when these foreign crops die in the uniquely pitiful Afghan soil."

"They go back to growing opium in a year, sometimes less," said Andrew.

"Ninety percent of the world's opium is grown here in Afghanistan, did you know that?" asked Greg, not waiting for an answer. "It's the backbone of the country's economy. Farmers grow it. Harvesters pick it. Manufacturers produce drugs. Distributors sell it. Money flows. Food is bought from other countries. It's an entire economy, little different from our own country."

"You learn that in business school?" asked Morgan.

"Just facts, that's all."

Ahead, a squat village was coming into view. Greg slowed the Suburban and pulled towards the side of the road.

"Pit stop?" asked Morgan.

"More like a point of interest on the guided tour," said Greg. "I think there's something you ought to know."

"What's that?"

"My name's not really Greg Baker. And this isn't Andrew Carlisle."

* * *

John Vitters parked the Suburban on the side of the road. He turned back to face Morgan.

"We also know a few things about you."

Morgan looked at David Freer, who was now holding a Sig .45 pistol in his lap. He eyed Morgan cautiously.

"What's the gun for?" asked Morgan.

"Just a precaution," said Freer.

"I thought we were getting along just fine."

Vitters smiled, looking at David Freer. "See, I told you he was a cool customer. These CID boys always are."

Morgan winced with disappointment. Vitters held up a hand.

"It's okay, Morgan. We know you're CID. There is no need to get yourself riled up, though. I've only brought you here to make you a business proposition. But, before I let you look under our dress, I want to give you one last chance to back out. If you're the kind of guy who has a conscience that would get him killed, the kind of person that would make a mistake in a tense situation, then maybe it would be best if we just sent you up the road to Jalalabad and let you find your own way back to Kabul."

Morgan said nothing.

"If, on the other hand, you are willing to consider our sales pitch, then I am willing to provide information in exchange. We know who killed your fellow CID agent. And we know why. At least hear my offer and decide for yourself. I can assure you that I will have you back in Kabul safely, whether you agree to do business with us or not."

Morgan once again said nothing.

Vitters looked at Freer. "Scout's honor, right?" Freer nodded in agreement. They both looked back at Morgan, waiting for an answer.

Morgan said, "I've come this far. I'd like to hear what you have to say."

"Good," said Vitters. "I am Captain John Vitters, U.S. Army Special Forces, Retired. And this is one of my three business partners, Staff Sergeant David Freer, U.S. Army Special Forces, Retired."

Vitters turned back into the driver's seat and put the Suburban in gear.

Freer did not turn back towards the front windshield, instead remaining focused on Morgan, the gun held calmly at the ready.

They traveled the last ten minutes to the village in silence.

Chapter Thirty-Three

As the Suburban pulled into the center of the village, Morgan saw a series of low, mud walls running in each direction, forming a grid. Behind these walls were fields lush with poppy plants, growing tall and steady in the hot Afghan sun.

Waiting in front of a large hut were two men in their mid-thirties, dressed in jeans, T-shirts and baseball caps. Neither of the men were local Afghans.

Vitters parked the Suburban and signaled with his hand for Morgan to exit the SUV.

As Morgan stepped into the dust-covered track that ran through the village, the two men in front of the hut strode towards the Suburban, seemingly at ease with the entire situation.

Vitters gestured towards the older, white man with stubble and said, "This is Warrant Officer Ethan Griggs, U.S. Army Special Forces, Retired."

Morgan shook hands with Ethan Griggs.

"And this is Captain Alexi Farrat, U.S. Army Special Forces, Retired."

Again, Morgan shook hands with the man.

Vitters looked at Morgan and said, "I'm sure you have a lot of questions. But, if you will indulge me, I'd first like to give you a tour of our operations. I think it would help you to understand the big picture."

"Lead the way."

Vitters gently put a hand on Morgan's shoulder and led him towards the closest poppy field. The other three men fell into step behind Morgan and Vitters. In another world, they could have been middle-managers following a senior executive through a manufacturing facility.

They passed through an archway in the mud wall, which led into the poppy field. Here, men of all ages were tending to the field: pulling weeds, checking plants and performing other agrarian tasks that Morgan didn't immediately recognize.

"When my business partners and I decided to return to Afghanistan in order to start this venture," said Vitters, "we chose this district, just south of Jalalabad for two reasons. It was productive, but not so much as to be highly desired. The other reason we picked it was because this region was at the time no longer under Taliban control, but rather under the iron grip of a local warlord."

"Was he a warlord or just the leader of this village?" Morgan asked, hoping the intention of his question wouldn't be lost on Vitters.

Whether Vitters recognized Morgan's slight or not, he continued unfazed. "Political systems in Afghanistan are much more complex than most people in the West give them credit for. The concept of the 'warlord' in Afghan tribal dynamics is more akin to how we would regard a strong community leader in our country. A person who leads a tribe or group of tribes through the gravitas of their character and measured by the might of the forces who follow."

"So you showed up and this local warlord was so impressed by your presence that he just handed over his villages? I doubt that."

"True. We had to lean on the one marketable asset we had: our experience in guerilla warfare."

"Then you took it upon yourself to drive out this warlord by force? What if the locals preferred him over you? It's not very democratic, you know."

Vitters smiled, ignoring Morgan's verbal jabs. "Warlords rise to power, they're not chosen. Some – not all, but some – are beloved by their people. The warlord who was in charge of this village was exceptionally ruthless. He took everything this village produced and gave back little to the villagers. He stole wives and enslaved children. To put it bluntly, he was a major asshole."

"And the thankful townspeople rewarded you by making you town sheriff?"

"Funny," said Vitters, "but no. We knew many of the village elders in this area from our rotations through here. We made them a business offer. They accepted."

"A business offer?"

"We provide protection to the village and arrange the sale of their products in return for a percentage of the sales. It's a business relationship. Nothing more."

"We have a word for that back in reality. It's called extortion."

Vitters shook his head. "The village chooses to grow poppies, because it is the most profitable business they can engage in. We protect their operation and ensure they receive the best market price for their goods. The added gross profit that we secure for them through negotiating better sales prices means that – even after our cut – they're making more per kilo of opium than ever before. It's what they call 'win-win' in the business world."

"So, what you mean to say is, it's not extortion. It's a protection racket."

"No. The villagers are free to govern themselves or to end our business deal at any time. We will walk away if they ask us to. Though, I doubt they would ask."

"Why is that?"

"We offer superior service. We take only our cut and nothing more. We do not steal their women. We do not enslave their children. We do not meddle in their politics. We only provide a business-to-business relationship that improves their lives."

Morgan looked into the distance at the men patrolling the village. He noticed several boys among them.

"If they are free to do as they wish, why the armed guards? Seems more like a prison camp."

"Part of our cut covers a 'services fee'. That fee goes to pay for security. The men you see are our employees, you might say.

They're paid to guard the village, unlike in the days of the warlords, when they worked for free or faced execution."

Morgan looked around. "And you're turning a profit on this, I assume?"

"We're happy with the returns, yes."

"If the villagers told you to hit the road tomorrow, why would you willingly leave if you're making such good money?"

"Our business model has been incredibly successful. We started here in this village, which is essentially our headquarters. Since then, we invite other village elders to come visit and see how it all works. They speak with the men and women who live here. The response is always incredible. We now have ten villages as part of our network. If one village wants out, we can just pick up shop and move to another."

Morgan found himself stunned by the scale of Vitters' operation. He said, "How do you control such a large swath of territory?"

Vitters pointed to his men. "My trusted business partners make daily calls to each of our franchises. We see each village three times in a week. The seventh day, of course, being off on a rotating basis among us. At each village, our trained security forces man the perimeter and keep the village safe."

Morgan scoffed. "What about other warlords or the Taliban? Certainly they haven't taken this development very well?"

Vitters smiled. "Oh, you're right about that. The problem for them is, we're highly trained and experienced Green Berets. We know a thing or two about mounting retaliation strikes. There have been tests. We haven't had too many repeat visitors."

Morgan looked out among the villagers, absorbing the scene before him.

Vitters stood by, letting Morgan take it all in.

Chapter Thirty-Four

Morgan followed Vitters into a hut in the center of the village. By comparison to the other huts, it was by far the largest in the village.

Inside was a pile of what looked like faded, ragged tennis balls. Morgan knew from a briefing prior to leaving for Afghanistan that these were the heads of the poppy plant.

Vitters pointed at the pile and said, "These were some early blooms that have been harvested. They are small compared to the harvest we'll take later this year, but some plants inevitably get damaged and we take what we can from them before they die."

Vitters grabbed a strange tool that looked like a cross between a three-pronged knife and a lemon zester. He scratched the surface of a poppy head. Within moments, a black ooze, similar to rubber, leaked from the cut edges of the bloom.

"That," said Vitters, pointing at the ooze. "That is our black gold. Raw opium. Ready to be made into a variety of products on the world market. Morphine. Codeine."

"And heroin," said Morgan.

"As with most drugs, it started with good intentions. Doctors trying to find a better way of delivering pain relief realized that heroin was very powerful. The human body converts heroin into strong, uncontrolled doses of morphine. It's this uncontrolled conversion that makes heroin so dangerous. The medical community soon realized it was incredibly addictive, as well."

"How much of the stuff do you personally use?"

"Heroin is a dangerous product and extended use can be hazardous to one's health. We all agreed to forgo such pleasures in the pursuit of this business venture."

"I hope you notice the irony in making a product that you yourself wouldn't use."

"I'm sure that the people who work in a Twinkie factory don't eat Twinkies, either, after they see what is used to make one.

Those things will kill you."

"Not quite the same, but I see your point."

Vitters led Morgan forward to a series of large stone slabs. Above each slab, a chimney led through an opening in the roof.

"This is the heart of the operation," said Vitters. "Here the raw opium gum is converted into heroin. We dilute the gum into water and boil it, which creates unprocessed morphine when strained. Then we introduce a series of chemicals. Magic happens and we get pure heroin."

"You do all that here?"

"Most villages ship out their raw opium gum to be made into heroin by either the Taliban, a warlord or a few independent operations in Afghanistan that operate similar to a drug cartel. By controlling this step in the process, we make our margins significantly better."

"How do you get the heroin out of the country?"

Vitters smiled. "Well," he said, "that has been the biggest problem for us. We're working on some new solutions that might alleviate that problem by the next harvest."

"I'm not going to help you move this shit. You know that, right?"

The men all laughed. Vitters put a hand on Morgan's shoulder. "No, I didn't expect you would. It's not why I brought you here today. We have other plans developing for moving our product out of the country."

"I'm confused. How is it you think I can help you?"

"We have a different proposal for you. First, let's have some lunch."

* * *

Morgan and Vitters sat on the carpeted floor of a hut that appeared to be a sort of office or command post for the operation. There were a variety of maps, materials and communications equipment, much of which had been covered to keep them from Morgan's view.

It was now just Morgan and Vitters. The others had departed their company when Morgan and Vitters had entered the hut.

Lunch, it turned out, was a very simple dish of Afghan rice with cooked meat, nuts and dried fruits. Vitters ate with gusto. Morgan ate more slowly, wanting to remain alert.

"Is food part of the deal, too?" asked Morgan.

"Yes, it is part of our contract with this village. When given adequate provisions, the local women here are excellent cooks. Afghan food is, in my opinion, one of the more unrecognized cuisines of the world. Afghanistan shares borders with India, China and the Middle East: it should be no surprise that those three culinary traditions would marry well."

Morgan felt impatience creeping in on him and took a deep breath to maintain his temper. He said, "I would love to hear your proposal and be on my way."

Vitters nodded politely, put down his plate and wiped his face with a cloth he had at hand. "Do you remember the warlord I mentioned earlier?"

Morgan nodded.

"He was not the only one who had an interest in controlling of this region."

"The Taliban?"

"No. Other interests. American interests."

Vitters stood and walked over to a table. He pulled out a large, digital photo camera, which he handed to Morgan.

Morgan looked at the display. It showed an obese Afghan man, standing on the edge of a village in broad daylight. He was surrounded by a group of armed Afghans who appeared very much like the *Arbakai* that Morgan had seen throughout the country.

"Do you see the photo of the man on the phone?" asked Vitters.

"Yes."

"That is the warlord we deposed. Alil Katmed. Scroll through the photos until you get to the one of Alil shaking hands."

Morgan forwarded through the photos, each focused on Alil. Then an SUV came into the photos. Then two men who were obviously Westerners, wearing civilian clothing. Alil shook hands with one of the men. Morgan stopped and held up the photo for Vitters to see, who nodded.

"Those men that Alil is greeting," said Vitters, "are with the CIA."

Morgan regarded the photo for some time, then said, "So? I'm sure the CIA met with lots of warlords throughout the country."

Vitters reached over and grabbed a piece of fruit from a plate, which he popped into his mouth. "The CIA exists in a strange netherworld. They are a secret organization in a country founded on governmental transparency. On one hand, we Americans have a desire to have a powerful intelligence agency capable of spy craft of the highest order. On the other hand, we have a compelling belief that every organization – even the CIA – should have civilian oversight. The problem is not that we want oversight of the CIA. The problem is that the CIA realized early on that it didn't want to be overseen."

Vitters looked to Morgan to see if he was following. Morgan said nothing and Vitters continued. "The lifeblood of bureaucratic departments is money. Oversight is how our government controls that lifeblood. Therefore, if you want to avoid oversight, it stands to reason that you need free access to money. With uncontrolled money comes uncontrolled freedom. The CIA developed a solution to this problem that maybe you've heard of?"

"Right. Shell companies, private planes, shadow corporations. I've heard all this."

"That's right. The CIA has a vast network of businesses – some even legitimate – that give it a war chest bigger than most countries' national budgets. All of it in the dark and covered in a shroud marked 'national security'."

Morgan shrugged. "I guess at a certain level, it would make sense for the CIA to have their own money. You wouldn't want them using tax dollars to buy hookers for the president of Bolivia."

Vitters shook his head. "If it were that simple, I think we could agree that it was merely the cost of doing business. Unfortunately, one of the tenets of good spy-craft is that the left hand should never know what the right hand is doing. In order to facilitate that, the CIA is not so much a unified organization led by the head of the CIA, but rather a series of independent cells that exist within vacuums. Most are well-known and under complete control by the CIA. Others are more loosely controlled, effectively creating a layer of distance for purposes of establishing plausible deniability when their actions are extra-legal."

Vitters looked at Morgan again to make sure he was following along. Morgan realized to his own surprise that he was indeed fully engaged with what Vitters was saying. Vitters had that sort of magnetic quality that enraptured people in daily life.

Seeing that he had the attention of his audience, Vitters continued. "The portions of the CIA that run the various shadow corporations and laundering enterprises are the most uncontrolled aspect of the whole agency. No one knows which person or group at the CIA is responsible for the accounts. It might be that no single person is in charge of it. The teams that run the CIA's businesses are the oldest ongoing parts of the organization and the best connected. They operate on their own, making decisions and running their operations as they see fit. This has led to some questionable business decisions, but since there is no oversight to speak of, their brazen disregard for international law has grown in scale over the years."

"What are you talking about?"

"The CIA is heavily involved in the drug trade. And I don't

mean in stopping it. I mean they are actively running a profitable drug ring, a habit they picked up in the Vietnam era. The CIA is making money faster than they can count it by pumping drugs around the world."

Morgan looked at Vitters, a bit incredulously. "How do you know all this? It's not like you had insider access to the CIA."

"Ah, but we did. When the war in Afghanistan started, the CIA was all over this country. There was going to be a power vacuum in Afghanistan as the U.S. pushed out the Taliban. Afghanistan, coincidentally, produces almost ninety percent of the world's opium. As we pushed the Taliban out of power, someone was going to gain control over the largest heroin supply in the world. The CIA moved fast to make sure they got a big piece of that pie. You know how they did it?"

Morgan shook his head.

"Access to the world's most powerful military."

Morgan had heard rumors of this type while in Iraq. He said, "I always thought that was just bullshit bored grunts told each other to keep things interesting. You have proof that there is something to it?"

"Securing the poppies was priority number one for the CIA. American Special Forces were grafted into that project on the auspices of denying the Taliban any access to the flow of money from the drugs. In reality, U.S. Special Forces were being co-opted by the CIA to take control of the world's supply of heroin. Me and my men – and several other units that I know of – were tasked with securing the opium fields. When a series of local warlords wouldn't cooperate with the CIA, we took them out on orders from CENTCOM. That was, of course, in addition to pushing the Taliban out of the drug trade all together."

Morgan looked at the photo on the camera, buying time as he considered Vitters' words.

Vitters pointed at the image of Alil on the camera display. "Alil was one of the CIA's most reliable strongmen. My unit and

I were tasked with keeping him in power. We rotated through this area under the operational illusion that we were here to secure the Pakistan-Afghan border against uncontrolled incursions. What we were really doing was training locals who were then forced into serving Alil. We were effectively ordered to prop up a local dictator who raped twelve-year-old girls in a society that would then kill those girls for being raped."

Vitters had grown angry, his voice gaining in intensity. Morgan said nothing.

Vitters took a breath, then said, "When we drove out Alil from this region, it wasn't just a business decision. It was about freeing these people from a tyrant. From the yoke of the CIA, which was using these people as a personal agricultural-collective to grow drugs, filter them through Alil and reap the profits for their global network of money laundering."

"If what you say is right, then certainly the CIA didn't take it well when you ousted Alil? They wouldn't just respond with a strongly worded memo."

"No memo. Instead, they tried sending other warlords. They even tried a raid using Pakistani Special Forces. We beat them all back with ease."

"Why not send the Army or the Marines in after you?"

"Times have changed here in Afghanistan and in the halls of CENTCOM in the later years of the war. The watch word in the military chain under McChrystal is to maintain the economic livelihood of the Afghans, even if they are making a living selling drugs. The days of burning the poppy fields are long gone."

Morgan said, "So, you took the CIA's cake and there was nothing they could do about it? No offense, but what you've taken is probably just a minor fraction of their entire holdings. They'll eventually forget about you."

Vitters gently took back the camera.

A woman came into the room with tea for both men. They watched quietly as she put the tea down on the floor. Vitters poured for both men while the woman cleared the dirty dishes. As she left, Vitters handed Morgan a cup of tea.

Vitters then said to Morgan, "Have you asked yourself why the Army has sent you here?"

"I know why I'm here. To find you."

Vitters nodded. "That is what I was afraid you were going to say."

Chapter Thirty-Five

Vitters drank his tea for a long moment in silence. He then stood and walked towards the door.

"It's stuffy in here. Take a walk with me?" asked Vitters.

Morgan felt comfortable enough due to the relaxed state of affairs to join Vitters in the doorway. Nobody had yet frisked Morgan or disarmed him. Morgan wondered if it was bravado that had led them to leave him with his gun or that their intentions for him were truly benign. In either case, Morgan found himself being led from the hut by Vitters and back into the sun of the early afternoon.

As they walked out of the hut, Morgan noticed that Griggs was standing outside with a watchful eye on them. Griggs gave a questioning look to Vitters, who raised his hand in an appreciative wave to indicate that everything was under control.

Vitters led Morgan down the dirt track towards the south end of the village, where they had a clear view of a small mountain chain that sat a short distance away.

"I have given you a lot of information about what we're doing here and our history," said Vitters. "Information that very much exposes us, considering our line of work. I wonder if you might feel compelled to answer some questions in return?"

"I don't usually answer questions."

Vitters nodded. "I believe we have a mutual interest in sharing notes, so I'm going to ask. Your mission was to find us. Why?"

Morgan thought for a while, then said, "Your organization was the subject of an investigation into a series of murders in Kabul, including a friend of mine. I was assigned to the case."

"I assume we're accused of killing the CID agent and possibly Martin Lansley. Who else are we accused of killing?"

"Two MPs at KAIA. They were found to be in possession of a large amount of money in their barracks. More than an MP would reasonably be expected to have at hand."

Vitters nodded. "How did that lead CID to us?"

"My friend, the dead CID agent, turned up rumors on base of U.S. Special Forces posing as contractors and running a drug ring, smuggling the drugs out through KAIA. That is how we got to Martin Lansley."

"Didn't it strike you as odd, then, when Martin turned up dead and your agent went missing?"

"Rumors, money and dead bodies often point to truth."

"There is some truth there, yes. You've been made a pawn in a bigger scheme."

"What makes you say that?"

"We didn't kill those MPs. We didn't kill your friend either. We certainly didn't kill our own business partner, who till his death was critical to our operation."

"I'm sure anyone would say that. But, why should I believe it?"

"Think about it from our perspective. Martin was the only person who could have verified that we had nothing to do with those two MPs. He's dead, but only after CID got the hint that we were responsible for killing two MPs, as well as Martin Lansley. You're left with a trail that seemingly points at me and my men. How neat and tidy."

"It makes a compelling case."

"The CIA has been painting a picture for you. I know exactly who at the CIA has been doing it and I'm willing to trade that information for your help."

By now, they had walked a good distance away from the village and Vitters was turning them back towards where they had come from.

Morgan said, "John, you know that what you're doing is illegal, right? You're never going to go back to the real world again."

"We're taking advantage of the white space in the market."

"You're playing a game that has no exit strategy."

"On the contrary, we have a well-defined business plan for that. Our long-term goal is to become wealthy enough that we can buy off a few politicians in a civilized country and live like kings for a long time to come. Breaking the law as a businessman is very easy if you grease the right palms."

"That doesn't make what you're doing right."

"Business ethics are all very grey."

Morgan shook his head.

Vitters continued. "We know who killed Jason Milner and those MPs. That has to be worth something to you."

"What kind of help do you want?"

"Young businesses have problems that are sometimes best solved by a consultant or lobbyist. People with sway. We know who you are. We know who you represent. We want you to report back to the Army that you've found nothing here."

"If you knew me better, you would know I can't take that deal."

"You can. We'll give you the name of the person who killed your friend and the MP. You can follow up on the name and when you're satisfied that we told you the truth, you can clear our name with the Army in return."

"Why would you trust me to do that?"

Vitters looked at Morgan for a long, long time. The sun beat down between them. In the distance, one of the villagers working the poppy fields hummed a melodic tune.

"How many times in history has a policeman like yourself looked the other way on a small crime in order to punish the bigger one?" asked Vitters.

"I only do those kind of things for just causes."

Vitters stopped their walk about fifty yards from the village. "I served seven tours in the Army, fighting from Iraq to Afghanistan and a few, discreet stops in between. When I left the Army, there was nothing for me in the U.S. There were no victory parades. There was no expedited services at the VA. There was no job market for former soldiers, no career path for West Point graduates. Just a constant deluge of come-ons from 'for-profit universities', which wanted to milk me of my GI Bill money, then spit me out into the job market with a worthless degree. The same awaits you, if you ever leave CID."

"So? Life is tough," said Morgan.

"Life IS tough. But, we served our country. What did the country offer back to us? What real opportunities are there for those of us who serve? The U.S. economy is long past needing skilled labor, which is all that we are. We're just chaff to be used up so that people can spend freely on useless crap. You say that what my business partners and I are doing is 'illegal'. I say, we gave more than could ever be expected of us and now it is time for us to collect something on that investment. What's happened to us – you included – isn't 'fair' in any sense."

Morgan said nothing.

"Everyone on the top has stuck their hand into this country and run off with a million dollars. We haven't murdered any Americans, Morgan. We're just doing a dirty business in a complex country and trying to get on with our lives. All I am asking you to do is to see if what I'm telling you is the truth and, if it is, to return the favor by giving us a running start."

Morgan looked at the mountains in the distance, then said, "Alright. Give me the name. If I can prove that he was the one behind all this, I'll fail to mention you in my report. If not, then all bets are off."

Vitters smiled. He pulled a piece of paper from a cargo pocket. Morgan paused before taking it.

"In addition to the name, I want full names and serial numbers for you and each of your men."

Vitters gave Morgan a curious look and then said, "It's a deal." Vitters handed the piece of paper to Morgan. "I am going to trust you at your word."

Morgan took the piece of paper and they shook hands. Morgan then read the small slip of paper. "You've got to be kidding me."

Vitters said, "Come on, I'll get someone to give you a ride home."

Morgan crumpled the paper into his pocket. He wouldn't need it to know who James Poole was. Or where to find him.

Chapter Thirty-Six

Just after 8:00 p.m., Morgan arrived back at the Intercontinental Hotel, road weary and still trying to process the day's events. True to his word, Vitters had delivered Morgan back to the relative safety of Kabul unharmed and unhindered, though it had been Griggs who had driven Morgan to his hotel.

As Morgan walked into the lobby of the hotel, he immediately sensed that someone was watching him. He stopped within a few feet of the door and scanned the open space. He then realized that sitting in a chair was Victoria Solano, wearing civilian clothes, her face a mask of worry.

Morgan sat down in the chair opposite. "What are you doing here?" he asked.

"I got tired of waiting for you to call."

Morgan leaned towards Victoria. "I'm concerned for your safety is all. You might be taking a risk to see me like this."

"No one is going to care about me, Morgan."

"Let's go somewhere we can talk in private."

* * *

Morgan opened the door to his hotel room and Victoria stepped inside. He closed and locked the door behind her.

"How long were you in the lobby?" Morgan asked.

"About an hour."

"Was anyone else in there that long?"

"One or two people."

"Anyone that stood out to you?"

"Am I being questioned?"

"More like an extra pair of eyes."

"Yeah, there was one guy."

"What did he look like?"

"A local, dressed as a businessman in a tan suit."

"Good," said Morgan. "I'll have to check on him."

"Am I free to go?"

"Funny. Sure, you can be released on your own recognizance."

"First, I have something for you."

Victoria reached into her purse and pulled a sheet of paper out. She handed it to Morgan.

"What's this?

"I'm good friends with the pharmacist at the embassy. I worked a little magic and found out that James Poole filled a prescription for Clonidine."

"What's Clonidine?"

"Blood-pressure medicine. Also used sometimes to treat ADHD, but I doubt that James has an issue with ADHD."

"So, he has high blood pressure. No surprise there, considering his line of work."

"What's weird is that it was the first and only time he has filled the prescription. Usually, if you're on a medication like that, you would be filling it on a regular basis."

"Maybe he brought a large supply from home?"

"Possible," said Victoria. "But, there is something else you should know. Clonidine is notorious for being used to induce an overdose in suicide attempts. It causes low blood pressure, leading to death when taken in large quantities, as well as pooling of blood in the deceased."

Victoria could see Morgan's eyes computing the information, so she said, "Have you gotten the toxicology on Jason, yet?"

Morgan shook his head. "Nothing."

Victoria eyed Morgan for a moment, then said, "I don't want to sound crazy, but the U.S. Embassy's medical staff has long talked about a suspiciously high number of Clonidine overdoses. So many that it has become routine. Now, one could take the argument that this is a high-stress environment, with people prone to suffering from such issues as depression that would lead to suicide. On the other side of the coin, we're a pretty tight-knit community at the embassy. And there have been a few too many jokes from the intelligence officers about 'suiciding' people they don't like."

Morgan took this in, then said, "I don't think that's crazy. Could you write down that prescription name so I get it right?"

Victoria took a small pad of paper from Morgan and wrote down the drug name. As she handed it back, their hands brushed again. They both stopped and looked at each other.

"Morgan, I want to ask you something."

"Okay."

"In another world, we were friends, right?"

"We still are friends."

"Right. I know. What I mean is, things have changed. A lot. And, well, I wanted to know if you feel weird seeing me. Here, that is."

"If what you're asking is whether I am worried what Laura will think, the answer is no, I'm not worried. She's engaged to someone. I'm more worried about your friendship with her."

Victoria nodded, then said, "I know, but something about living here has reminded me that life is short. I want to ... I think ..."

Victoria stumbled through her words, then pierced Morgan with a hard look. She then darted in quickly with a kiss that took Morgan by surprise.

Victoria pulled away, blushing.

Morgan smiled at her.

"We should go slowly," said Victoria.

"You're the one who kissed me," said Morgan, smiling.

Victoria laughed and then stood. "I mean, I probably should head home."

"You got a ride?" asked Morgan.

"The State Department would pick me up if I call, but a cab should be fine."

They looked at each other for a while, then kissed again. A

short, simple kiss. Then Morgan walked Victoria down to the lobby.

As she stepped into a cab, they held hands for one long moment, then she departed into the night.

Chapter Thirty-Seven

At just past eleven at night, Morgan returned to the lobby. The only people in the lobby were a handful of contractors who were taking advantage of the time difference to conduct business back in the states via international cell phone.

Morgan scanned the room for the man that Victoria had described earlier in the evening. As a pretense for walking through the lobby, he headed towards a table on which was an English-language newspaper.

As he picked up the paper, Morgan saw the businessman in the tan suit. He was seated in the far corner, doing a poor job of pretending not to watch Morgan.

Morgan didn't want to take the chance that the man was in the employ of the CIA. Yet, it was also possible that the man was in Vitters' pay, or even someone else. In either case, Morgan now wanted to shake that tree to see if something came down to the ground.

Morgan walked to the front desk. The man behind the desk smiled at Morgan with a polite grin. Morgan looked at the man's nametag, which read 'Nigel' and said, "Nigel, I'm wondering if you can help me with something?"

"Surely, sir, how may I help you?"

"You see the man sitting in the corner?"

Nigel looked across the room, then turned back to Morgan and waited patiently for Morgan to continue.

"He reminds me of an old friend, but I don't want to embarrass myself by asking his name. Can you find out his name for me?"

"His name is Jelal."

"Are you sure? I think I know him. Can you tell me what room he is in so that I can drop by later?"

"I'm sorry, I can't do that."

"Why not?" asked Morgan. "I won't tell him how I found

out."

"Because he is not a guest."

"Oh. Well, if he is not a guest, then why is he allowed in the lobby?"

Nigel shrugged and then stared at Morgan passively, waiting for him to continue.

Morgan smiled. "If I were to speculate that Jelal has paid you to let him stay in the lobby, would I be wrong?"

Nigel said nothing.

Morgan nodded. He then pulled out a large amount of Afghan currency and discreetly counted off close to two hundred American dollars. He slid them to Nigel.

"You take this gift from me and ask Jelal to leave for the evening. He can come back tomorrow if he likes, but tonight I think it would be better if he went home and got some sleep."

Nigel looked at Morgan for a long time, then subtly put his hand on the money and slid it into his coat pocket.

"I will see what I can do," said Nigel.

Morgan walked to an open chair and sat down with the paper. Nigel made a pretense of wrapping up some paperwork at the front desk, then walked toward Jelal. When Nigel was close enough to whisper, he spoke in rapid, hushed tones to Jelal.

As Nigel spoke, Jelal became more and more angry. He shot an angry look at Morgan, who ignored him by keeping his nose in the paper.

Finally, Jelal quietly walked out the front door under the watchful eye of both Nigel and Morgan.

Morgan nodded in appreciation towards Nigel as he resumed his position at the front desk.

After reading the paper for five more minutes to be sure that Jelal had left, Morgan folded the paper under his arm, then walked towards the phone booths.

Morgan called Ben Ferguson's personal cell phone from memory. After a few rings, Ferguson's voice came through, sounding as if it were at the end of a tube into the ocean.

"Ben Ferguson."

"It's Huntley. I've got some new names for you."

"Okay, but first: someone else has called here looking for you."

"Who?"

"You know a Colonel Kzaltry in Defense Intelligence?"

"Yeah. He called you?"

"Direct, looking to get in touch with you. Said it was urgent."

"Did he say how he got your number?"

"I asked him that. Said it was a DIA thing, which really pissed me off."

"Did he say what he wanted?"

"No. Only that he needed to get in touch with you ASAP. I told him I only had your cell number at hand."

"Ben. I'm out of the country at the moment. Copy that?"

Ben was quiet for a while, then said, "Okay, yeah, I get it. Why didn't you tell me sooner?"

"I couldn't. Too dangerous."

"I told you to be careful."

"Does anyone else know that Kzaltry is looking for me?"

"Not that I know of, though he could have called anybody looking for you."

"Shit," said Morgan. "Okay, I'll deal with that as soon as I get off the phone. In the meantime, I need full backgrounds on four men, all supposedly retired U.S. Army Special Forces. You ready to copy?"

"Go ahead."

Morgan read the names, ranks and service numbers of Vitters and his men to Ben Ferguson, who copied them back. When he was finished, Morgan said, "Create a new email account and put the info there. I'll call back late tonight your time and you can give me the login."

"You know I'm not supposed to put Army records onto a

private email account."

"Don't worry, I'll delete the account when I'm done."

"That doesn't destroy the data."

"Hey, the NSA and the Chinese have all this stuff already, so what else can really go wrong?"

"Good point. Call me on this number tonight after 2200 local."

"Will do. Thanks, Ben."

Morgan depressed the receiver, then called the number for Col. Kzaltry. The line rang and Morgan prepared himself to leave another message, when he heard a clear voice come through on the other end.

"Hello?"

"Kzaltry? It's Morgan Huntley."

"Thank god, Morgan. You're in a lot of shit."

"Don't I know it?"

"I'm not sure that you do. Are you still in no-man's land?"

"Affirmative. How come you're dialing half the Army to find me?"

"You talked to Ben Ferguson, huh?"

"He wasn't happy about how you may or may not have obtained his number."

"Just old-fashioned spy work. I've got a lot of news for you on the Franklin issue if you're ready to copy."

"Go ahead."

"Franklin intends to hang you out to dry."

"I had a feeling."

"It's worse than that. Apparently the Afghan drug ring is a real thing."

"I've confirmed that myself, just today. How did you get that info?"

"Franklin had hard facts from other sources long before he sent you there. The real problem is, these guys have got it out for you, Morgan."

"How the hell did you get that information?"

"I can play dirty pool with the best of them."

"What do they have planned for me?"

"I couldn't get that out of them. Whatever it is, it's not good, I can tell you that. What's the status on your case?"

"I've got a lead on a suspect."

"Is it solid information?"

"I'm not sure if I trust the source, but I am going to follow the lead and see where it takes me."

"I think it's time you got out of there, Morgan. I've talked with some of our friends in British OSS and they're willing to help me put together an operation to get you back to the States post-haste."

"How long do I have to accept that offer?"

"I can have things together for you in twenty-four hours. Just say you'll do it now and let's get you out of there."

"Not yet. I still have work to do."

Kzaltry was quiet for several seconds, then said, "Alright, but if you were my subordinate, I would have you out of there tonight."

"That's why you're a good man, Bill. For now, just keep the Brits warm until I get out of here."

"Be safe."

"Thanks, Colonel."

* * *

Bill Kzaltry ended the call. He made sure to delete the record from his phone, so that no casual inspection would show the recent conversation. He then left his office to see if some caffeine could help with what he sensed was a growing headache.

What Bill Kzaltry didn't realize was that a little less than fifty miles away, a copy of his call had just been recorded at an NSA processing facility.

Army CID's Col. Franklin had gotten to the top of his

profession by having a few friends who owed him less-than-legal favors. One of those was a high-ranking staffer in the NSA. Ever since the conversation with Kzaltry, Franklin had put a request in with his old friend for a copy of all conversations that Kzaltry made on his cell phone.

Within an hour, the conversation between Morgan and Col. Kzaltry had been tagged, recorded, transcribed and flagged for immediate distribution.

Ten minutes after that process was complete, a fresh copy of the transcript was in Col. Franklin's hands.

Chapter Thirty-Eight

Morgan found it difficult to sleep and roused himself from bed early the next morning. Knowing that the lobby of the hotel was no longer secure, he eschewed his usual payphone location at the Intercontinental and instead caught a cab to the nearby market. Most markets in Kabul had one or more payphones that were marked by a plastic, yellow hood. While there could be a line to use one in the late afternoon, Morgan had his choice of three phones at this early hour.

He pulled out his calling card and, after checking to be sure that he was alone, called Ben Ferguson.

"Ferguson."

"It's Morgan. Are we ready with that account?"

"Of course. Ready to copy?"

Ben read the new email account and password to Morgan, which he entered into the webmail service link on his Blackberry.

"That work for you?" asked Ben.

"Yeah, I'm in."

"Don't forget to delete the damn things when you're done."

"I won't."

Morgan ended the call and took the Blackberry towards a small café that was at the edge of the market.

* * *

Accessing the internet from his Blackberry, Morgan drank a cup of poorly brewed coffee in the café while he read the emails within the new account set up by Ben Ferguson.

The first of these was just a note from Ben Ferguson, saying that he had no problems finding the records for the four men and that there were no oddities that made him worry about tampering with the files. The next four emails each contained an attached copy of the Army's file that corresponded to the names that Morgan had provided to Ben.

The first file was for David Freer. David had come from a small suburb of Oklahoma City, volunteering for the Army straight out of high school. High scores in marksmanship landed him in a combat unit that was on its way directly to Iraq after his graduation from infantry school.

In that first tour in Iraq, David Freer was wounded badly in a roadside ambush, a bullet passing through his upper bicep. His unit's medical team didn't treat the wound as seriously as they should have and the wound became infected, causing David to have to undergo a brief hospitalization.

From there, Freer's career showed no other notes of interest, other than continually high praise from commanders. He joined Special Forces and served several rotations under Vitters' command in Afghanistan and Iraq. Freer's next opportunity to re-enlist was 2009, but he chose an Honorable Discharge. The file ended by noting that the forwarding address on file for David Freer was no longer correct.

The second file was for Alexi Farrat. Alexi's parents had been Egyptian-Americans who lived in Florida, where they were employed as civil engineers. While majoring in foreign languages at Florida State, the Army ROTC had piqued his interest. His native ability to speak Arabian, which he had learned from his parents, and his ability to quickly learn foreign languages made him a natural for a fast track into the Army's Special Forces. He served several rotations with other units until meeting up with Vitters in 2007. He, too, chose a discharge in 2009.

Warrant Officer Ethan Griggs of Tennessee had joined the Army in 1995 after dropping out of an associate's degree program at a local community college. His long career in the Army had seen him first serve with an infantry unit, then the Rangers and then on to Airborne qualifications: a classic career path to Army Special Forces. He had joined Special Forces in late 2000 and was an active Green Beret before September 11th, 2001.

Ethan then deployed repeatedly between Afghanistan and Iraq, rotating in and out of a head-spinning series of deployments until he left the Army in 2006. However, his discharge was cancelled soon after his end date and a note was entered that – after being in civilian clothes for two weeks – Ethan had wanted back into the Army. Morgan recalled that the Army had been desperate for all the help it could get around 2006, so likely the Army had been all-too-happy to bring Griggs right back into the fold. Upon his return to the Green Berets, Griggs was assigned to Vitters' unit.

All told, Ethan Griggs served nine rotations through various war zones. In 2009, he was once again eligible for re-enlistment. This time, he officially resigned from the Army, just like his other compatriots.

The final email contained the file for Captain John Vitters. John was born in Abbeville, South Carolina, the son of a local attorney and a housewife. Vitters' father, Mr. Roland Vitters, had also attended West Point and served as an officer during the Vietnam era.

John Vitters' time at West Point was without much comment. He finished middle of his class, with several notes in the file about his engaging personality. His first assignment out of West Point had been in command of a combat fire team that participated in Operation Iraqi Freedom. Not much information was provided about his performance during the invasion, but his promotion to first lieutenant noted that he was beloved by all who served with him. From there, his career took him to Airborne school, then a jump straight to the Green Berets, where he received high marks for his leadership skills in Special Forces School.

Vitters, like his men, then served a series of tours and assignments within Iraq and Afghanistan, the sum of which had left him gone for much of the years from 2006 through 2009. Towards the end of 2009, a review by his last commanding officer had noted:

> *Captain Vitters is no longer showing the same enthusiasm for his assignments. I have recommended that he consider whether he is invested enough in the mission to continue to be an effective leader.*

Morgan scrolled through the file. His eye caught on one other interesting piece of information. Apparently, at least when he was discharged from the Army in 2009, he had still been married. Morgan remembered their conversation in the SUV when Vitters had been posing as Greg Baker and wondered if Vitters had been telling a tale about divorcing his wife or if that had indeed been the truth.

Morgan deleted the files in the inbox and then shut down the email account, ending what he hoped would be any future access to it by prying eyes.

He then logged into his corporate email account. He had two messages there. One from Stan indicating that the check from GenetiGreen to the village was ready to be picked up.

The other was from Chief Thompson. It was a stern reminder that Morgan had not reported on his progress to Thompson for the last two days, a break of strict operational protocol.

In order to pacify Thompson, Morgan wrote back quickly that he would file an updated briefing soon. Morgan didn't want to give Thompson a sense of what was happening quite yet, until Morgan was certain that he understood the entire situation.

Morgan then paid the bill and went into the street to find a taxi.

It was, after all, long past overdue for Morgan to visit James Poole.

Chapter Thirty-Nine

Outside Washington D.C.

Just after six in the morning, Colonel Kzaltry left his home in the Quantico area, headed for Andrews Air Force Base, where he was scheduled on an early-morning military flight to MacDill Air Force Base in Florida. Once at MacDill, Kzaltry would be meeting with the head of Army operations for the U.S. Military's Central Command, more commonly called CENTCOM: the joint command responsible for the combined combat effort in Afghanistan.

The reason for the trip had been kept a secret from even Bill Kzaltry's bosses. That was because Kzaltry had decided to bring several commanders whom he trusted up to speed on what he had learned about Franklin's actions in their theatre of operations. While Kzaltry wasn't sure what their reactions might be, he knew well enough that his own bosses at DIA wouldn't want to share his information with CENTCOM before it had first impressed the top brass at the Pentagon. Doing that would ultimately expose Morgan, which was not Bill Kzaltry's intentions.

Within twenty minutes of leaving his home, he was on the Interstate, running ahead of schedule. As he cruised through the sparse traffic towards Andrews AFB, Kzaltry noticed a black SUV several times in his rearview mirror. He thought nothing of it for the first few miles. Yet, now, just minutes away from his exit, Kzaltry couldn't help but notice as the SUV closed on his bumper and flashed its brights, indicating that it wanted to pass.

The exit for Andrews Air Force base was nearing, so Kzaltry eased into the right-hand lane, figuring the SUV would pass.

As he made his way into the exit lane, to Kzaltry's surprise, the SUV stayed right on his bumper.

The exit ramp was long and built with gentle curves as it

meandered towards the highway, designed originally for the heavy military vehicles that regularly make the trip towards Andrews Air Force base.

The same design, however, allowed lighter vehicles to maintain high speed as they exited. The SUV took advantage of this, getting within inches of the back end of Kzaltry's car.

In another time in Kzaltry's life, he would have tapped the brakes, hoping for a fight in which he could break the other man's nose. Now, though, Kzaltry was hoping to see his career go to the top levels of Defense Intelligence: a fist fight with a civilian over driving etiquette wouldn't serve that purpose well.

Kzaltry swallowed his pride and pulled slightly to the side, his passenger tires riding the shoulder of the long off-ramp, hoping that the SUV would finally pass by him.

The SUV's engine roared and it came abreast of Kzaltry's car. Kzaltry looked up towards the windows of the SUV. He could see nothing inside the car.

Then the passenger window of the SUV rolled down. The barrel of a handgun came into sight.

As Kzaltry's brain recognized the imminent danger, he tried to slam on the brakes. The gunman, however, was too fast. The gun peeled off a series of shots that slashed into the sedan at a downward angle, hitting Kzaltry in the neck, the shoulder and twice in the legs.

The shock and the impact caused Kzaltry to involuntarily jerk the wheel, sending the car careening off the edge of the raised off-ramp. Kzaltry's car dived nose first into a field just below the embankment.

As the car landed in the field, Kzaltry's head slammed hard on the inside edge of the door frame, knocking him unconscious.

The SUV slowed for a moment, its occupants taking note of Kzaltry's slumped, unconscious and bleeding form. Then it raced back onto the highway, disappearing from sight within seconds.

Less than a minute later, another car came down the off-ramp, slowed, then stopped.

Its passengers rushed to Kzaltry's car and called for the police.

Chapter Forty

For most of the day, Morgan had been sitting in a cab, just within view of the entrance to the GenetiGreen offices. Due to the late-afternoon sun, the cab was now hot and stuffy. Morgan was hoping that the increasing discomfort would pay off soon in the form of visual confirmation of James Poole as he exited the GenetiGreen offices.

Just before five in the afternoon, Morgan finally got what he wanted. James Poole exited the building at a casual pace and hailed a cab using the security staff outside the building.

Morgan leaned forward to speak with his own cab driver, Afil, whom Morgan had hired for his knowledge of English. "Follow him and be sure to stay back out of sight."

Afil slowly inched the taxi through Kabul's afternoon traffic, the dense streets helping Morgan's cab to stay safely behind James.

Morgan waited patiently as Afil did an admirable job of keeping just within sight of James Poole's cab. Morgan had learned to like the mid-thirties driver, who had a profound love of his two children and British Premiere League soccer. Morgan had already paid Afil for the full day and planned to give a large tip once James Poole arrived wherever it was he was going.

Twenty minutes later, they were in a part of Kabul that Morgan had never seen before. "What part of Kabul is this?"

"Safe neighborhood. Old Russian neighborhood, now filled with many European business people."

"Any Russians left?"

"No."

"You speak Russian?"

"It is an ugly language spoken by ugly people."

A few minutes later, James's taxi pulled into the entrance of a hotel. James exited the car and passed through the guards who stood in front of the building. James quickly disappeared inside the hotel as Morgan watched from afar.

Morgan said, "I'll get out here."

Morgan paid Alil and gave him an extra tip. They shook hands, then the cab drove off into the Kabul traffic.

An Afghan store with tables and a sign advertising coffee in English was across from the hotel. Morgan headed into the shop, ordered a coffee and picked a table within view of the entrance to the hotel.

The coffee came in a chipped porcelain cup and saucer, but was freshly brewed. In fact, it was one of the first decent cups of coffee that Morgan had tasted in this country.

* * *

Ninety minutes later, James Poole re-emerged freshly changed and showered from the hotel. He hailed another cab, which he was able to catch quickly. Within mere moments, he was inching away into the last rays of the smog-choked afternoon sun.

Morgan watched all this from the café and waited another ten minutes before paying his tab. He then crossed the street to James's hotel.

The lobby of the hotel was done in an ironically fake Middle Eastern motif, with a pair of fountains. It had an airy, open feeling that the Intercontinental lacked.

Morgan approached the man at the front desk, who wore no name tag. "Hello."

"Hello, Mr.?"

"Harrington," Morgan said, using a false name he often defaulted to when it was needed on a case. It was a little lie that most investigators kept on hand for various encounters with the public.

"Yes, Mr. Harrington. How might I help you today?"

"I have a friend staying here at the hotel and I wonder if I might find out what room he is in?"

"If you give me his name or room number, I can ring him."

"I'm not sure of his room number. But, the name is James Poole."

The front-desk attendant picked up a phone and dialed. They exchanged glances as the man waited for someone to answer, then he put down the phone.

"I'm sorry, sir, there is no answer. Can I take a message?"

Morgan smiled, then said, "Darn. James had a shirt of mine that I wanted to get for tonight."

"I can leave him that message."

Morgan reached into his pocket and produced a stack of afghanis. He put them under a document on the counter, then slid it across. "Any chance I could go look for myself?"

The man eyed Morgan warily, then said, "You have five minutes. Then I will send someone up after you."

Morgan nodded. The man craftily extracted the money from under the document, then gave Morgan the room key.

* * *

Morgan quickly found the room, which was on a corner of the third floor. He held his breath as he inserted the key into the door, which easily turned and opened the deadbolt.

The room was actually a full suite, with a separate living room and bedroom.

"CIA," Morgan muttered to himself, "they always have the nice things."

There was a desk in the living room and Morgan shuffled through the drawers, finding nothing of note. Atop the desk was a laptop, but it was password protected, preventing easy access. Morgan left the laptop alone. A failed series of password attempts might tip off James to his presence in the room.

Morgan continued to hunt through the suite, but came across nothing of interest in the living room or the kitchenette.

During a careful inspection of the bedroom, though, Morgan found a small file box placed under a laundry hamper, which he opened carefully. Inside was a Heckler & Koch P30 handgun, a small 9mm model that easily fit under clothing. Morgan picked up the gun using a dirty shirt in the hamper so that he could examine it more closely.

The small pistol smelled like it had been fired recently and hadn't been cleaned since. Morgan checked the magazine, which was full. He carefully pulled a round out of the magazine and inspected it for its manufacturer's stamp, which was marked with the letters **GECO** on the bottom of the bullet casing. It was a small detail, but Morgan had learned from older agents that such information could quickly provide a key thread in an investigation.

Morgan put the round back into the magazine, then returned the gun and file box to their original location.

The only remaining room in the suite was the small bathroom. Quickly assessing the various items, Morgan found a small, plastic sandwich bag with a half-dozen blue pills in the medicine cabinet.

He opened the bag and took one of the pills. He didn't recognize the pill or the markings on it, so he pocketed it for further examination and hoped that James wasn't a fastidious counter of his pharmaceuticals.

With no other spaces in the suite to inspect, Morgan departed as quickly as he could to save himself from an embarrassing encounter with James.

Back down in the lobby, Morgan laid the keys on the front desk. The concierge took them with a deft swipe of his hand.

"Couldn't find the shirt," said Morgan.

"I presumed," said the man behind the desk. "Have a good day, Mr. Harrington."

* * *

As Morgan left the hotel and caught a cab back towards his hotel, he didn't notice that standing just two blocks away, smoking a cigar and watching Morgan carefully, was James Poole.

After Morgan's cab struggled into the ever-present traffic, James walked back to the hotel.

"You were right, Mr. Poole," said the front-desk man, "you were indeed being followed."

"I told you. Sixth sense."

James doubled the tip that Morgan had paid, then returned to his room.

Chapter Forty-One

In the back seat of his newly hailed cab, Morgan used the time in traffic to connect to the internet via his Blackberry.

The first thing he searched was the list of ammunition-manufacturer headstamps. He quickly found **GECO**, which stood for Gustav Genschow, & Company. According to a quick search, Gustav Genschow, & Company was the biggest German manufacturer of ammunition and provided rounds in all of the standard calibers.

Morgan then tried to find information on the pill he had found, which was blue, oblong and marked CL8. Unfortunately, there were no definitive answers on what the pill represented. What he needed, Morgan realized, was someone who might have a firsthand knowledge of prescription medications.

A moment later, Morgan had his Blackberry to his ear as he placed a call to Victoria Solano.

"Hello?" she said.

"This is Morgan. Have you had dinner?"

"I was just about to grab some at the embassy cafeteria."

"I need your help with something urgent. Can you catch a ride to the Intercontinental? We can eat there if you like."

Morgan heard her pause and thought she would decline, but then she said, "I'll be there in an hour if you can wait."

"Sure. Just come to my room when you get here."

* * *

A few blocks before arriving at the Intercontinental, Morgan spotted the ubiquitous yellow payphone near an intersection and asked the cab driver to stop. Morgan paid the driver and walked over to the payphone, where he used his calling card to dial Ben Ferguson's personal number. After a long delay, he was connected.

"Sergeant Ferguson."

"Huntley."

"I was beginning to wonder if I was a one-night stand. You get the files?"

"I did. Excellent work."

"And did you destroy the account?"

"Of course."

"You can't be too trusting in this Army."

"Tell me about it. Listen, I got one more research project for you."

"That's what they pay me for."

"Underpaid, I would say. Alright, here's what I need. Two Kentucky National Guardsmen were murdered in Afghanistan in February of this year. I need some details from their autopsy report."

"Sure. What were the names?"

Morgan read him the names and ranks of the men from memory.

"Just a moment," said Ferguson.

After a few minutes, Ferguson was back. "Okay, I've got them. What do you need?"

"Cause of death in each case?"

"Homicide. Violent trauma from a gunshot to the head."

"Was a bullet recovered from either body?"

"Both bodies."

"What were the forensics?"

"9 millimeter slug, flat nose."

"Any information on the manufacturer for either bullet?"

"No, the rounds were too disfigured."

"What about a chemical analysis?"

"They did that. Notes say that they were unable to draw anything conclusive from the analysis, but the bullets were likely of European manufacture."

"What did they base that on?"

"Quality of the lead. I don't know. Ions or some crap."

"Okay. Let me ask you a question, professional to professional, to make sure I am not out on a limb here. I've got a suspect with an automatic pistol loaded with ammunition that has a German headstamp, **GECO.** Forensics says the bullets in the Kentucky MP killings were European in origin. Does that connect the dots for you?"

"Sure does. What else have you got?

"Not much right now. But, I might have some more news after a meeting I have coming up tonight."

"Good luck. Did you get in touch with Kzaltry?"

"Classified."

"What isn't?"

"Thanks again." Morgan ended the call.

* * *

Morgan headed to his hotel room, where he showered, shaved and changed. He took extra care to bury the clothing he had worn all day and which reeked of a Kabul taxi.

Just as Morgan was putting his socks on, a knock came at the door.

Victoria was in the doorway, her hair pulled into an attractive knot at the back of her head. She was wearing cargo pants that fit perfectly. Morgan felt a slight shiver run down his back.

"Nice of you to join me," said Morgan.

Victoria reached out for Morgan's hand and gripped it firmly. "I'm starving."

A few minutes later, Morgan and Victoria were eating kebabs amid the cacophony of the rooftop pool deck.

"How was your day?" asked Victoria.

"That question sounds too normal. I feel like it should be something more reflective of life here."

"Okay. What horrible things did you see today?"

"Better," Morgan said, smiling. "My day was filled with bad news. How was yours?"

"I got to see a gentlemen with an advanced case of syphilis today."

"That's a highlight?"

"More like the sort of embarrassing detail that you wouldn't normally want to know about someone. Funny, though, when the patient is a big name at the embassy."

"Odd thing to contract in a country not known for its hot sex life."

"Embassy staffers around the world are notorious for dipping into each other's gene pools."

"Yeah? I bet that poses all kinds of problems."

"The biggest problem is figuring out where to stay. If both compounds have a "no guests" policy, where do you hook up?"

Morgan ate some grapes, then said, "You sound like you have personal experience in this."

"I've had a hot night destroyed by the rules of embassy life, yes. Does that bother you?"

"'Don't ask, don't tell', right?"

"Deal."

Morgan nodded and finished the last of his kebab.

"It's beautiful," said Victoria, "this roof. It feels like another world."

"It does. Unfortunately, I need to discuss a small bit of reality."

Morgan reached into his pocket and produced the pills he had found in James Poole's bathroom. "Are these Clonidine tablets?"

"Where did you get those?"

"I'm not sure you want to know."

Victoria held out her hand and took the pills. She reviewed them carefully. "I'm pretty sure. Without a druggist encyclo-pedia, I can't be one hundred percent."

"But your educated opinion is that they are Clonidine?"

"Yes. I would be shocked if they weren't."

Morgan put the pills back in his pocket. "I have another favor to ask. I need to talk to someone in the State Department. Preferably someone from State Department Internal Security."

"About what?"

"I've got a bit of a problem that I need some outside help with. A CIA problem."

"State Department hates the CIA."

"That's why I hope to get a friendly reception there."

"Is it James Poole?"

"I'm not sure you want to know."

"Well, you're already involving me by asking my help. I would like to be clued-in."

Morgan put his hand on Victoria's and said, "I think it's better if I left you in the dark about it. I really need the help and I'm only asking because I trust you. But, if you don't want to do it, I understand."

Victoria squeezed Morgan's hand again. He felt a current of electricity go through his body.

Victoria said, "One of my patients is in State Department Internal Security. I'll get you a meeting with him tomorrow."

Morgan smiled. Their hands stayed locked together. They looked at each other for a long time.

"Care to take an evening stroll around the pool?"

Victoria laughed. They stood and strolled, hand in hand, around the pool. Somehow, their conversation strayed to normal topics.

Somewhere, between the seventh and the eighth circuit around the pool deck, they headed into the stairwell and down to Morgan's room. From there, Victoria phoned U.S. Embassy Security and told them she would not be returning until morning.

Chapter Forty-Two

Quantico, VA

Ben Ferguson had grabbed his second cup of coffee of the morning and was now making his way through a stack of files that had been pulled for replacement. A knock on the door to his office broke his concentration.

Before he could answer, the door opened. CID Special Agent LeShaunda Collins stood in the doorway. Her face was the usual mask of impatience with which she treated all clerical errands.

"What can I do for you, Agent Collins?" asked Ben.

"I just need a personnel file."

Ben waved at a series of forms on a table and said, "Fill out the request and I'll have you on your way."

Ben logged on to his computer and waited for LeShaunda to finish the form. When she handed the request to Ben, he took a moment to review it. Then he reviewed it again to be sure he had read it correctly. "You sure you got the right name here?"

"Yeah, why?"

"I know Colonel William Kzaltry."

LeShaunda gave Ben a look of investigative curiosity. "How?"

"I shouldn't say I know him, I mean I've spoken with him recently. He was involved with a case that Agent Huntley was working on. Why is he on your radar?"

"First tell me his involvement in Huntley's case."

"Background information for Huntley. I spoke with him on the phone once or twice."

LeShaunda looked at Ben for a long time, sizing him up, then said, "Kzaltry was shot multiple times while driving to Andrews Air Force base."

"Jesus. When was this?"

"Yesterday morning. I'm working the case."

"Did he survive?"

"He's unconscious at Bethesda. Critical condition, but stable."

"Any suspects?"

"None yet. You know any?" LeShaunda gave Ben a rare smile.

Ben shook his head, his mind was racing. He turned back to his computer and accessed the Army's personnel database.

"Shit," Ben said. "His file has been security controlled."

"What's that mean?"

"It means that we have to ask a command-level officer to get the file."

"Not surprising. He is DIA brass."

"I think there might be more to it that just the usual DIA angle."

LeShaunda pierced Ben with a hard stare. "Sergeant, if you know something that you're not sharing, I will knock your teeth so far down your throat you're going to have to shove food up your ass to chew it."

Ben put his hands up in mock defense. "Easy, Agent Collins. I'm just thinking about how to explain things."

"Don't think. Just give me the straight info."

"Do you have plans for lunch?"

"I prefer older men, Sergeant."

"I mean, I need some time to put together some materials for you."

"Fine. Where do you want to meet?"

"I don't know. I don't do this very often."

"There's a small bar off base called Killarney Tavern. You know it?"

"Yeah, I've been there."

"It's deserted at noon. Meet me there."

* * *

Ben walked into the Killarney Tavern just after 12:30. The bar was dark and its windows were covered with cardboard advertisements.

As his eyes adjusted to the low light, he saw Special Agent Collins in the back of the bar. She was already on her second beer.

Ben sat down across from her and put a file folder on the bar.

"Is that what I think it is?" asked LeShaunda.

"It is."

"How did you get it?"

"Sorry, trade secret. But, I do have to warn you that someone might notice that I was able to get my hands on this information, so the clock is ticking for you."

Ben slid the file over to LeShaunda, who read it quietly.

"Have you looked at it?" she asked.

"I have."

"Anything that would explain why it was locked down?"

"Nope. It just says that he's an Army spook."

"I take it, then, that you know something that is not in here?"

Ben reached over and took Agent Collins' beer. He drank a long swig from it, then said, "What I'm going to tell you can't come back on me, okay?"

"You got my word."

"I spoke with Colonel Kzaltry not more than a week ago. On the phone."

LeShaunda took out her notepad, but Ben waved her off. "Regarding what?" she asked, putting the notepad down on the bar.

"He was looking for Morgan Huntley."

"Huntley is on administrative leave."

"No, he's not."

"What do you mean?"

"Huntley is overseas, working the Jason Milner case. Not on admin leave."

"How do you know that?"

"I just know."

Ben recounted the call from Morgan and the information he

had researched for Huntley. He then said, "I don't know if Morgan called Kzaltry and I don't know what they spoke about. I only know that Kzaltry wanted to talk to him."

"And now Kzaltry is in the hospital, barely alive," said LeShaunda.

They sat in silence for a moment, then LeShaunda drained the beer.

"Thanks, Ben. I'll take it from here."

Ben grabbed her arm. "No mention of this conversation and of where you got the file, right?"

"I wouldn't burn the only lead I've got, would I?"

Chapter Forty-Three

Morgan arrived in the reception area of the U.S. Embassy shortly before ten in the morning. Victoria was waiting for him with a visitor's pass marked in yellow. As agreed upon early that morning, they did not risk any sign of affection in the crowded lobby.

"You have a meeting at 10:15 with Nathan Foss," she said. "His official title is Deputy Director of Embassy Security. Really, he's the State Department's Intelligence Officer here at the embassy."

"You trust him?"

"Nathan's a good man from what I can tell. He'll give you a fair shake."

Morgan nodded and said, "Thanks. You better get back to your office before anyone gets interested in us."

"Can I see you tonight?"

"I was just trying to figure out how to ask you that. The best I could come up with was 'my place or yours?'"

Victoria looked around, then said, "With all the rules here, it will have to be your place again."

"Come by the hotel around seven and we'll have dinner at the restaurant downstairs."

They said goodbye and Morgan watched as Victoria headed into the medical wing.

At 10:15, Morgan approached the security personnel and asked to be shown to Nathan Foss's office. One of the security men, a heavily muscled man with a badge that read 'Ortiz', took Morgan's visitor's badge. He reviewed it and checked a computer terminal to verify Morgan's appointment.

Ortiz then led Morgan through a secured hallway with several barricades. They stopped in front of an unmarked office door. Ortiz knocked and from within a voice said, "Come in."

Ortiz opened the door and pointed to Morgan. "I have

Morgan Huntley here to see you for your 10:15 appointment."

The room was windowless as part of an effort to keep it free from eavesdropping. The man behind the desk was in his mid-forties, a pair of thick glasses framing a perfectly manicured patch of thick, brown hair. He was working from a computer screen that Morgan couldn't read due to an attached privacy screen on the monitor.

Nathan Foss waved for Morgan to enter. Morgan did so and Ortiz closed the door behind them.

As Morgan sat, Nathan Foss offered a firm handshake. "Nathan Foss. Victoria Solano is a good friend of mine. She told me you needed help with something very touchy. So we're clear, I usually only deal with matters of embassy security. Victoria assured me this wasn't a waste of my time, so I would like you to bring me up to speed as quickly as possible."

"I understand that you represent State Department Intelligence here?"

"I want to hear about your background first."

"I'm Special Agent Morgan Huntley with the Army's Criminal Investigative Division. We're working a case in Kabul."

"Okay? So, what can the State Department do for you?"

"My case has run into a series of complications. Problems that have led me to believe that my life may be in danger from those within my own command structure."

"What kind of problems?"

"CIA problems. And problems in my own command structure. I believe the CIA is behind the killing of several American soldiers and I have good reason to suspect that members of CID brass may have been accessory to that crime. I have made arrangements to depart the country safely. I don't have the weight to bring down a CIA agent on my own. I thought the State Department might have an interest in putting a bag of flaming dog shit on the front door of Langley, as well as the Pentagon."

Nathan Foss leaned back in his chair and gave Morgan a long, critical look. Finally, he asked, "Is any of this verifiable by someone other than you? I mean, you're not even here in uniform, much less ..."

"What would you like?"

"First, confirmation that you actually are a CID agent. No offense to Victoria Solano, but is there anyone with enough rank and title that I can talk to who can make me feel comfortable about even listening to this story?"

Morgan thought for a moment, then said, "Colonel William Kzaltry at DIA."

Nathan nodded. "You got the number for his office?"

Morgan retrieved his Blackberry, but Nathan's desk line rang. He picked it up and said, "Foss."

Nathan Foss listened intently, muttering occasionally. He wrapped up the conversation with "Jesus, alright. I'm not happy about it."

Nathan hung up the phone and looked at Morgan.

"I'm sorry, but we'll have to end this conversation."

"What?"

"That was my own boss, calling me from the middle of the night back in the States. I'm not sure who you are, but I've been ordered not to touch you with a ten-foot pole."

Morgan fought back the urge to let his frustration show and tried to let logic win the day. "Nathan. This is the CIA playing games."

There was a knock on the door. "Come in," said Nathan. The door swung open and two U.S. Marines stood in the doorway.

Morgan looked from the door and back to Nathan Foss. "What the hell, Nathan? At least hear me out."

"I'm sorry, but embassy security was ordered to remove you from the embassy as quickly as possible. My hands are tied."

"No, they're not."

"I'm afraid they are."

The two Marines entered the room. Morgan looked over his shoulder and, realizing he didn't want to make a bad situation worse by grappling with a pair of armed Marines inside the U.S. Embassy, he stood.

"Hands behind your back, sir."

Morgan slowly moved his hands behind his back.

"Don't let the CIA do this, Nathan," said Morgan.

Nathan turned his chair and averted his eyes.

"You're playing their game."

"I wish you the best of luck."

"Call Kzaltry."

"I don't have his number."

"Look it up."

Nathan shook his head.

Chapter Forty-Four

Morgan was led by the Marines to the furthest perimeter of the U.S. Embassy and unceremoniously shoved into the street. The Marines stood there, waiting, as Morgan collected himself. He then grabbed his cell phone and dialed the number for James Poole.

After a few clicks and rings, he heard James steady voice come on the line.

"Morgan. Nice of you to call."

"Where are you?"

"Out and about, taking a couple of meetings."

"We need to talk."

"What about?"

"You know."

"I'm sorry. I'm not quite sure …"

"Stop the fucking game, James. We need to talk."

There was a pause on the phone and then James said, "I'm not sure what you're so upset about, but maybe it would be best if you calmed down before we meet."

"Fine. I'm calm. Where can we meet?"

"Look, I'm in meetings all day. How about first thing tomorrow at the office?"

"How about now?"

"I'm sorry, I'm busy."

"Then tonight. Dinner."

"No can do. I'll see you at the office tomorrow morning. Got to run, Morgan. Keep safe."

James ended the call before Morgan could say anything more.

For some time, Morgan stared at the phone, considering whether he should call back. He then decided on contacting a different person.

* * *

Morgan walked into the Intercontinental Hotel and scanned the lobby, looking for the man named Jelal whom he had run out of the lobby just two nights before. Morgan had decided it was time to take a risk.

When he had departed Vitters' village, Morgan had agreed to meet Vitters in The Brydon in five days. There were still two days remaining before that appointment, but Morgan wanted to talk to Vitters immediately. If Jelal had returned to the lobby, Morgan had a good sense that the man was at least not working for the CIA. The CIA used the FBI's technique of a wide rotation of observers in order to keep a suspect guessing as to whether he was truly being tailed or not: a practice honed to perfection during the Cold War. If Jelal was in the lobby, Morgan couldn't be certain who Jelal worked for, but he could deduce that it was unlikely to be the CIA.

Morgan found Jelal within moments, sitting in the corner of the lobby, his eyes locked on Morgan.

Morgan walked straight towards the man and said, "I'm Morgan."

Jelal stared at Morgan for a long time, then said in broken English, "Hello, Morgan. Is there something you need?"

"I believe we have a mutual friend. Captain John Vitters."

Jelal said nothing.

"Well, if I'm right, I need you to do me a favor and tell Vitters that I need to see him immediately."

Jelal still said nothing.

"Can you tell him that?"

Finally, Jelal stood and said, "I will see what I can do. Be here tomorrow at noon."

Jelal left the lobby and walked into the street. Morgan watched him go, then headed to the payphones in the back of the lobby.

He called the phone number for Bill Kzaltry. There was no answer once again, so he left another message. "Bill, this is

Morgan. I think it's time to call the Brits. Get in touch with me by any means possible."

He ended the call, then dialed Victoria's cell phone. She answered just before it turned over into voicemail.

"Hello," said Victoria.

"It's me."

"What happened? Foss told me he had to end your meeting short."

"That's one way to put it." Morgan thought about complaining to Victoria, but stopped. "I'm fine. I'm worried about you now."

"Why is that?"

"I think we should cancel our date for this evening. It's for your own safety."

"Shoot. Maybe tomorrow?"

"I have a feeling I am going to be back in the States in the next forty-eight hours. I'm sorry."

Victoria was quiet, so Morgan said, "I don't want things to end between us. Things are spinning out of control in my case. I would feel terrible if you got caught up in this. Once I'm back in the U.S., we can talk about how to see each other again."

"I guess. I guess that makes sense."

"This isn't a blow off, I promise."

"Okay. Thanks for calling."

"That sounds like you don't believe me. I promise I will call as soon as I am back in the States."

"Alright. I believe you. Be safe."

"You too."

Morgan put the receiver back in the cradle. As he did so, he was reminded of just how much less painful it was to press 'end' on a cell phone.

Chapter Forty-Five

Several hours after speaking with Victoria, Morgan was back in his room, his belongings packed into his suitcase. Prior to packing, he had made sure to clean his handgun with a small, travel-sized cleaning kit.

Morgan had just taken off his shirt and run a hot shower when there was a firm knock on the door. He left the water running and grabbed his pistol from the edge of the sink.

He stepped towards the front door slowly, careful to not let a heavy footstep betray his location to whoever was on the other side of the door. Once within reach of the doorknob, he knelt to reduce the chance that a bullet fired on the other side would strike him.

"Who is it?" Morgan asked.

A familiar voice called out from other side of the door. "It's me."

Morgan reached for the doorknob, but before grabbing it, he asked, "Are you alone?"

"Of course."

Morgan opened the door and let it swing towards him. He then leaned out quickly in a crouch, aiming the gun into the open doorway.

Victoria stood there with an overnight bag in her hand, a look of bemusement on her face.

"I know you told me you wanted to cancel, but I didn't think that meant you would shoot me for coming here."

Morgan leaned out into the hall. He checked both directions and, seeing that it was safe, gave Victoria a kiss before quickly pulling her into the room.

"You shouldn't have come over tonight," Morgan said.

"I couldn't let you leave Kabul without seeing you one more time."

"I think you should go back to the embassy."

"I can't. I'm starving. By the time I get back to the embassy, I'll be skin and bones."

"I'm serious."

"You don't want to see me?"

Victoria stepped closer and wrapped her arms around Morgan. He tried to resist, but then fell victim to a long, slow kiss from Victoria.

"Not fair," he said.

"I know."

Victoria dropped her overnight bag on the bed next to Morgan's suitcase. "I'm not wasting my last night in the same country as you, Morgan."

Morgan shook his head, then said, "Alright, come on. Let's go get some dinner. Mind if I shower first?"

"I'm about to eat my own hands I'm so hungry. I wouldn't care if you smelled like an abandoned Army outhouse."

Morgan stuffed his gun into the back of his pants, then put on a shirt.

He caught Victoria eyeing the gun.

"It can be tough to get a table."

* * *

Morgan led Victoria to the ornate, formal dining room attached to the hotel lobby. The well-dressed host led them to a table, which was covered in threadbare linen.

They were offered tea and juice. For a quiet moment, they considered the menus, which were printed in several languages.

The host returned, apparently working also as the waiter. "What would you like this evening?" he asked in his heavy, British accent.

Morgan looked at Victoria and asked, "Would you be alright if we let the kitchen take care of us this evening?"

Victoria put down her menu and smiled, "I think that's a great idea."

"Can you bring us three or four courses of whatever the chef recommends?"

"Certainly, sir."

The host disappeared into the kitchen, leaving Morgan and Victoria alone in the dining room except for a pair of tables attended by Western businessmen.

Victoria was looking hard at Morgan's face, so he said, "You seem like something is on your mind."

"Just questions."

"I'm not going anywhere."

"Do you still have feelings for Laura?"

"Oh. You wouldn't rather talk about Afghan cuisine?"

"It's a serious question."

"You mean romantic feelings?"

"What other way of asking that question is there?"

"I've moved on from my marriage. She has, too."

"What did you think I was asking?"

"Whether I still care about Laura."

"Do you?"

"She was a big part of my life. I still worry about her. I think I will always feel a tinge of sadness that it didn't work out."

Victoria took this all in, but said nothing.

Morgan said, "Is that a bad answer?"

"No, it's the kind of answer I should expect from a decent person, I guess. I wanted to hear your side of things."

"I was surprised you even wanted to talk to me when you saw me in the embassy. I thought you hated my guts after the divorce."

"She never really badmouthed you. It was the marriage that wasn't working for her."

"I suppose that is comforting."

"I know what Laura thinks, but what did you think was wrong with the marriage?"

"What makes you think I thought there was anything wrong with the marriage?"

"I mean, Laura said it was her or the Army. You seemed to pick the Army."

The host arrived with the first course: a dip that looked like hummus, flatbreads and pickled vegetables.

Morgan waited for Victoria to serve herself. When he had taken his own food, he said, "We got married young. We both changed. I know she told you that she was tired of the stress at the hospital. She never wanted to say it, but all those burned and missing body parts gave her nightmares after a time. She needed to get away from it."

"She did."

"Were you tired of it, too? Is that why you joined State?"

Victoria chewed on a piece of flatbread, then said, "I remember one day, in Iraq, I was on rotation to a base near Basra. We received a lot of bad cases there. A young soldier came through. He had been hit by a roadside bomb. His nose had gotten sheared off. He had no nose, just bandages across his face and burns all around it. I was changing his bandages and I asked him, 'How are you today?'"

Victoria took a moment and drank some water from her glass. "And he said, 'It's my birthday.' So I asked, 'Oh, how old.' And he said, 'Twenty.'"

Victoria paused then continued. "Meanwhile, as he said it, I was looking at his face. He had a lifetime of facial reconstruction coming. And I knew the odds of him having brain trauma were pretty good."

Victoria started to choke up, so she drank a little more water. "His life was ruined while most of the people his age – what is it, 97% of Americans his age? – were out having a good time on their own birthdays, like none of this was even happening. He was in the hospital with no nose and not much of a life ahead of him. It took everything I had not to cry in front of him, but I cried that night for over an hour. I don't think I carried it home as much as Laura did, but I was done with all of that when my time was up."

Morgan nodded.

Victoria pierced Morgan with a hard look. "I guess what I'm asking is, how come you never wanted out of the Army?"

"All those things that were bothering Laura were bothering me, too. The stress. The trauma. She wanted out. I thought about leaving. I realized the one thing holding me together was the Army. If I left, I was going to be not only useless as a husband, but as a human. I needed the Army so that I could hold it all together. She wanted me to leave it behind. I couldn't for both of our sakes."

Victoria looked at Morgan for a long time in silence. "Is it working?"

"Mostly."

"Did you ever tell Laura that?"

"By the time I realized how to say it, things were already over."

The next course arrived.

Morgan said, "You never told me why you joined State instead of leaving government work altogether."

"I guess I still wanted to do my part."

"I get that. You like the State Department?"

"It's a different vibe. Same bureaucracy, just as much politics, if not more. But the mission feels different. More justified. More of a representation of what I thought we were as Americans."

"More money, though, in civilian nursing. How come you didn't go work at a civilian hospital?"

"Not everything in life is about making money."

"That's not a very American thing to say."

Victoria scoffed. "I'm well within my rights to not want to make money."

"Oh, a ripe communist in the State Department."

"No. Just, it's not like I was going to get rich being a nurse. I could make good money and maybe someday I'll go that route. For now, I'd rather my life's work go to something bigger than myself."

"If my father heard you, he wouldn't know how to place that statement against his belief that everyone under thirty is a self-centered narcissist who is waiting for a free ride."

Victoria shook her head. "Then what does he think of you?"

"I'm not sure anyone our parents' age can connect very well with what we do day-to-day."

"Mine do. They're very proud."

Morgan nodded as he ate his chicken. "This conversation has gotten a little heavy, huh?"

"It started weird."

"What was weird?"

"I asked about Laura."

Morgan shrugged. "It was an important question."

"Why?"

"Because, we probably needed to clear the air on that."

Victoria smiled. "What happens after tonight?"

"I need to get out of this country in one piece first. Then, how about a week-long date somewhere with tropical drinks?"

"Deal."

Chapter Forty-Six

Jelal Entim had returned to the lobby of the Intercontinental for his evening shift. He had communicated Morgan Huntley's desire to meet with his bosses earlier that day, though he had expected them to refuse. Instead, John Vitters had replied that he would be coming to the hotel personally the next day.

A little past nine in the evening, he watched as Morgan Huntley and a woman left the hotel's restaurant together, then headed towards the elevators. The woman had her arm draped around him in a very familiar manner. She carried a large, brown purse, similar to those worn by many American women in Afghanistan. There was some mistaken belief shared by the Americans that carrying a brown purse would draw less attention to the object, seemingly forgetting that many women around the world had no such accessory and it was the act of carrying one that itself drew attention.

Jelal grabbed his cell phone and reported to Vitters' men that Morgan had headed to his room.

Folding a copy of the day's paper, Jelal prepared to burn the last few hours of the evening waiting in the lobby. He was certain that he would not see either the man or the woman again tonight. Still, he was paid to stay until midnight and he needed the money, so stay he would.

* * *

Just as Jelal was becoming absorbed in the newspaper, he noticed a Westerner in the lobby that he had not seen there before. Why the man stuck out to him, he couldn't say. He looked like many of the other men in the lobby, dressed in cargo pants and a polo shirt, a cell phone attached to his belt. His eyes, though, belied a certain aggressiveness that Jelal instinctively noticed.

Jelal kept his eyes on the man, who did not appear to know

that Jelal was observing him. He walked out several times from the lobby on the pretense of getting a breath of fresh air or making a cell-phone call. While outside, the man would smoke a cigarette, which was a very American habit, since men here would simply smoke within the building, rather than walk outside to do such a thing.

Just before midnight, the man left, disappearing into a cab on the street. Five minutes later, Jelal also ended his shift, the last person remaining in the lobby. Normally, he would have a sixteen-hour break and his assistant – Paiman – would be in the lobby early tomorrow for the morning shift. With tomorrow's plan for a meeting, however, Vitters had asked if both Paiman and Jelal would be at the Intercontinental early to make sure things ran smoothly.

It would make a short night of sleep for Jelal. He hoped it also would mean that tomorrow would be his last day standing around in this hotel.

Chapter Forty-Seven

The first rays of sunlight were coming through the cracks in the heavy curtains in Morgan's room. Victoria was tightly wound in the sheets and as her eyes came open, she realized she was alone in the bed. She turned to see Morgan sitting in the corner of the room, his pistol on the bedside table. Their eyes met.

"How long have you been there?" she asked.

"All night."

"Nervous?"

"Cautious."

Victoria sat up. "What time is it?"

"Just after six in the morning."

Victoria nodded. "I should probably catch the early shuttle to the embassy and let you get on your way, huh?"

"I think it would be best if we got you back to a safe place as soon as possible."

Twenty minutes later, after getting dressed and attending to a rushed morning routine, they stood near the door, holding each other in a long embrace.

"I don't want to go," Victoria said into Morgan's chest.

"I know. We'll see each other soon. I promise."

Victoria craned her neck upwards for a kiss, which they held for some time.

Finally, Morgan reached for the door. "Ready?"

"Yes."

Morgan took his pistol into his hand and opened the door into the hallway.

Instantly, three armed men rushed through, knocking Morgan to the ground as they careened into the room.

The men swarmed on Morgan, forming an angry cloud of grasping hands and sweeping kicks as he tried to bring his gun to bear. Someone hit Morgan's wrist with the butt of a pistol, causing him to lose control of the weapon, which then clattered to the ground. Within seconds, the melee of men had quickly pushed the gun from Morgan's reach.

Victoria dropped her things to defend herself. Before she could consider a plan of attack, one of the men had already rushed towards her, a pistol trained towards her face. In perfectly clear English, the man said, "Get down."

Morgan was trying to wrestle free from the grasp of the other two men, but they had already tied his feet together with a pair of plastic zip ties. The seeming ease with which they had subdued Morgan spoke volumes of their practice in taking hostages by force. Morgan looked towards Victoria and saw that she, too, had been handcuffed already with plastic zip ties.

The other two men finally succeeded in pushing Morgan's wrists together close enough to put plastic zip ties around his hands, forming ad-hoc handcuffs. With his feet and hands bound, Morgan was effectively incapacitated. He could see that Victoria had also been laid prone on the floor, her hands and feet tied in the same manner as his.

With Morgan and Victoria subdued, the men began an evaluation of the room, seeking weapons, personal belongings and other items of interest, collecting all of these on one of the beds in the room. As they did this, James Poole strode through the door, smug and happy.

"Nice work," he said, looking at the men. They all gave small, professional smiles. One of the men pulled out a roll of duct tape and stretched off a piece, then put it over Victoria's mouth.

Morgan stared at James and said, "What the fuck is this?"

"You've screwed with the wrong people, Morgan."

Morgan opened his mouth to say something, but the man with the duct tape had already slapped a piece over Morgan's lips. Morgan shook his head in a vain attempt to disengage the tape, but received only a smack on the back of the head from the man behind him.

"Sorry, Morgan," said James, "but the time for comments is

over."

James pointed at Victoria's shoulder bag and Morgan's duffel. "Grab their things."

The men scraped all of the loose items in the room into the two bags, including Morgan's gun. They then put the bags over their shoulders.

James nodded at the men. Two of them grabbed Victoria by her arms and ankles to carry her. James and the third man grabbed Morgan in the same manner.

In unison, they carried Morgan and Victoria from the room.

* * *

As requested, Jelal had arrived early at the Intercontinental after his late shift the previous evening. Arriving just before six, he was dismayed to find that Paiman had not yet come to the hotel. Jelal doubted that the young man had gotten as little sleep as he had and cursed his tardiness.

He ordered a coffee at the hotel's café – the one Western habit he had adopted since beginning his freelance work for the Americans – and took the cup towards the lobby, where he watched the early-rising guests go through their morning routines.

Halfway through his cup of coffee, he heard a loud commotion among the security people outside the hotel. Jelal left his coffee on a side table and walked through the front door into the already-hot morning air.

He immediately saw what was causing the problem. Past the security checkpoints for the hotel, a van had pulled alongside the hotel. The security men were yelling at it to move.

A moment later, four men burst out of the stairwell doors that led out of the hotel. They were carrying two people with them, but at the distance and with the speed they were moving, Jelal could not be certain who they were.

Until he saw the brown purse. He then noticed that one of the men was the same Westerner with the long beard that he had seen the night before. He was carrying a man, who looked uncomfortably familiar to Jelal as well.

By the time Jelal had put the entire puzzle together, the four men had shoved the two people into the van, ignoring the shouts from the security personnel outside. The van roared away as quickly as it had arrived, leaving behind the security personnel on radios and cell phones as they tried desperately to contact supervisors and the Afghan police.

Jelal picked up his own cell phone and called his boss, hoping that the man was awake. And ready to hear bad news.

Chapter Forty-Eight

Morgan and Victoria sat cross-legged on the floor of van, each with a gun pointed at the back of their head, facing the rear cargo doors. The ever-present gun barrel pressed firmly into the base of their neck prevented each of them from looking towards the front of the van, which was darkened by a curtain that partly obscured the cargo bay from the front seats. The rear windows were also covered with curtains that gently danced as the van drove onward.

The only person who wasn't behind Morgan was James Poole, who was sitting on the wide wheel-well of the van, studying information on his smartphone. He must have sensed Morgan's piercing glare. He turned to face Morgan with a grin on his face.

"You're going to miss work today," said James, looking at Morgan. "And you, too, Miss Solano."

Neither Morgan nor Victoria could respond, as their mouths were still covered with duct tape.

James waved his handgun around as he emphasized his talking points.

"In fact, Miss Solano, I find not only your decision-making to be questionable, but also your choice in men. You do know this man was your best friend's ex-husband, don't you? Maybe I just have better values than that."

James looked at Morgan.

"And your performance here in Afghanistan has lowered my already dangerously poor opinion of Army CID."

The van slowed, then stopped. James looked over Morgan and Victoria's heads to see through the front windshield.

Morgan attempted to turn his head to catch a glimpse, but the man behind him pressed the muzzle of his gun hard into the back of Morgan's neck, encouraging him to return his gaze towards James.

The sounds of men at a checkpoint filtered through the van

and a few moments later, the checkpoint had been passed. The van was once more bounding along the rough Afghan roads.

James said, "This country is an amazing place. So impoverished as to be completely corruptible by any currency in the world. American dollars go far, but they're just as happy to take rubles, yen or any other currency. So long as it's cash and enough of it. Really, I think it's an inherited genetic memory of when this was a key route on the spice trade. They don't care who comes through and what business they're in: so long as you pay for transit and don't make a mess."

Victoria tried to shift. The man behind her gave her a shove as a reminder that she was not supposed to move.

"Try to relax," said James. "We're only another hour from our destination. You will be very, very busy for the rest of the day."

James smiled his crooked smile again. He pulled out the smartphone once more, focusing on the screen.

Morgan wasn't sure that he could risk moving his head again, but the distraction of James's smartphone gave him a moment to search the van with his eyes.

In addition to James, Morgan counted four other men in the van: two guards, a man in the passenger seat, plus the driver. He knew the men who had abducted him were armed. He could only assume the driver was armed as well.

Stacked in the back of the van was a pair of duffel bags. Morgan had no idea as to their contents, but they looked soft and under-filled. Finally, there was the luggage from Morgan and Victoria's hotel room, which the men had thrown into the van with them. James had searched both bags as soon as they had departed the hotel. He had found both Morgan and Victoria's cell phones and thrown them from the vehicle.

There was one other weapon in the van that Morgan knew of and that was his own pistol. James had emptied the magazine of the gun, then placed it in his own waistband. It could obviously be useful, but Morgan would have to go a long way to get it from

James.

So, by Morgan's count, it was him against five armed men, plus at least one extra weapon and possibly a few loose items in the van. Of course, he would need a pretense to have his restraints loosened, which he couldn't vocalize through the duct tape on his mouth.

Still, James was now working on his smartphone and completely distracted. Morgan had the sense that the guards were likely to be relaxed by their boss's attitude, so he risked a slight look at Victoria.

Victoria's eyes were closed. Her face looked pale, but she wasn't trembling or showing any outward signs of fear. Morgan was glad that she had served in the Army, which was hopefully giving her the confidence to remain calm. He hoped that he could think of a way out of this mess before she lost that control.

Morgan heard the engine of the van decelerate and felt the momentum shift as it slowed.

James looked up from his smartphone towards a small gap in the curtain that separated the front cab from the bay. He then quickly exchanged his smartphone for the pistol. He asked a question in Pashto of the driver, who replied in rapid, tight sentences.

The atmosphere in the van grew increasingly tense. James knelt at the back, his gun ready. Morgan heard a round being chambered by someone in the front.

They glided to a stop. The driver spoke with a person outside. The sound of money being counted floated in the air.

Then the sound of counting money stopped. The conversation took a harder tone. The man behind Morgan shoved him to the floor of the van, then knelt beside the sliding door. Within seconds, Victoria had been shoved down alongside Morgan.

Seconds later, gunfire erupted from outside.

A combination of blood and glass sprayed through the curtain from the front of the van. Morgan and Victoria involuntarily hugged the floor. Morgan could hear Victoria screaming through the duct tape that covered her mouth: a strange, smothered cry that barely registered over the echo of gunfire.

The man who had knelt behind Morgan fired through the sliding door, while James scrambled forward towards Morgan and Victoria.

A hail of bullets laced through what was left of the front windshield, catching the man behind Victoria in the face, who then crumpled into a heap.

Morgan heard the dead-man's gun clatter down on to the floor beside him, but was in no position at the moment to reach for it, as his hands were still pinned behind him.

James was now hovering over Morgan and Victoria, one knee dug into Morgan's back and his handgun pointed at Victoria's head, pressing her face roughly against the floor. He was shouting something in Pashto to the only remaining man of his entourage when gunfire from behind blew out the two darkened windows on the back doors. The flood of light was akin to a blinding lamp being turned on in the cargo bay of the van.

The attackers took the momentary pause caused by the blinding change in light to point an automatic rifle into one of the destroyed windows, from which position they shot James's last remaining guard.

A hand came through the second window of the van in search of the door lock. James fired, catching the man's arm with a bullet.

What James had not accounted for or at least forgotten about in the moment, however, was that Morgan was still very much alive at his feet. Morgan wrenched his back upwards in an arc, catching James's knee and sending him off balance. Within seconds, James had fallen over onto the body of one of his fallen men, the slick blood slowing his attempts to reorient himself.

Morgan pulled his own legs up and rolled. Once on his back, he lashed out at James with his feet, catching him in the arm as he tried to block the blow and causing James to lose control of his pistol for a moment.

Just as James was about to regain his balance and his grip on the weapon, the back and front doors of the van were ripped open. Within seconds, three armed Afghans were in the van, pointing AK-47 rifles with extended magazines at James, screaming at him to drop his gun.

James looked at the men, then at Morgan. Finally, he complied, dropping the handgun to the floor.

The men unlocked the side door of the van and slid it open. Outside were another four men, plus a man that Morgan recognized: Vitters' interpreter, Joseph. Parked on each side of the road were outdated SUVs of a make that seemed to have originated in India.

The men roughly pushed James out of the van, where he was instantly surrounded and escorted to one of the two vehicles.

Joseph entered the van slowly. He knelt near Morgan and Victoria, then pulled the duct tape gently from Morgan's mouth. "Are you alright?"

"Yes," Morgan said, the word catching strangely in his throat after so much time with tape over his mouth. "I'm glad to see you."

Joseph nodded, then looked at Victoria and asked, "Is this your friend?"

Morgan nodded and asked, "Can you remove the tape from her mouth and our restraints?"

Joseph pulled the tape from Victoria's mouth. He then used a knife to cut free the plastic ties that bound both Morgan and Victoria's feet. He did not, however, loosen the restraints on their hands.

"Please follow me into the van."

Victoria sat there, momentarily at a loss for words, then said, "I am a member of the U.S. State Department."

Joseph said nothing, but waited for them to follow.

Morgan nodded and looked at Victoria. "It will be okay," he said.

"How do you know?"

"I've met Joseph before. And his boss. Come on."

Morgan pulled himself to his feet and exited the van. He then assisted Victoria through the door.

As the armed men prepared to leave, they doused James's vehicle with gasoline and set it ablaze, turning it into a funeral pyre for the dead men who still lay inside.

Chapter Forty-Nine

The SUV bounced off the main highway and onto a dirt road, then headed through the hot afternoon sun into an expanse of desert, followed closely by the second SUV that had come to rescue Morgan and Victoria.

Morgan leaned forward from the back seat and asked Joseph, "Can we stop for a bathroom break?"

Joseph glanced back, then said, "We will arrive soon. You can use the bathroom there."

Morgan continued, "Where are we?"

"I cannot tell you that."

"Can you tell me how far we are from Kabul?"

"Two or three hours."

"By car?"

"Yes."

"What direction is Kabul from here?"

"If you do not know, I cannot tell you."

"Why not?"

"I am paid to keep this location a secret."

"Why not blindfold us?"

"I was told it was unnecessary." Joseph glanced back. "Was that correct?"

Morgan leaned back into his seat. Victoria looked tense, so Morgan flashed a smile at her, which she acknowledged by pursing her lips into a thin smile.

Ten minutes later, an abandoned fortress appeared in the distance. It was built of local mud and stone, its walls crumbling in numerous places.

"Is that where we're headed?" asked Morgan.

"Yes."

"Doesn't look in the best shape."

"It is safe," said Joseph. "There are many abandoned forts in this country. This one was built by the British. Good builders.

Not like the Soviets. Their bases rust over and crumble. They are useless after several decades."

"After Stalin died, the Russians stopped killing people for low-quality work," said Morgan.

Joseph said nothing in reply to this.

Victoria pushed her leg against Morgan to get his attention, then whispered in his ear, "Enough."

Morgan smiled. "It'll be fine."

Victoria didn't look like she believed him, but she returned her gaze to the passing terrain outside of the SUV.

* * *

Several minutes later, the two SUVs had arrived at what appeared to have once been the main gate of the fort. Several of Vitters' armed *Arbakai* stood outside the gate and watched diligently as the SUVs parked just in front of the fortress.

Joseph opened his door and exited, then opened the door for Victoria. Another man opened the opposite door for Morgan.

As they were escorted towards the gate, Morgan looked back towards the parked SUVs. James was on his feet outside one of the vehicles, surrounded by three men with automatic rifles. They were obviously waiting for someone to give them instructions on what to do with their captive.

For one moment, James and Morgan made eye contact. Then Morgan entered the fortress.

The fortress was centered on a large courtyard, with a series of archways in the center that led into a maze of hallways and rooms. Vitters and his men were waiting in the courtyard, dressed in U.S.-issue camouflage. Vitters was carrying only a semi-automatic pistol in a holster on his belt, but the other three had automatic rifles slung across their backs.

Vitters walked straight towards Joseph and the two spoke in hushed tones. Vitters then pulled Griggs aside and said something to him that was unintelligible to Morgan. Griggs headed towards the parked SUVs.

Vitters then approached Morgan and Victoria. He stopped several feet from them and asked, "How was your trip?"

"We're ready for a restroom break."

Vitters laughed and pulled out a knife. He cut loose the plastic straps holding Morgan and Victoria's hands.

"Freer will show you to the facilities. They're not much, but the British did at least build a cistern to collect waste and prevent disease. It's functional, you might say."

Freer nodded for them to follow him.

"Good. After that, I'd like to have a brief meeting and be on our way," said Morgan.

"Sure, sure. Civilized matters first."

Morgan and Victoria followed Freer into the maze of hallways within the walls of the fortress, where they quickly lost sight of the men in the courtyard. After several twists and turns, Freer pointed them to an open doorway that led into a pitch-black room.

Morgan looked at Victoria and said, "Ladies first."

Victoria peered into the dark room, then said to Morgan, "I would prefer if you scoped it out for me."

Morgan shrugged. He entered the room, dimly lit by a narrow slit at the top of the wall. A mud bench with several holes was just off the ground. Morgan finished the necessary tasks and found Victoria safely waiting for him outside.

"No washing your hands and no toilet paper, but it'll do."

"No toilet paper?" asked Victoria.

Freer reached into a cargo pocket and produced a flattened stack of toilet paper. He handed it to Victoria.

"What a gentleman," she said.

Victoria entered the room.

Freer looked at Morgan and said, "Quite a good-looking friend you have."

"More than a friend."

Freer nodded.

A few moments later, Victoria re-emerged and Freer led them deeper into the honeycomb of crumbling hallways.

They were shown into a large, windowless room, which was lit by several electric field lanterns on tables. Vitters was sitting in a chair, drinking from a green Camelpak. He waved for them to take a seat. Freer remained near the doorway, his rifle still slung over his shoulder.

"Can I get you something to eat?" asked Vitters.

Morgan looked at Victoria, who nodded in agreement. "Sure."

Vitters walked towards a cooler, from which he grabbed two apples. He handed them to Morgan and Victoria, then sat back down. "We'll hustle up some MREs for you in a little bit."

Around a mouthful of apple, Morgan said, "Quite a place you got here. Who pays the rent?"

"This is within the territorial control of our outfit. One of the perks of the recent addition of a nearby village to our network."

"How's the neighborhood?"

"Parking is easy."

Morgan snorted. "And plenty of room for guests?"

"More than we need."

Morgan finished his apple and put the core on the table. "How did you know we were in trouble?"

"The same way you got in touch with me. My man in the lobby, Jelal, witnessed your abduction and contacted me immediately. Having worked with the CIA in the past, we knew that you were being taken to one of two possible locations, so we had our assets in the area set up roadblocks on both routes. We got lucky from there."

Morgan nodded. "Where is Mr. James Poole?"

Vitters feigned an indignant look. "Not even a 'thank you'?"

"Thank you," said Morgan. "We were certainly in trouble."

Vitters smiled. "Yes, Mr. James Poole. On that matter, I

wonder if you and I might be able to talk in private, without Miss Solano present."

Victoria looked at Morgan.

Vitters interjected. "Now, before you object, I would point out that you are still covered in blood and we have a field shower set up here. Certainly, it wouldn't hurt to refresh yourself and get the more unpleasant aspects of your day behind you. It's a cold shower, but having been in the Army, I figure you can tough it out."

"The embassy will be looking for me by now," said Victoria. "It might be best if we got back and you two can have your conversation another time."

"I do apologize," said Vitters. "But I think Morgan will agree that this is something we need to deal with immediately. We'll have you back with a cover story to the embassy as soon as we can. If that's alright with you, dear?"

Victoria looked pissed, then said, "It's Sergeant Solano, if you must. I'll take that shower in the meantime, but make your meeting quick."

Vitters picked up a radio, then called for Freer to bring soap and towels for Victoria.

Chapter Fifty

Morgan waited as Victoria left with Freer, then looked back at Vitters.

"I looked into the tip you gave me. You were right. There is some connection between the CIA and my bosses. They intend to use me, lose me and kill you. I tried talking to the State Department for an assist, but the CIA scared them off."

Vitters nodded. "I read about your little Wooster case in our research on you. Must have pissed off the wrong people at CID for them to want to get you killed out here."

"I wouldn't play ball with CID brass. Apparently they took it personally."

Vitters grabbed a cigar from a box on the table and offered on to Morgan. He declined, so Vitters said, "What was your intention for the meeting you requested with me?"

"When I asked to meet with you, I thought I would need your help in arresting James Poole. Now, he seems to have fallen into our laps."

"Does that mean you've decided to help us?"

"I'm not sure, yet."

"Well, what I will and won't do with James Poole is likely going to hinge on that decision."

Morgan rubbed at the sore spots on his wrists where he had been bound by James, then said, "I need more information if I'm going to help you and your men."

"Ask away."

"Why did you and your men all leave the Army in 2009?"

"Our commitments had ended."

"It's unusual for four men in the same unit to all retire at the same time. Did the Army question it?"

"Not so unusual for Green Berets. The lifestyle leads to a very close bond. Many times, whole teams will leave the Army at once."

"Your file made it sound like something changed after your last tour."

Vitters looked at Morgan and adjusted the cigar in his mouth, then said, "In a way."

"What was it?"

"I'm not sure it would make much sense."

"Was it your wife? The first time we drove out to that village, before you told me who you really were, you mentioned that you had gotten a divorce. Yet, your Army file shows that you were still married when you ended your service."

"In reality, we're divorced. In the eyes of the law, I guess we're still married. She left me for another guy while I was on deployment in 2008. When I got back, she had the papers ready for me, but I couldn't sign them. Still can't, but I think she's alright with it. I guess I am, too. She's still getting half my pay, which is probably the same as if we had gone to court and made it formal."

"You still talk to her?"

"Nah."

"Why?"

"Just gone. She made the right choice. Her husband was in the house for maybe two total years out of six. Shitty pay, shitty life, shitty bases, surrounded by women who were losing husbands, and I don't mean just to death. I mean men coming back as hulled-out shells of themselves. Missing arms. Missing legs. Mostly, missing personalities. If I had died in the field, she could have moved on and still had a life. But, if I came back a disabled or a mentally ill, she would be a prisoner to me. She left rather than wait to find out what would be left of me after this war."

Morgan sat there, visions of his own marriage and fears for what might become of him if he ever left the Army floating through his head. He pushed them aside and asked, "Is that why you left the Army in 2009? Your marriage?"

"No. The marriage was already toast by then."

"Then why leave?"

"You ever see a ghost?"

"Not that I'm aware of."

Vitters nodded. "We had another member of our team, Cade Sanderson, one of our Weapons Specialists. He had been through a lot, served a tour in Iraq for the invasion, and then a few years with us. He had a wife and kid at home. He left at the end of his commitment in 2008 to start a new, civilian life. We gave him a big farewell party while we were back in the States at the time. Then we were on rotation out here for six months. During that rotation, we were joking about how easy it would be to come back here and make some money, do right by the people. But, it was all talk, you know: guys talking about big ideas, but everyone knows that you aren't really going to follow through on it."

"Sure. I know what you mean."

"Anyway, the four of us, we all knew we were up for re-enlistment when we got back. We all just figured we would do another few years. But, when we got back, Sanderson got in our heads."

"How so?"

"He and his wife had moved home to Cincinnati and rented a place. He started having these sort of episodes, like losing his temper and throwing things. Got a little rough with the wife. He couldn't find work for a long time. Finally took a job at a gas station. Then one day, he just lost his mind while at work and punched a customer over something. I don't know what for. He lost the job. He knew he had a problem, so he tried going to the VA to get help, but he was put on a six-month waiting list. Six months to see a doctor. They said he should try to get a job that provided insurance."

"Too many stories like that."

"Right. Anyway, it was too late for Sanderson. Things got out of hand and a week later, he used a handgun to blow his brains out in the kitchen. Kid was still home."

"Kid alright?"

Vitters nodded. "I went up to visit his wife at her parents' place. We talked for a while. She asked if I wanted to see the note."

Vitters looked at Morgan to see if he understood, then continued. "He wrote about how, at night, he still had dreams about being here. About being in the field, about Iraq and Afghanistan and all the other places. How even during the day, sometimes things from back here would superimpose over what he was seeing, like a movie running in front of his eyes. That he no longer felt like a man or a part of society there in that gas station. He talked about how useless and pointless his life had been."

"A lot of lives are on hold these days. Civilians and military."

"On hold. But not like ours. Ours are imprisoned. Forever, maybe. I read that letter and I saw myself in it. I have those same dreams. I went berserk in front of my wife a couple of times before she left me. It's inside me, too, you know? I'm more stable here. This is my life now. When I came back from that trip, I brought a copy of Sanderson's letter for the guys."

"They all felt the same way?"

"More or less. We got to talking and after a few weeks, we agreed that maybe the best thing would be to strike out on our own, here in Afghanistan. Apply the only skills we have for life in a place where we're normal."

"That was 2009?"

"Yeah, that was 2009. We handed in our papers."

"How did you get here?"

"We applied for jobs with a contract company looking for truck drivers in Afghanistan. False names and all. Then we disappeared on them when we arrived."

Victoria returned from her shower and stood in the doorway, wearing clean, but oversized Army camouflage. Vitters and

Morgan looked at her, then back at each other.

Vitters said, "I don't know if you've made up your mind or not, Morgan, but consider that we haven't done anything to betray our country here. No one here thinks what we're doing is a crime. We're just locals now. If anyone here is the victim, it's us. We just want to be left alone to make something out of what he have left."

Morgan sat in the chair across from Vitters, wrestling with his thoughts.

He looked Vitters in the eye and said, "I'm willing to make the deal."

Chapter Fifty-One

Vitters waved for Victoria to enter and have a seat. She did so slowly, sitting at the folding table in the room and looking at Morgan. "What's going on?" she asked.

Morgan waved at Vitters. "This is Captain John Vitters, U.S. Army Special Forces, retired. He now runs heroin into the United States for a living. I'm going to help him hide away here in the desert. And he's going to help me with my problems."

Victoria looked confused, but before she could ask another question, Vitters said, "Okay, you know what I want. I want to know what you want in return."

"I'm going arrest Poole for kidnapping, murder, terrorism and misuse of Army resources."

"The last charge sounds a little pointless."

"You'd be surprised. He might get out of murder, but you don't mess with the Army's supply chain."

"You really think you can waltz into the Pentagon with James Poole on a leash?"

"That's not going to happen, no. I need you to hold on to him until I can make a case back home, then for you leave James Poole at a location that I specify for pick-up by the Army."

"The CIA will never let you put one of their own on trial. You know that."

"I don't give a shit. He's been playing games with the lives of U.S. soldiers. If this makes life uncomfortable for them, so be it."

"It's career suicide."

"I'll deal with that later."

Vitters took a large puff on a cigar. "Alright, you got a deal. I'll hold Poole for up to a month and then dispose of the garbage as indicated. But, if you can't make a deal in thirty days, I'm clearing the books. Take it from me, you don't want a CIA man with a grudge wandering around free in your life."

Morgan raised a hand. "I'll get the Army to at least extradite him back to the U.S."

Vitters seemed impressed, then said, "Okay. I need one thing from you. Then you can leave."

"If you have a WORLDSAT phone, I'll call it in right here and now."

"No, not good enough."

Vitters stood and retrieved a laptop, which trailed a black Ethernet cable that extended out of the room.

"We have internet hear via a satellite uplink. I want you to put a report in writing to the Army ending any speculation of our actions here."

Morgan looked at Victoria, then said, "I would prefer to just call it in."

"I need a written document. The kind of thing that will stick around in the Army in case you want to go making a stink."

Victoria leaned over and said, "Can we talk?"

Morgan nodded and said to Vitters, "Mind if we step into the hall to discuss?"

"Go right ahead."

Morgan and Victoria stepped into the hallway and she said in a low voice, "What's going on?"

"I'm playing jailhouse lawyer."

"Poole's not worth this. Just get us out of here."

"I was about to write the email."

"They're never going to put Poole on trial. Let's go home and live to fight another day."

"No."

"Why?"

"Because of the body count."

"Jason wouldn't want you to ruin your career over this."

"It's not about what Jason wants. I swore an oath."

"To an Army that is more than willing to crush you in order to protect itself."

"Sorry, with the oath comes unconditional subservience to my duty and the Army. I'm bringing Poole home in cuffs."

Victoria put her hand on Morgan's arm. "Please. I want to get out of this place."

Morgan smiled at Victoria and said, "We'll be headed home soon."

Victoria didn't look happy, but said, "You promise?"

"I promise."

Morgan and Victoria walked back into the room. Vitters was smoking the cigar slowly, his eyes half-closed in pleasure. "Have you reached a decision?"

"I'll do it. Then I need to place Poole officially under arrest. I would like us to be safely on our way within an hour to the U.S. Embassy."

Vitters stood and offered his hand. Morgan took it and shook. Vitters then pushed the laptop towards Morgan.

Morgan logged in to the online portal of his work email and drafted a report to Thompson. When he was done, he showed it to Vitters:

TO: Chief Warrant Officer Thompson
FROM: Special Agent Morgan Huntley
RE: Completion of Investigation
In pursuance with orders to investigate the deaths of CID Special Agent Jason Milner, as well as two U.S. Army National Guardsmen at KAIA, I have arrested CIA employee James Poole on suspicion of murder, conspiracy to murder, kidnapping, terrorism and misuse of Army Resources within the AO of CENTCOM.

Through my investigation, I have collected evidence and testimony that indicate that Mr. Poole was responsible for organizing and/or directly participating in the murder of the aforementioned victims. These killings were conducted to create the impression that retired U.S. Army personnel were conducting illegal activities – including drug smuggling – within CENTCOM AO. This plot was developed to protect Mr. Poole's illegal business interests within CENTCOM AO and was intended to lead the Army into using its various resources to protect Mr. Poole's own operations.

I have arrested Mr. Poole and placed him under detainment here locally. I will require assistance in transferring him to U.S. Army custody.

During my investigation, I uncovered no direct evidence of U.S. Army personnel involved with either the killing of U.S. Army personnel, or involvement in Mr. Poole's operation. Based on this, I have deemed further investigation into a drug ring composed of retired U.S. Army personnel to be of no further use to the Army.

I will file a complete debrief and all evidence, statements and other materials required by Army CID upon my return.

Special Agent Morgan Huntley, 501st MP, Army CID

Vitters read through the report quietly and then said, "That will be fine. Mind if I hit send?"

Morgan smiled. "As long as you don't giggle when you do it."

Vitters clicked the 'send' button on the computer screen, then closed the laptop. He said, "Hungry?"

Morgan shook his head. "I would prefer we just be done with talking with Poole and then be on our way."

Chapter Fifty-Two

James was held in a featureless room set well within the fort. He was tied to a chair using plastic zip ties, his clothes soaked through with sweat and blood.

Griggs stood guard outside the room, chewing tobacco methodically.

"How is our guest?" asked Vitters.

"Real pleasant," said Griggs.

Vitters stepped to the side and said to Morgan, "He's all yours."

Morgan nodded and approached James slowly. Victoria and Vitters followed into the room.

James was awake. He eyed Morgan with something that measured between bemusement and disdain. James nodded at the blood stains on Morgan's shirt. "I see they haven't given you a fresh change of clothes, either."

"I wanted to talk to you first."

James chuckled and gestured to the room using his head. "Just like the office, huh?"

"Not quite."

"I don't know what they've told you, Morgan, but these are criminals. Plain and simple."

"I know plenty about criminals. That is my line of work, after all."

James looked at Victoria and said, "You better watch your backside in this place, sweetie. These guys haven't seen a real woman in some time."

"Go to hell."

Morgan stepped in front of James and said, "I'm placing you under arrest and having you hauled up in front of an Army Court-Martial. I just wanted you to think about that while you sit in this stinking hole for the next week or two."

James laughed. Morgan watched, impassively. James said,

"That's the funniest shit I've ever heard. I'm under arrest? For what?"

"Kidnapping and murder, among other charges."

James's face took on a staged look of seriousness. "I wasn't kidnapping you, Morgan. I was transferring you to a CIA facility for your own safety. As for the other things you said, I'm not sure I know what you're talking about."

Morgan said nothing. James cracked another smile and said, "Then again, it doesn't matter. We're both dead men. Maybe your girlfriend will get lucky and they'll only rape her."

Morgan took a step towards James and punched him in the gut, knocking the wind from him.

James coughed and sputtered, then took several long, sucking breaths. Soon, his gasps turned to laughter. "See," he said, "I told you."

"Told me what?"

James nodded his head towards the door. Morgan turned around.

Freer and Farrat were holding Victoria in a tight, restrictive grip, her arms pinned behind her back. Freer's hand was held over her mouth, while Farrat held a pistol to her head.

Griggs was standing to the side of the door, his own sidearm pointed at Morgan. Vitters was standing to the side of the room now, a tripod and video camera in hand.

"What's going on?"

Vitters stepped close to Morgan and put a hand on his shoulder. "I'm sorry, Morgan."

Morgan looked from Vitters to Victoria, then back again. James was laughing harder in the background. Morgan said, "We had a deal, Vitters."

"As they say, a deal is only as good as the paper it's written on."

Vitters stepped towards the corner of the room and opened the tripod, then mounted the video camera atop it.

"See, I've got a problem," said Vitters. "I like you Morgan. I even trust you a little. I'm still willing to let you walk out of here with Victoria and go home. But, the problem is, trust only goes so far. And my men, especially Griggs – who is a wise old owl – they disagree with me. They think I should at least take out some insurance."

"What kind of insurance?"

"James Poole is not going to stand trial back in the U.S. You know it. I know it. Hell, even he knows it. Isn't that right, James?"

"Fuck yourself," said James, half smiling.

"I never figured out where James is from, but with that kind of language, I'm betting on New York. What do you think, Special Agent?"

Morgan just stared at Vitters.

"Oh, right," said Vitters. "The point. I've got a business to think of here and people who depend on me. I can't let James Poole slip out of my hands. You know too much, Morgan."

"We had a deal, Vitters."

"I had my fingers crossed the whole time." Vitters held up his left hand, on which his fingers were crossed. "See? Didn't count. I needed you to write that letter and had to tell a little bit of a lie. Our deal isn't quite what I represented it to be, though you do still have a chance to walk out of here."

"I don't play games."

"No, no. Not a game. Don't you want to go home with this nice young lady? All in one piece? I just need insurance. And I need James Poole dead. So, you're going to kill him."

Vitters pointed at the camera in the corner. "I'm going to film it. A gruesome video, to be sure. But, one that I feel will provide the kind of indemnity against you opening your mouth once you leave here. The way I figure it, you would end up with at least life in prison if a video of you killing a CIA officer in cold blood ever surfaced. That should probably keep you from ever spilling the beans on what I've shown you."

"What's my other choice?"

"Not interested?"

"I at least want to know what my other choice is."

Vitters smiled and said, "Your other choice is … less pleasant. I won't kill you. I don't think that's fair considering that you've been a straight dealer."

"Then what do you have in mind?"

"Business relationships are complex. Parked out front at this very moment, I've got a pair of Taliban lieutenants. They want a high-profile hostage. Someone they can taunt the government with. Me? I need to move heroin. The Taliban is willing to get my product to Europe. As with any business deal, however, I have to give them something that they want in return. I wouldn't say that there is any love lost between the Taliban and us, but it is a win-win partnership."

"Why not just give them James?"

"James and his little rat bastard friends in the CIA have all kinds of dirty deals. I'm not taking the risk that he is 'besties' with some Taliban commander. He dies here and now."

"What if I kill James? If you let me go home, then who does the Taliban get instead?"

"They're willing to take cash instead. They're not picky."

"You're better than this, Vitters. Don't go this route."

"I did fool you, didn't I? I'm running a drug ring, Morgan. Something about doing this kind of business just sort of forces you into a certain lifestyle."

"You're such a fucking moron," said James, still chuckling to himself.

"Shut up, asshole. You're dead either way."

James laughed. "You never know."

Vitters hung his head in a feigned sign of contrition and said, "I am sorry, Morgan. But, I figure, he killed your best friend. For what it's worth, I am offering a bit of vengeance. Certainly you won't be the first CID agent who has killed a man during an interrogation."

Morgan looked at Victoria. Her eyes were cold and set on him. He knew her vote without having to hear her say it.

Morgan turned towards Vitters. "Give me the gun."

Griggs laughed.

"I'm sorry, Morgan, but I'm not handing you a live weapon in this situation. You're on your own to figure this out. I am actually curious to see what you'll do."

Morgan looked at Vitters, then at James.

"Don't do this, Morgan," said James. "You'll regret it."

"I guess I'll have to deal with that later."

"What if I'm not guilty? How will that look on your record?"

"Then tell me. Are you guilty?"

James and Morgan stared at each other for a long time. Then Morgan pulled off his shirt. He spun it into a makeshift rope and walked behind James.

Vitters said, "Quiet on the set," and turned on the camera.

Morgan slung the shirt over James's neck, pulling it snug against him, but not yet constricting. He could hear James squirm in the chair.

"Tell me," whispered Morgan.

"What good would the truth do you?"

Morgan squeezed tight on the shirt. James's body arched against the pressure on his windpipe. The sound of his mouth sucking for air filled the tiny room.

Victoria turned her head.

James was turning a pale shade of blue. Vitters and Freer watched impassively, their eyes meeting Morgan's.

Morgan released the shirt and James's body made popping sounds as he sucked in air.

The color returned to James's face. It looked as if James was about to say something, but Morgan drilled another punch into James's kidney, driving the air from him once more.

"No more bullshit," said Morgan. "The next time you catch your breath, I want an answer to my question."

James finally caught his breath and looked up at Morgan. For a moment, a look of fear flashed through his eyes, followed by anger. He drew back and spit on Morgan.

"At least I had the decency to enjoy killing your friend."

Morgan drove a punch into James's face, then flung the shirt around the CIA agent's neck once more. Morgan quickly hauled back with an anger that threatened to break the man's neck long before he would choke.

The room watched quietly as Morgan choked the last breaths from James Poole.

Chapter Fifty-Three

Morgan dropped the shirt next to James's body, then watched as Vitters shut off the camera.

"Well done," said Vitters, "Let's go."

The entire entourage walked into the hallway, leaving James's body uncovered on the chair.

Freer had removed his hand from Victoria's mouth, but he was still holding her arms behind her as they walked through the hallway. Their eyes met, but she said nothing to Morgan.

Morgan walked in front of Griggs, who held his rifle stiffly against Morgan's back, cajoling him ever forward.

As they entered the courtyard, the last rays of the afternoon sun had faded and only the indirect lighting of dusk was left. At the entrance to the courtyard, a quartet of armed Afghans were standing around a large, dirty four-door sedan. Amongst them, they had a hodge-podge of automatic weapons, all from the Soviet era.

"Your ride, Mr. Huntley," said Vitters.

"I would prefer if you took us to Kabul yourself."

"No, I don't think you understand." Vitters turned to face Morgan. Freer and Farrat continued to lead Victoria towards the other side of the courtyard, away from Morgan and the entrance. "I'm not going to Kabul. And neither are you."

Victoria realized before Morgan that they were being separated. She tried to wrest herself from the clutches of Freer and Farrat, kicking Farrat's shin and spinning her wrist.

"Morgan!"

For a moment, it looked like she might free herself, but the two men quickly re-established control.

Morgan took two steps towards her and found himself face-to-face with the muzzle of Griggs' rifle. Morgan tried to move, but Griggs pushed the muzzle firmly under Morgan's chin.

Vitters clucked his tongue in disappointment. "Morgan,

consider this a lesson in dealing with the Devil. If it comforts you, it is my understanding that the Taliban will keep you alive for as long as possible in order to embarrass the U.S."

Morgan lashed out with his left wrist, sending Griggs' rifle barrel into the air. Morgan's next move was to grab Vitters' collar, his other hand searching for Vitters' sidearm.

Vitters was taken by surprise, but responded quickly. He grabbed Morgan's free hand and bent it around. He then then kicked the back of Morgan's knee, which sent him sprawling to the dirt.

"I told you that you were getting old and slow," said Griggs with a smile to Vitters.

"I'm not slow. He's fast."

Morgan pulled himself to his feet. "You're a piece of shit, Vitters. Not some modern-day Robin Hood. Just trash."

"That hurts. I would like to think that in another life, we might have been friends."

"I doubt it."

Vitters looked at the ground for a moment in thought. He then looked up at Morgan and slowly pulled his pistol from its holster. Morgan tensed for what he thought would be the sound of the gun as it fired towards him. Instead, Vitters threw his pistol to Griggs, who caught it one-handed.

"Fine. Let's settle this the old-fashioned way. Hand to hand. No holds barred."

"What do I get if I win?"

"Just satisfaction."

"How about you let the girl go?"

Vitters looked at Victoria, then said, "Win first and then we'll deal."

Vitters moved quickly towards Morgan, not waiting for a response.

Morgan stood his ground, his hands at the ready. As Vitters moved closer, they began to circle, each looking for an opening.

Vitters snaked a fast jab towards Morgan's jaw, which Morgan dodged.

Morgan replied with a kick towards Vitters' knee, hoping to tear something vital. Vitters, however, was much too well-trained in hand-to-hand combat. He not only stepped out of the way of the kick, but in one motion delivered a stunning blow to Morgan's neck.

Morgan fell to one knee, his vision blurred by an explosion of pain. He tried valiantly to block the blows that were coming at him, but Vitters was a trained specialist; Morgan, merely an Army cop. He had been in a few fistfights, yet nothing had ever prepared him for an assault by a perfectly practiced Green Beret.

Finally, Vitters delivered a punishing kick to the back of Morgan's head, sending Morgan sprawling to the ground, blood dribbling from his mouth. Morgan could literally see stars. The whole world felt as it if was racing below him on ball bearings.

Vitters stood over him, breathing hard and smiling. "I'm sorry, Morgan. I truly am."

Vitters then waved for the men near the car, who walked over to Morgan. As they picked up Morgan to carry him to the sedan, he finally succumbed to the beating and passed out.

* * *

Victoria watched in horror as the Taliban's men carried Morgan towards the sedan and threw him into the trunk. They then entered the car and drove off into the growing darkness, windows down and cigarettes freshly lit in triumph.

Vitters stood before Victoria, "I don't want you to be scared, Miss Solano. You are a captive, but I hope you will be a working one. We hope to leverage your nursing skills to assist our sick locals and improve the lives of those who work for us. It's essentially a two-year contract, maybe less if I can further solidify my position before then. If you cooperate, I promise that no harm will come to you. Work hard enough and I'll give you a cut of our profits. Am I clear?"

Victoria just stared at him.

Vitters smiled and said, "We'll be leaving in an hour for our main operations post. I know it's not what you would want. Considering the circumstances and what we could have done to you, I think it's more than fair."

Chapter Fifty-Four

The inside of the sedan's trunk was pitch black.

As Morgan slowly returned to consciousness, it was hard for him to determine whether his eyes were open or closed due to the perfectly dark confines. It wasn't until a momentary glimmer of the taillights through the edges of the trunk that Morgan was able to confirm to himself that his eyes were indeed open.

Morgan's head was pounding. With little warning, the motion of the car and the lack of visual references formed a wave of nausea within him. To combat it, he laid his head back down on the floor of the trunk.

Moments later, Morgan passed into unconsciousness once more.

* * *

When Morgan regained alertness, it was still dark within the trunk and the car was moving over rough terrain.

The pounding in his head had subsided slightly. His eyes had adjusted to the darkness, which allowed him to make out the outline of the trunk without the aid of the taillights. Panic welled in his throat as he thought of being locked in the trunk once the sun rose, but he fought it back by searching softly with his hands.

His hands finally found what had once been the emergency-release latch within the trunk. It was shaved to a metal nub, rendering it useless. The thought crossed Morgan's mind that these were professional kidnappers and not just one-time delivery boys.

Morgan cautiously rolled over and considered the seat backing that faced into the trunk. Through those cushions were presumably the four men who had abducted him. If he had a pistol or a knife, he could work his way into the main cabin of the car and possibly fight his way out. In his current condition, however, and without a weapon, it would be a silly gesture that would result in the four men realizing he was awake.

For the next few minutes, Morgan searched through the trunk for any type of object that could be of some aid, but found nothing. In a country where junk and discarded items seemed to proliferate in every open space, he had been locked into a trunk picked clean of any useful item to the human hand.

With nothing to do, he laid back and tried to clear the fog that still hung in his head.

He had no sense of how long he had been in the trunk or how far they had traveled. He remembered a Special Agent training seminar that had discussed the importance of tracking time and distance to prepare for an escape. That opportunity was long lost.

Moments later, the car slowed to a crawl, then came to a stop. The motor shut off with a resounding series of rattles.

Morgan heard the passenger doors to the car open from within and then heard the voices of the men as they came around the car. He also heard the bolt on an automatic rifle snap back and forth, loading a round into the chamber.

The trunk was flung open. Morgan was surprised to find himself blinded by the scant light outside after so much time in the perfectly dark trunk. He could barely see the men and their rifles. He didn't dare move without clear sight.

Morgan heard a voice say, "*Dzem,*" which he knew to mean 'go' or some rough equivalent, having heard it several times at checkpoints.

Somewhere in his brain, his mind connected the word with another phrase he had heard several times at those checkpoints, which meant something along the lines of "Can I pay a fine," so he said, "*Os təsha jurmaana darkəm?*"

The men all laughed. Now Morgan could see that the oldest of the men was the one who was talking as he said, "*Dzem,*" again.

Morgan put his hands out in front of him and slowly emerged from the car. He felt the barrel of a rifle in the back of his neck prod him forward, urging him onto his unsteady legs.

Scanning the darkness of the desert, he could see that he was near a small set of huts at the base of a range of mountains. No lights were to be seen for miles around. He could hear a chicken rustling somewhere in the background.

The men led Morgan into a hut.

"*Kseenem.*"

Morgan didn't understand the word, but the eldest of the four repeated it again. "*Kseenem.*"

"I don't understand."

One of the men walked behind Morgan and kicked him in the back of the knee, forcing him to fall forward. Morgan took the hint and kneeled.

A captor with a long, light-brown beard, entered the hut and immediately set to handing out bottles of water from a pack he carried. Morgan reached forward and took the water bottle. He drank from it, emptying it within moments, then held the bottle out and said, "More."

One of the men took the bottle and handed Morgan another, which he again drained, this time more slowly.

The eldest of the men gave a small smile, then nodded at the man with the backpack. He pulled from it a stack of flatbread wrapped in wax paper. The ration was handed out equally, Morgan receiving his last.

The men took turns watching Morgan and eating their bread. Morgan ate his share slowly, not wanting to cause himself a sick stomach. When all of them had finished their bread, the youngest of the group grabbed a rope from the pack and walked behind Morgan.

The older man said something that Morgan didn't understand, then made an example of what he wanted Morgan to do by pantomiming his wrists held together behind his back.

Morgan held his wrists back and felt the young man roughly tie his hands together. He then felt the young man urging him to his feet, so he stood.

He was led outside the hut to a small ditch. The young man reached forward and slipped down Morgan's pants and waved his hand, then turned his back. Morgan relieved himself into the ditch, then the young man returned Morgan's pants to their original position.

Several minutes later, the three older men were asleep in the hut. The youngest moved Morgan to the corner and indicated with a free hand that he should lie down. Morgan did so.

The young man was on guard duty first. He kept his eyes and his rifle on Morgan, doing an admirable job of preventing their captive an unsupervised moment to escape.

Outside the hut, the first rays of sunlight were rising on the horizon. Just 48 hours before, Morgan had been a relatively free man moving about Kabul at will. Now he was a captive of the Taliban in a small hut in god-knew-where Afghanistan.

His mind drifted back to the State Department pamphlet he had read:

"Be patient, as hostage negotiations are often difficult and time consuming. Remember, your chances of survival increase with time. Most episodes of kidnapping or hostage-taking end with no loss of life or physical injury to the captive. Eventually you will probably be released or rescued."

Morgan doubted anyone on earth knew where he was, about as sobering a thought as he had ever experienced. The Army likely wouldn't begin looking for him for another few days, assuming that Thompson or anyone else even wanted him to be found. He was supposed to turn up dead, he recalled, so maybe Thompson and Franklin would insist on finding him in order to complete their little story. On the other hand, his email regarding his implication of James Poole had likely tipped them off that the gig was up, so he wasn't entirely certain they would actually care if he fell off the face of the earth.

After an hour, Morgan realized the young man who sat across from him was a diligent guard and not likely to fall asleep. To spite him, Morgan did the only thing he could do: he rested, hoping that at the least it would irk the young man to watch someone sleep while he had to force himself to remain awake.

Tomorrow, he would search for an opportunity to escape. If that opportunity came, he would need all the rest he could get.

Chapter Fifty-Five

Victoria awoke inside a mud hut, her bed a simple pile of blankets on the floor over a thin layer of straw. Her head hurt fiercely from stress and poor sleep. She felt disoriented and lay still for several long minutes, trying to establish in her mind that this was indeed reality.

Sitting up slowly, she surveyed the humble surroundings.

An Afghan woman in her late thirties entered through the archway that led from the room to the center of the hut carrying a platter of tea and flatbread, which she placed on the floor. The woman then pointed to a pile of clothing, which had been laid flat on the floor beside Victoria.

* * *

Ten minutes later, Victoria was dressed in the clean clothes and standing in what amounted to the front doorway of the hut. Outside, several young boys were playing with a soccer ball. She could see a field of poppy flowers behind a mud wall, which were being attended to by several adults. In the distance, she could see Afghan men with rifles patrolling the edges of the village.

Her eyes then met with Alexi Farrat, who was smoking a cigarette a few feet away. He appeared to be waiting for her. He stubbed out the cigarette and walked towards Victoria.

"Good morning," he said, "I hope you slept well."

"Do you have some Advil or Tylenol?"

Farrat nodded and reached into his tunic, then produced a prescription bottle. "I figured you might need that."

Victoria took the bottle, looked at the pills and said, "Codeine?"

Farrat shrugged.

Victoria used a bottle of water she had found with the fresh clothing to wash down the pills. "Where are your compatriots?" she asked.

"Out and about. Much to do after returning from a business trip."

Victoria nodded with a scowl. Farrat said, "Don't be so glum. You get a chance to work with the locals."

"You're all lunatics."

Farrat clucked his tongue. "That's what I get for helping with your headache?"

Victoria said nothing.

"As it stands, we have a young man in the village who is very ill. I think it is time you started earning your keep."

Victoria looked at Farrat, unsure if he was giving her a line or telling her the truth. Finally, she asked, "Where is he?"

* * *

Victoria entered the darkened hut with Farrat and scanned the interior. There was a small wooden bed, hand-carved, on which a young Afghan boy was curled into the fetal position. A woman, presumably his mother, sat near the boy holding a wet towel to the boy's head.

Victoria approached and, not knowing what to say to the woman, turned to Farrat.

"Ask her if it is okay if I examine her son."

"It's okay. Go ahead."

"Please ask her first."

Farrat asked the woman a question in Pashto. She replied and stood, then smiled at Victoria.

"It's still okay," said Farrat.

Victoria glowered at Farrat, then approached the boy. He was pale, covered in sweat and unconscious.

"How long has he been like this?"

Farrat translated the question and then listened to the

mother's answer, which he repeated. "Almost three days."

"Do you have a medical kit here?"

Farrat pointed at an Army medical field kit, which appeared to have been brought in ahead of time. Victoria opened the kit and within a few minutes had a variety of medical instruments at hand.

She began a thorough examination of the boy. As she did this, Vitters entered the hut unannounced.

Victoria continued her inspection of the boy, lifting his clothes and examining his body.

The mother asked a question and Farrat translated. "She wants to know what you are looking for."

"A scorpion sting or some other bite. His blood pressure is very low, which is a symptom of toxicity."

Farrat translated and the mother replied. "She says that she has checked him and he was not bitten."

Victoria ignored the woman and continued to evaluate the boy's skin. On his leg, she found a long series of scrapes.

"What are these?"

Farrat translated and then said, "He cut his knee playing soccer. They fixed that wound right after."

Victoria leaned in closer, then waved over the mother.

"These wounds are infected. Not with traditional gangrene, which offers the telltale green bacterial growth, but with what we commonly call a staph infection. The boy is having toxic shock as a result of the infection."

Farrat said, "We gave him antibiotics."

"Staph is nasty. It needs the strongest antibiotics available, which aren't in a field kit. Someone needs to go get a strong dose of an amoxicillin derivative."

"Captain, tell her we'll send one of our vehicles right away," said Vitters from behind them.

Farrat translated and the woman grabbed Victoria in a hug.

Victoria turned and saw Vitters for the first time. The woman hugged everyone in the room, then rushed out. Farrat followed.

Vitters approached the bedside of the little boy.

"Not even here twelve hours and you're already making a big impact."

"Go to hell."

"He would have died without you."

Victoria was quiet. "He may still, but his chances are helped by the fact that children his age can generally bounce back quickly if given help."

"I'm sorry about this. I really am," said Vitters.

"Save the bullshit."

"Don't worry. Stockholm Syndrome will eventually kick in."

"Is that your idea of a joke?"

Vitters shrugged and walked back towards the entrance to the hut. "Don't go getting cute. There's two-dozen armed men on the perimeter of this village."

Victoria picked up the wet rag and held it to the boy's skin. As she tried to cool him, she kicked the bottom of the bedframe in anger.

Chapter Fifty-Six

When Morgan awoke, it was daylight outside. The young man who had been charged with guarding him in the night had obviously been given a break, as he was now asleep on the floor. The man with the brown beard watched Morgan, his automatic rifle trained on him.

His guard noticed that Morgan was awake and said something to the other men. As they all looked at Morgan, the eldest man said something in reply and the man with the brown beard stood. He walked behind Morgan and helped him to his feet.

The man untied the rope on Morgan's hands and guided him outside to the ditch. Knowing the drill, he took care of the necessaries, then allowed himself to be marched back to the hut. As they walked, he tried to take advantage of the daylight to get his bearings.

The sun was high in the sky, giving no indication as to the cardinal directions. Worse, the hut was at the base of a large mountain range that Morgan didn't recognize, not that he was an expert on Afghan geography. He could see little other than a continuing stream of mountains in the distance.

They re-entered the hut. Morgan was given a bottle of water and a piece of flatbread. He consumed both eagerly, then allowed himself to be sat down once more on the ground. This time, his hands were not bound together, though two men watched him at all times with rifles ready.

The next few hours dragged by. The men rarely spoke. Morgan tried to rest.

He paid attention to the habits of his captors, as well, using the time to issue each of them a simplistic name. He learned that the young man, who he called Youngest, was the most dedicated of the men, rarely taking his eyes off of Morgan when it was his duty to watch him. Eldest was less concerned and would often take a short walk during his stretches of guard duty. The other two men – Brown Beard and Shorty – were more attentive than Eldest, but by no means as dedicated as Youngest. Both of them could be distracted at times and Shorty in particular had a bad habit of leaving his hands too far from his weapon when he was on guard duty.

Through this time, the men took turns praying to Mecca in accordance with their faith. It was discordant to Morgan that these men should be so fundamentally sound in their religious zeal as to remember to pray four times a day. Yet here they were in a hut in the desert, holding a man at gun point, presumably with the intention to kill or illegally imprison him for years to come.

* * *

The sun was sinking below the mountains in the distance when Morgan's captors handed out the evening ration and began preparations to leave the hut. Despite the lack of calories, Morgan didn't feel hungry. Instead, a mixture of adrenalin and anticipation of what lay ahead fought for control within his body.

Morgan was led from the hut and the men cut his bindings then retied his hands in front of him. Shorty walked to the sedan. Morgan had the impression that he was going to be once more thrust into the trunk. Instead, Shorty started the car and drove away, the other three men waving a brief goodbye as Shorty headed into the desert.

So far, there had been little to feel good about in the last twenty-four hours. The departure of one of his four captors was a glimmer of fortune for obvious reasons. Morgan hoped that it was a permanent change in manpower and not just a temporary errand from which Shorty would return.

Morgan was gently pressed towards a path that led from the huts towards a narrow trail into the mountains. As they walked,

Brown Beard and Youngest stayed behind Morgan, each holding automatic rifles. Morgan quickly understood the reason they had tied his hands in front of him. Walking uphill on a difficult trail in the dark would be hard enough: doing it with a person's hands tied behind their back would be nearly impossible.

Eldest led the way through the dark. He hummed quietly to himself as they traversed the difficult mountain trail, which at times was incredibly steep. Morgan found the lack of food and water over the last few days had enfeebled him. Several times, he lagged in order to catch his breath, but was immediately pushed ever forward by the rifle barrels of his captors.

* * *

Somewhere after the first two hours, they came upon a small stream and stopped. Eldest waved Morgan towards the water. Morgan didn't quite understand, but the two younger men took the cue and drank.

Morgan followed suit and drank deeply of the cool water. A moment later, as he stood, Youngest tapped Morgan on the shoulder. The young man had a wry look in his face and crooked his finger for Morgan to follow him.

They walked several paces off the trail until Youngest pointed at something in the darkness. Morgan stepped closer and realized that he was staring at the body of a man. The deceased was dressed in the sort of clothing that Western contractors wore throughout Afghanistan. From the look of things, the dead man had been shot in the back of the head.

As Morgan turned away, Youngest smiled and made a pantomime with one palm and his opposite hand's fingers to indicate a person running, then pointed at the dead body. He followed up the entire demonstration with a wag of the finger in the universal sign of 'no'.

Morgan nodded in understanding and Youngest led him back

to the others. A moment later, the march up the mountain resumed.

Since the start of their journey up the mountain, Morgan had been considering whether this was a good moment for an escape attempt. He had finally been able to determine north, south, and so on from the setting sun. Yet, even with that information, Morgan knew this was not quite the right moment to bolt. Identifying north and south was important, but he still had no true bearing on where civilization might lie or where he was within the country. Morgan was now hoping that the opportunity afforded him by such a high vantage point might give him a sense of where the nearest city or base might be located.

Already, his chances had improved with the reduction in the number of his captors from four to three. Whether they would be joined by others further along their trek, or how circumstances might change was a wild card that could reverse those gains at any moment. His steadily declining fitness and health reduced those odds further. In short, he was now gambling for a better window of escape in the hopes that it wouldn't shut before he realized it.

Chapter Fifty-Seven

Victoria listened to the silence of the village around her as she lay in her straw bed inside the hut. She had never realized how much she took for granted the ever-present clocks in Western civilization. It was disorienting to exist in a timeless space, as if she was locked into an open-air jail cell.

Through the day, the memory of an Army instructor named Franks and his repeated invective that it was every soldier's duty to escape if captured had been roaring in her head. As she lay there in the dark, she felt determined to heed that advice. The village had reached the stillness of the late evening and Victoria decided that this moment was probably as good as any chance she could take if she were going to escape.

Victoria stood softly and made her way to the door. Peering out in the darkness, she saw no movement in the center of the village. She stepped out of the hut, hugging the wall as tightly as she could.

With all the grace she could summon, she worked her way across the village in soft, halting steps. She knelt beside the last hut, then searched the darkness that lay beyond.

By the light of the moon, she could see several men making their rounds in the distance. Two of them had wandered near each other to share a cigarette. The result was a hole in the line of guards just wide enough to make her way through and on into the desert. She didn't know if she had the survival gear for the challenges that might await her if she got away: whatever those were, Victoria was willing to risk it to escape the prospect of years of imprisonment.

She rushed into the darkness, aiming for what she perceived to be the space between the guards.

As she approached an earthen wall that demarcated a field, she slowed and knelt near it. She could see the next clearing from her position near the corner of the wall. Ahead of her was a stand of small trees, near which was a small shed for tending the fields.

Checking her surroundings and seeing no guards, Victoria raced for the cover afforded by the trees.

As she was about to reach them, Griggs stepped out from behind the shed, held up a rifle on which was mounted a night scope, and said, "Good evening, young lady."

Victoria skidded in her attempt to stop and she fell on her rear. Griggs slowly approached to within a few steps of her and said, "On your knees."

She slowly moved to her knees and used her eyes to follow Griggs as he slowly stepped behind her. An instant later, Victoria saw stars and felt searing pain race through her body as Griggs crashed the butt of his rifle down on the back of her head.

The blow had been hard enough to daze her. When she regained her sense of consciousness, she found herself face down on the dirt. Behind, she could feel Griggs kneeling over her, his face close to her ear.

"Get off me."

"I don't think anyone is asking."

Victoria tried to roll out from under Griggs, but the dizziness and the strength of his grip prevented her from doing more than feebly rocking from side to side.

Terror and anger welled within Victoria. "You're a piece of shit, you know that?"

Griggs slammed her face into the ground. She felt her nose break and blood run from it. Seconds later, Victoria drew her breath as the utterly distinctive coolness of a large knife pressed against her throat.

"Who am I kidding?" growled Griggs into her ear. "I told Vitters to quit messing around with you. Close your eyes and I'll make this fast."

Victoria tried to wrestle herself away, but Griggs was too strong. Then, without warning, the weight of Griggs body was lifted off her as if by a crane. She heard footsteps scuffling near her and then the weight of a man hitting the ground.

Victoria rolled over and saw that Vitters and Freer were standing over Griggs.

Vitters looked from Victoria to Griggs, then shook his head. "Griggs, I'll have a word with you in my office in twenty minutes."

Griggs nodded, then stood and walked off into the dark.

Vitters knelt beside Victoria and said, "As for you, I hope this is a lesson as to why you should never leave the safety of my camp."

Freer roughly grabbed Victoria under the armpit and lifted her back on to her feet.

As if in a dream, she slowly walked with the men back to her hut.

Chapter Fifty-Eight

The first rays of dawn were rising on the horizon. Morgan was exhausted. His captors had led him deep within the mountains. They had reached the first crest of the range several hours earlier, but continued climbing through the night.

As Morgan had hoped, when they attained the crest, he had been able to make out the silhouette of mountains in three directions from their location due to the brightness of the moon. In the distance, back along the way from which they had come, Morgan could make out the lights of a mid-sized city, as well as a smattering of small lights speckled throughout the countryside. Undoubtedly, there were more villages interspersed in that region, which could not be seen in the darkness due to a lack of electrical infrastructure.

Looking to the southwest, the mountain range ended several miles further away, with the pink haze of a city faint on that horizon.

They had not rested on the crest for long, however, and they had followed the trail deeper into the mountains, descending for a long stretch of time, then climbing once more as they made the next ascent.

By the time they stopped near dawn, Morgan's legs were quivering and his head pounding with dehydration. His captors were winded as well, but seemed to be regaining their breath with ease.

Eldest led Morgan into a small cave in the side of mountain. It seemed that this must be a common stopping point for these men, as there were pre-arranged packages of food, water and clothing waiting. Morgan was given more water and flatbread, which he once again ate slowly.

The men had left Morgan's hands tied in front of him for the entirety of the climb. Now Brown Beard cut loose these bonds and once more retied Morgan's hands so that they were behind

Morgan's back. Brown Beard then indicated that Morgan should lay on the ground, which Morgan did without complaint, happy for the respite.

Morgan's first guard of the evening was once again Youngest. The other two men fell quickly into a deep sleep.

This time, however, Morgan was determined to only pretend to be asleep so that he could understand the patterns of their shift changes. He closed his eyes.

To keep awake, Morgan replayed in his mind the anger and frustration of seeing Victoria hauled away by Vitters' men.

* * *

After what seemed to be an eternity, Morgan heard the sounds of someone shuffling to their feet. Morgan slowly opened one eye. It was daylight outside of the cave, but the other two men were still asleep. Youngest was still awake, but had stood and now had his back to Morgan.

Youngest walked outside of the cave. A few moments later, Morgan heard the sound of the man relieving himself.

Several minutes later, Youngest re-entered the cave and shook Brown Beard awake, who was clearly unhappy about taking his turn at guard duty. Brown Beard slowly stretched, then took the rifle from Youngest and moved over to guard Morgan.

The day continued on like that, with Morgan pretending to sleep until Brown Beard relieved Eldest and the old man started his shift covering Morgan.

With Eldest now on duty, Morgan felt that he understood the pattern of his guards. It had cost him dearly in the form of a night – or day, rather – of sleep. Yet, he now felt certain he knew the flaw in their tactics. Satisfied that he had learned all he could, Morgan allowed himself to fall into a heavy sleep.

Chapter Fifty-Nine

Several hours later, Morgan was awoken by the smell of an orange. The old man was eating the last segment, the rind in a pile at his feet. Their eyes locked on each other. Finally, Eldest said something in Pashto to the other men.

Brown Beard stood and brought a piece of flatbread to Morgan. The last rays of sunlight were filtering through the entrance to the cave. Morgan's body was tired from the irregular hours and he felt stiff all over. He ate the flatbread, which by now was stale and tough.

An hour later, as the sun set, they once more took to the mountain path. Morgan marked the location of the sun in the sky relative to their direction of travel and noted that they were heading southwest. In his mind, he tried to triangulate the location of the city lights he had seen the night before.

They hiked in silence, traveling further into the mountains. Tonight's sky was covered in clouds and the darkness was oppressive, almost disorienting during the points where they passed steep cliffs along the trail.

Morgan used the time to think through his plan. If the men kept their regular schedule today, Morgan was sure he knew the moment he could make a move.

* * *

An hour further into the mountains, Morgan detected the scent of a burning fire. The other men sensed it, too, and their conversation became excited.

As they rounded a turn on the mountain trail, a complex of caves on a small plateau came into view in the darkness. A fire was burning in the entrance to one of the caves and six men were preparing to roast a spit of chickens.

One of the men saw the approaching group and said

something to the others on the rocks, who stood and waved. Eldest cracked a big smile, slung his rifle over his shoulder and greeted the men.

Morgan's heart sank. He had prepared himself mentally for an escape, but that plan had been predicated on escaping from three men in an isolated cave in the mountains. How he would get away from a whole cadre of Taliban was beyond him. With the weight of a thousand stones on his heart, Morgan realized he had waited too long.

Eldest was talking animatedly with the other men, pointing at Morgan. They were engrossed in his story and one of them even came close to Morgan for a better look.

After a few minutes of this, Eldest said something stern to Youngest, who gave a small glower of dissatisfaction, then disappeared alone into the cave. The other men continued talking until Youngest re-emerged with a fresh stack of flatbread. He broke the load equally among himself and Brown Beard.

Eldest continued to talk, then said what looked like a 'goodbye' and walked back to Morgan.

Within a few seconds their little troupe was once again back on the trail, leaving the encampment behind.

Morgan felt relief wash over him as they continued, the cave complex falling further and further behind them. Silently, he vowed to himself that tonight would be the night that he escaped, lest he lose his chance altogether.

* * *

The rest of that night's march was a hard slog across rocky, unforgiving terrain. The trail was just a barely discernable, thin ribbon of flat earth along the mountains. Several sections were along sharp drop-offs and Morgan was certain that – if they had attempted these passes in daylight – none of the men, regardless of their experience, would have wanted to make the crossing.

The darkness at least offered the bliss of not knowing just how long and painful a death lurked with every step.

Once, as they cleared one of these steep sections, they came across what appeared to be a patrol of two men, armed with automatic rifles. These men smiled and greeted the others, giving little more than a cursory glance to Morgan.

Apparently everyone on this mountain was in the same business, Morgan thought.

Morgan's group then proceeded through a steeply walled pass cut into the crest of the mountain range. This eventually led out into a junction of multiple trailheads.

Morgan tried to keep track of the bearings as they veered off onto a new trail.

* * *

Not long after they had passed through the junction of trials, as dawn was rising in the distance, they stopped near the entrance to yet another cave. This one had no pre-delivered accommodations waiting for them and was sparse by comparison to the cave from the previous night.

After they had settled in, the captors shared the flatbread they had acquired at the cave complex. Morgan was given a small apple, which he ate in five bites. It was tart and almost unpleasant, but the coolness of the fruit gave Morgan a chill on his back.

With the first rays of dawn mounting outside, Morgan lay down and pretended to fall asleep as quickly as he could. He hoped his captors would allow him to keep his hands tied in front of him, which would offer more freedom in an escape attempt. Unfortunately, he felt a foot nudge him in his side and he looked up. Eldest was waving at Morgan to stand.

Morgan followed the command and, a moment later, Brown Beard untied his hands. He then retied them behind Morgan's back.

Morgan tried to hide his dismay. Eldest smiled slightly at him as they finished restricting his hands, as if he could sense Morgan's thoughts.

Morgan lay back down on the ground and closed his eyes. Within ten minutes everyone in the cave was snoring except Youngest, who once again was the first on watch.

As day broke outside the cave, Morgan continued to keep still and breathe slowly, sneaking glances through half-shut eyes at Youngest. He felt his body stiffen with the waiting. Several times his skin raised in goose-bumps as the thought of his impending escape attempt caused adrenalin to course through his body.

As he waited, Tom Petty's "The Waiting is the Hardest Part" bubbled into his head from some deep memory. He had to stifle a laugh born of both comedy and stress at such a strange thought coming into his head at just this moment.

* * *

After what seemed like an eternity, Youngest slowly, quietly stood.

Morgan watched him quietly make his way towards the entrance of the cave. Morgan had rehearsed the next sequence of events in his head a thousand times during the last few hours. Yet, as Youngest stood to exit the cave, he did something that Morgan had not expected.

Youngest reached for Brown Beard. Morgan watched in horror as it appeared that Youngest was waking Brown Beard for the next duty shift. Morgan's plan had depended on only one of these men being awake. Within moments, Youngest would inadvertently foil that opportunity.

To Morgan's relief, though, instead of shaking Brown Beard awake, Youngest gently grabbed the collection of thin paper the men used for bathroom tissue.

A moment later, Youngest was outside the cave and Morgan was alone with the two sleeping men.

Morgan quietly turned over on his back. He pulled his knees to his chest and worked to slip his hands under his feet. As part of CID training, he had undergone a class in which they had learned firsthand how prisoners might escape by practicing techniques such as sliding handcuffed wrists from back to front over their feet. Now those sessions were paying off in a literal life-and-death situation for Morgan, who found that with some minor scraping of his hands, he was able to pull his arms in front of him.

Morgan sat up and held his breath. He could hear Youngest urinating somewhere outside the cave and the slow breathing of the two other men. Morgan moved to his knees, then his feet. His legs felt stiff and unusable.

Both men slept with their rifles at hand. It was too perilous to grab one without waking someone. Morgan instead tiptoed towards the entrance to the cave and spent a moment listening. Somewhere in the distance, he could hear Youngest pulling his pants down.

Morgan chanced a look outside the cave and found that Youngest was about 30 yards away, with his back to him. Morgan looked towards the ground and saw what he wanted: a rock about the size of a baseball. He slowly knelt and took the rock into his hands, then worked his way, step-by-step, until he was within five yards of the man, who still had his pants around his ankles.

Morgan rushed the last few yards, the young man turning in surprise in time to see Morgan launching a kick towards his face.

Morgan's foot caught Youngest in the jaw. The combination of the force of the kick and the fact that Youngest still had his pants around his ankles caused the young man to fall over onto the ground face-first. Before the Youngest could make another move, Morgan was on top of him and brought the rock down on the man's head as hard as he could, striking him in the temple.

The blow stunned Youngest and he gave a small, guttural groan as he lurched towards the ground.

The realization that his own freedom was at hand flashed through Morgan's mind. Instantly, he brought the rock down several times in rapid succession Youngest's head, stopping only when he saw bone. Morgan knew there was no chance the man was getting up again, so he stopped.

Standing up, Morgan grabbed the automatic rifle that lay nearby and walked towards the entrance to the cave. The rifle was awkward in his still-bound hands, but at the short range, he doubted he would need the accuracy afforded by having his hands free.

As Morgan entered the cave, he saw that Eldest's eyes had opened and he was staring at Morgan. They both looked at each other for a long moment.

Then, Morgan pulled the trigger.

The three-round blast from the rifle echoed like a cannon within the confines of the cave. Eldest was killed instantly. Brown Beard sat up in a blur, but Morgan had already aimed at the man and pulled the trigger once more. The second flurry of bullets struck Brown Beard in the chest. The man sat there and looked at his wounds, then slumped forward and moaned.

Within seconds, Morgan was searching Eldest's pockets and found the knife that he had seen him using to cut the orange the day before.

Morgan freed his hands by sawing through the rope, then searched both bodies for a cell phone. He found nothing of use on either man other than the knife and a few coins.

Morgan walked back to the body of Youngest and pulled it into the cave, dragging it unceremoniously across the ground in a rush. He dumped it next to his dead compatriots.

The evidence hidden as best as possible in a short amount of time, Morgan grabbed the satchel filled with food, water and ammunition. An instant later, he departed the cave at a flat run.

Chapter Sixty

The mixture of late-morning sun and cool mountain breeze tasted sweet in Morgan's mouth. He could not stop, though, to savor the sensation of freedom that was washing over him.

Morgan knew that the first hour after an escape was critical to an escapee. In an hour, a typical person could cover about four to six miles, depending on fitness and health. This six-mile radius in any direction led to an ever-expanding complexity of options that the escapee could utilize to evade pursuit.

For Morgan, maximizing the distance from the point of his escape would be made difficult by the rugged terrain, limited trails and by the armed patrols in the vicinity. Whether anyone had heard the shots fired was a guessing game. He hoped that the strange ways in which sound traveled in the mountains would help obscure the location of the shots to anyone who had happened to hear them.

Morgan paralleled the trail on which they had traveled the night before, returning towards the junction of trailheads they had passed just recently.

In the distance, he could see what had previously been obscured by the darkness of their night marches. The mountain range was wide and filled with several lines of mountains, which rolled outwards like waves in a sea of giants. It was unforgiving and cragged, with merely scrub at the highest elevations for cover. There were no obvious shortcuts, passes or roads. Morgan would have preferred to get off the trail where he was less likely to be seen or tracked, but the trails were likely the only routes through and across the imposing terrain.

Morgan finally found the junction of trails. There were a total of four options, discounting the trail from where he had just come. He also discounted the trail that he had traversed the evening prior, which he knew would lead him past the cave complex several hours ahead.

Of the remaining options, one was well worn and descended along the side of a ridge, disappearing into the small, elevated valley formed between two lines of mountains. The problem with this, though, was that Morgan could see no means of escaping from the valley other than to travel back into the mountains at some point in the future. The additional factor of the trail's well-traveled appearance led him to believe that movement along it would bring a high risk of encountering a patrol or an unfriendly civilian.

The remaining two options were little-worn and thus had the enticement of possibly offering a low risk of encountering enemy combatants. One seemed to curve back, angling downwards along a cliff that transited below the trail he had come from. Morgan disliked the idea of traveling in that direction, even if it led lower from the mountains, so he eliminated this choice as well.

That left the fourth and final option, which followed a similar elevation to the one he was at now, but looked as if it curved around the backside of the mountains he had traveled along the previous night. This had the theoretical benefit of moving behind the encampment in the caves, but like the others, he had no real idea where it might end up. Among four poor options, it seemed to Morgan that this trail was the least terrible of the choices. It was not how he usually liked to evaluate a decision, but he found no means by which he could describe any of his options as 'good'.

To help dissuade any possible trackers, Morgan started by walking onto the steep, well-worn trail, stamping his feet hard into the soil to leave imprints. He then slowly lightened his step and edged off the path and into the scrub. He gently made his way back to the junction of trailheads through the scrub. Once there, he walked along the side of his preferred trail until the narrowness of the passage forced him back onto the pathway.

With the desire to make the best time possible, Morgan broke into a steady jog. He tried to balance his desire to leave the area quickly with a need to move quietly, so he fought the impulse to run at a full-out sprint. Several times, he thought he heard voices in the distance and stopped to take cover. Each time, he saw no one approaching.

The sun was high in the sky and beat down on him. Sweat soon poured from his body. His head ached with lack of sleep and inadequate food. The pack was like a heavy millstone on his back.

Morgan put all of these from his mind and kept putting one foot in front of the other.

* * *

After running hard for what he thought was about forty minutes, Morgan felt forced to rest by the ever-growing heat. He ripped into the backpack, found a bottle of water and guzzled half of it. It wasn't nearly enough to slake his thirst, but the water had to be rationed out of caution.

As he wiped the sweat that was rolling across his head, he heard something further down the trail. He quietly put the bottle of water into his sack and prostrated himself into a firing position.

He aimed the AK-47 down the trail, his ears picking up the sound of footsteps. He rested his finger on the trigger and waited.

Two boys about the age of twelve appeared on the trail. They held stacks of flatbread tied in twine, similar to how a schoolboy would carry books in a leather strap. They also each had a Soviet-era automatic rifle slung casually across their backs, the guns nearly as big as the children. As their eyes came to rest on Morgan, they both dropped the flatbread.

Morgan stared at the boys, who were clearly unsure of what they were to do. Morgan stood slowly, then walked towards them, his rifle pointed at the taller of the two.

Using the tip of his barrel, Morgan waved for them to unsling their rifles and put them on the ground. One of the boys understood and slowly lowered his rifle down. The other boy followed suit.

Morgan then came closer and grabbed both rifles. He disconnected the magazine from each and cleared the chamber, putting the ammunition in his satchel. He took one of the stacks of flatbread and shoved it into his own pack.

Walking backwards, Morgan passed the boys in the direction they had come from, his gun still trained on them.

Within a few seconds, Morgan was at the edge of their sight. He turned his back to the boys and ran down the trail as hard as he could.

A moment later, in the distance, he could hear the boys yelling for help.

Chapter Sixty-One

Morgan rushed down the loose trail. The boys' yells for help had faded into the distance and the only thing he could hear now was the pounding of his own footsteps as he rushed ahead.

The path was leading him towards an elevated valley between two mountains. As Morgan moved along the trail, he realized that the two boys had been carrying fresh food up the mountain, presumably towards the men at the camp.

Morgan slowed to a stop.

If the boys had been carrying food along this trail towards the camp, it probably meant that this trail was likely to pass near a village. One that would likely be unwilling to help him.

Worse, while the trail did make for easy travel, it was headed in the opposite direction from either of the cities he had seen the previous night from his vantage point on the mountain.

Morgan listened for a moment, but could hear nothing. Still, he was certain that the two boys had at least garnered the attention of a patrol, if not made it to the camp in the mountains by now. There would surely be armed pursuers, possibly from both directions if they had cell phones or other communication devices at hand.

Morgan considered his alternatives. The mountains on his left were steep and unforgiving, but he could see a line of ascent towards a saddle at the top. He wasn't sure if he had gone far enough to pass the encampment on the other side, but from the top of that mountain, he could likely pick a path of descent that would keep him clear of it. What's more, he might be able to observe the movements of his potential pursuers and find a gap in their search net.

Morgan took a long swig of water, then began the climb through the scrub up the side of the mountain.

The going was slow. His hands were quickly cut and scraped by the need to scramble over numerous, steep sections. And his head still pounded a dull, throbbing pain.

* * *

Halfway to the saddle in the ridge, Morgan finally saw seven armed men rushing along the trail below him. Morgan took cover amid a pair of low bushes, aiming the rifle at the group.

He watched the men approach the point at which he had exited the trail. One of the men was scanning the hillside and for a moment Morgan was certain that his eyes had swept across him.

The man continued his search, however, apparently not seeing Morgan's hiding position.

To Morgan's relief, the party of men continued on past the point at which Morgan had exited the trail, not seeing the evidence of his climb. In a hurry, they were soon out of sight, around the next bend formed by the mountains.

Morgan waited another moment, then continued his climb. The time he had to reach the peak was now fixed by however much time it would take those men to reach the end of the trail, whereupon they would certainly learn that Morgan had never arrived. They would then likely double back and begin searching for him in earnest on the edges.

He had one choice: to get across the crest before the searchers returned.

* * *

An hour later, Morgan was nearing the top and the gap that crossed the mountain. He was exhausted, filthy and bleeding. It was here that his luck ran out, as well.

As he scanned down the mountain face once more, he saw the group of men returning along the trail. They were carefully searching above and below the trail this time for signs of him.

Morgan's position was the most exposed it had been along his climb. There was little scrub to hide him from the naked eye and he was sure that he could be clearly seen against the rocky crags of the peak.

Morgan looked up. The saddle in the mountain that he had been aiming for was one or two minutes of hard climbing from him. He still had no idea what was on the other side, but he had a huge head-start on the men behind. Even if they saw him now, he might be able to close the gap and cross to the other side, out of range of the automatic rifles that he could see held at the ready below.

He decided his best option was to attempt to hide once more, despite the poor cover. Trying to clear the remaining distance in the open would make him an easily identifiable, moving object in an exposed section of mountain. These men had been unable to locate him the time before. Perhaps with the added distance, they would once more fail to see him.

Morgan lay down on the ground and slowly rubbed his face and arms with dust, hoping to obscure his skin tone. He watched as the men continued to search the terrain around the trail. Morgan felt his heart lifting with hope as they kept moving forward.

Then, the same man who had previously seemed to scan over Morgan's hiding place was once again looking right at him. Morgan's gut twisted as he sensed that this man was thinking the same thing that Morgan had from the trail: that this approach up the mountain was at least passible.

Morgan watched the man slow his pace. He seemed to be looking directly at Morgan.

The man stopped walking. He said something to one of his companions, pointing in Morgan's direction. The men all stopped and stared towards the top of the peak, looking at where Morgan was hiding.

Then the men became excited. Morgan saw one of the men

aim a rifle at him. Its muzzle erupted with flashes that for a moment were soundless at the great distance. Luckily, the angle and deflection of the shot caused the bullets to land harmlessly short of Morgan's position.

Still, Morgan involuntarily ducked, hugging the earth. The movement was all the men needed to confirm their suspicion that they had found their target.

As two of them began to rush up the mountain towards Morgan, he broke cover and scrambled for the gap in the crest of the mountains.

He worked his way towards the top of the mountain, hearing gunfire and shouts from below. Several bullets sailed in the air past him. He thanked the forces of physics for making a rifle shot up the side of a steep mountain one of the most difficult in all of marksmanship.

As Morgan reached the top of the saddle, he felt a bullet knick the top edge of his shoulder. The force of the impact threw him forward and he fell flat on his chest, sliding back down the path he had just come about seven feet. The rocks beneath him scraped and burned along his arms and something – a rock or a root – cut deep into the top of his right thigh.

Morgan cried out in pain, but neither the glancing wound on his shoulder or the cut in his thigh was debilitating. A moment later, he regained his footing and reattempted his ascent, sharp pain wracking his body.

As Morgan crossed the top, he blindly scrambled onto the small, flat spot on the crest, out of sight of his pursuers.

Once there, he surveyed his wounds. The cut on his thigh was ragged and bloody, proving to be the worse of the two. He ripped off the bottom of his shirt and wrapped it around his leg to assist with the bleeding.

Morgan then scanned the downward face of the mountain and thought about the options it presented to him.

To his left, he could see the trail that he had traveled the previous evening as a captive. A thin wisp of smoke arose from somewhere in the distance and he presumed this to be the cave complex.

Beyond the base of the mountains below him, spread out in the distance was the expanse of the Afghan plain. Maybe ten or fifteen miles from the base of the mountain range, he could see a paved road snaking into the horizon.

From the angle of the sun, Morgan judged it to be several hours past noon. He would have another four or five hours of daylight before reaching the safety offered by darkness. If he could make it to the road by morning, he hoped that from there he could possibly hijack a car or some other vehicle that passed by. It wasn't a very good plan, but it was the best one he had at the moment.

The shortest distance off the mountain was a ravine that traveled downward from the saddle. There were sections that looked as if they might be tough going, but this also offered the benefit of slowing his pursuers.

Morgan began the hard scramble down the mountain ravine. Twice he stumbled and fell, sliding on his rear, cutting his clothing in several places.

His mouth was dry with fear. His shoulder and his leg cried out to him in agony with every hard step. Yet, onward he churned, moving as quickly as he could downwards, hoping that he could put enough distance between himself and his hunters. There was now no turning back. Recapture would mean inevitable death, if not something worse just before it.

* * *

Much sooner than he had hoped, Morgan heard gunfire behind him, indicating that the men had crested the mountain. He still had the advantage of a head-start, but that dwindled with both his wounds and the speed of his pursuers.

Morgan turned back to review the situation.

Two men had reached the top of the mountain and were shouting, pointing at Morgan. Due to the steepness of the decent, he would soon be once again out of their direct line of sight, though he had no idea how close their friends at the camp might be. Whether they had radios or phones, or how those might work in this area, was all a mystery: one he hoped to never know the answer to.

With no other choice, he continued to work his way down the side of the mountain, hearing an occasional burst of gunfire and an echoed shout.

The descent along this section of the ravine was becoming more and more shallow as it approached the base of the mountains below. Just as he was finding himself able to pick up the pace due to the ever-easier descent, the sound of a nearby rifle ripped the air and a line of bullets cut the ground around him.

Morgan dove for cover, then looked back. Two men had gotten within fifty yards. How they had made up the ground, or if they were part of some patrol that had worked its way from the complex of caves, Morgan wasn't sure.

Morgan realized he had not reloaded since he had first fired at his pursuers from the top of the mountain. He grabbed a magazine from the satchel and worked it into the rifle as several bursts of fire crashed over his head.

With the weapon loaded, Morgan raised himself to take aim.

The men had split apart, coming at him from two angles. Morgan switched the rifle to single fire and cranked off several rounds towards the man on his left.

The shots were all misses, but both men dove for cover.

The man on Morgan's right reappeared first, possibly sensing that it was a good opening for him to return fire. As he took position, though, he made himself an exposed and stationary target. Morgan, despite being an average marksman, was able to lace two shots into the man's chest, sending him to the ground.

The man on Morgan's left returned fire from a prone position. Morgan had no way of getting a good angle on him. The only thing Morgan could do, he decided, was to backup from his line of sight, hoping to force the man from his cover.

As Morgan did so, the man fired again. Several bullets whizzed dangerously close, but Morgan continued to work his way out of the man's line of sight.

The man realized that he had a terrible angle on Morgan and stood. Instead of pursuing Morgan, however, he ran to his dying compatriot. Morgan understood the impulse to check on a friend, but the man had just given Morgan the only opening he needed.

Morgan stepped forward back into the line of sight and fired at the man on full automatic, knocking him down into a crumpled heap.

He didn't think he had killed the man, at least not instantly: he was certain, though, that he had incapacitated him, which was all Morgan needed.

Morgan turned and rushed down the hill, his whole being yearning to find a way to reach the road in the distance.

Chapter Sixty-Two

The steep descent of the ravine had been incredibly dangerous, requiring Morgan to scale down several sharp, vertical sections. Yet, it had also brought him to the bottom of the mountain range much sooner than he had expected. As a result, Morgan was now running across the more flat expanse that stretched away from the base of the mountains and towards the open terrain that lay ahead.

Looking back towards the mountain, Morgan could see several groups of men still scrambling down the ravine, closer than he would like. With the new perspective of how his pursuers were spread, Morgan also had the growing sensation of being herded towards something in front of him.

As Morgan had descended, he had looked ahead for approaching vehicles. This time, as he looked out into the desert, he could see a trail of automotive dust cutting towards him in the distance, the vehicle still out of sight.

Morgan pulled the remaining ammunition from the satchel and drank a large gulp of water. He then dropped the bag, leaving himself with nothing but the rifle and the spare clips, unencumbered. In the open as he was, his only choice would be to fight. There was no cover, other than the occasional change in gradient or boulder.

Morgan set off at a jog, trying to create as much distance between him and his pursuers as he could before he encountered the vehicle that was steadily approaching. With every step, the searing pain in his thigh shot through Morgan's mind. He could hear occasional attempts at gunfire behind him, though whoever was shooting was likely doing so to continue to drive him forward.

The SUV that had been barreling towards him materialized into reality on the horizon, approaching from his left, roaring and bumping across a dirt road. The driver instantly caught sight of Morgan and the vehicle made an adjustment, blazing across the terrain towards him.

Morgan slowed, then kneeled in a rut and pulled his rifle to a shooting position.

Just as the SUV entered Morgan's effective range, he began a series of controlled bursts, attempting to hit the occupants through the windshield. He managed to lay a few shots into the glass, which cracked in several places.

The shots had the desired effect and the SUV skidded to a halt as it crested a small rise forty yards from Morgan. Two Afghan men jumped out of the vehicle, moving faster than Morgan could track with his sustained fire.

One of the men fired a long burst from an American-made M16 automatic rifle at Morgan. As Morgan fired a long burst in return, the man who had been driving the SUV shouted at Morgan in broken English, "Drop the gun!"

Morgan fired another burst at the man in response. The man ducked behind the SUV.

As Morgan reloaded, the realization of the opportunity posed by the SUV struck him. Getting to it would mean crossing open ground under hostile fire. Yet, he doubted that he could win a race on foot to the road in the distance. He wasn't going to out-run the men behind him forever. What's more, his pursuers would surely find another car soon.

Getting to that SUV at all costs was his last, best remaining option.

The two men from the SUV continued firing on Morgan, a round ripping the air perilously close to his ear. Down to his last clip of ammunition, he fired back slowly, trying to make each shot count.

Another long burst erupted from the direction of the SUV. As it ended, Morgan raised back into a kneeling position and saw that the man on the passenger side of the SUV was attempting to reload his rifle.

Morgan fired several shots in quick succession and hit the man in the leg. The man clutched at his thigh, trying to simultaneously stem the bleeding with one hand and keep his rifle pointed in Morgan's general direction. Within moments, he was on the ground and attending to his wound.

The driver wheeled around the front door of the SUV and fired a burst towards Morgan. Then Morgan heard the telltale *click* that signaled a jammed rifle.

Morgan fired his clip empty to force both men to take cover, then rushed headlong towards the SUV.

As Morgan closed the distance, the man on the passenger side of the SUV, who was still clutching his leg with one hand, fired a long, untrained burst, which missed wildly.

Morgan reached the driver, who had not realized Morgan was charging him as he tried to unjam his rifle, and buried his shoulder into the driver's mid-section, sending both of them to the ground. Morgan brought the butt of his rifle down in a slashing motion into the man's face, knocking him unconscious.

Morgan heard the wounded man reloading and shouting towards the men in the distance, who were now reaching a range at which they might effectively take aim on Morgan.

Morgan looked at the SUV: it was still running.

Almost from instinct, Morgan lunged towards the interior of the vehicle. As he leapt towards the driver's seat, however, the wounded man on the other side of the car fired his rifle under the chassis.

In a blinding instant, a bullet sliced through Morgan's left calf. He fell backwards out of the SUV with a howl of pain.

Morgan brought his rifle around and fired at the wounded man, succeeding in hitting the man several times in the torso. The man dropped his rifle and doubled over.

Bullets were now slowly raining down from the mountain as the men in pursuit came closer. Morgan dragged himself into the driver's seat, his left leg all but useless. He slammed the door shut, then pressed his foot to the gas. The engine roared and Morgan realized the SUV was not in gear.

A moment later, he had the SUV spun around, reorienting towards the road in the distance. Several bullets pinged into the back of the vehicle, fracturing the rear glass.

Morgan stomped on the accelerator. The SUV bounced and shuddered as Morgan drove it hard across the rough desert.

Within seconds, the sound of bullets ricocheting stopped. Morgan scanned the terrain in all directions, but no other vehicles were in sight.

A few minutes later, Morgan saw the road approaching ahead and he checked the dash. He had just under a half tank of gas in the SUV, which he figured would give him at least another 100 or more miles.

His leg was bleeding from the wound to his calf, though, and bolts of pain shot through him as the adrenalin began to ebb. Morgan wasn't sure if he personally had enough in his own tank for 100 miles.

He entered the roadway and rolled to a stop. The road ran perpendicular to his last bearings on a major urban area, which was problematic. He had no way of knowing whether traveling north or south would be the fastest route to an intersecting road that would allow him to cross over towards the city he hoped lay in the near distance. Of course, that assumed that Morgan would find someone friendly within that city, but at this point, there was no better option than to rely on luck.

He spun the wheel north in the thought that it placed his back most squarely to the men he had just left behind and crossed his fingers on top of the wheel.

Chapter Sixty-Three

Over the last several days, Morgan had struggled with the disorienting effect of living without clocks or a watch. His hopes of getting a time-fix from the SUV were dashed, however, since, as with so many things in Afghanistan, the clock was broken. Judging by the sun, though, it was late afternoon.

The road that Morgan found himself on was deserted and since joining with it, he had kept the speed just over sixty miles an hour. Based on distance traveled, he at least knew now that he had been driving for about forty minutes.

Worse, Morgan was still losing blood. For the last fifty miles, he had been hoping to cross paths with a friendly-looking vehicle so he could beg for help. But to this point, he had crossed paths with no cars, no cities and no other maintained roads. Just endless expanses in all directions and a few villages in the distance that appeared deserted.

For the first time since stealing the SUV, Morgan saw an intersection ahead, with a roadway sign marking distances. As Morgan approached it, he slowed.

The sign was written in Pashto and had kilometers marking distances. He recognized the Pashto script for Kabul, which was denoted as being another 200 kilometers ahead. With an arrow marking left, just 30 kilometers away, was a city name written in Pashto that Morgan had never seen before.

Morgan looked at his leg. It looked as if it had been dipped in blood.

He felt faintness creeping in at the edges of his vision and his motions appeared to him as if he was moving through a dream. There was no way he was going to make it to Kabul.

He turned left towards the unknown destination that awaited him 30 kilometers further.

* * *

As the kilometers clicked down towards the small city ahead, Morgan tried to keep his drifting focus on the road. At times he saw double. Patches of darkness were blurring his sight.

He looked at his odometer and realized he had forgotten how far back the intersection had been. A wave of unbridled panic washed over him, which he stifled by retraining his eyes on the road.

In the distance, a roadblock appeared, stretching across all lanes. At first, Morgan thought the roadblock was a mirage. With each growing second, though, he became more certain that he was indeed looking at a barricade.

Frustration welled within his heart. Not only did he have no cash, he was incapable of explaining in the local tongue why he was dressed in tattered clothing, carrying an assault rifle, driving a damaged vehicle and covered in blood. Morgan also knew that to veer away now would incite suspicion he could ill afford.

His best option was to drive to the checkpoint and let the chips fall as they may.

Morgan slowed the vehicle as he approached and tried to make a casual stop for the checkpoint, but instead awkwardly parked the SUV ten feet short of the barriers.

The men operating the checkpoint all wore Afghan army uniforms. They glanced at each other in confusion before slowly approaching the vehicle. One man wearing an officer's cap walked to Morgan's door and indicated with his hand for Morgan to roll down the window. Morgan did so slowly.

The officer – whose nametag read 'Ormurzai' – asked something in Pashto. Morgan shook his head and mumbled, "English."

The officer grimaced. "Identification, please."

Morgan shook his head.

The officer looked at the bullet-riddled car, then stepped back and said, "Please step out."

Morgan shook his head again. "I need a doctor."

"Step out. Now."

The officer waved for the men to raise their weapons. They

did so.

Morgan looked at the men and shook his head.

"I need a doctor."

The officer said, "Sir, step out."

Morgan felt himself passing out. His foot was searching for the gas pedal, but it was like he was watching someone else go through this experience. Somewhere in the edges of his mind, he heard what sounded like an intercom system.

Then he heard car horns.

The Afghan troops looked edgy and confused. There was shouting.

Morgan tried to look in his rearview mirror, but couldn't focus on the reflection it provided. He could see two men in uniforms approaching his SUV, but the words coming out of their mouths were foreign to Morgan.

The men stood before Ormurzai, who pointed at Morgan's SUV. One of the men approached Morgan. His nametag read 'LeGrange'.

The man looked in the SUV, scowling as he scanned the carnage within. "American?" he asked.

Morgan nodded.

"Are you in trouble?"

Morgan nodded again. "Need a doctor."

Morgan saw the French flag on the man's sleeve as he turned to talk with the Afghan. There appeared to be an argument, then the French officer turned to Morgan.

"They need you to step out of the vehicle. I will help you."

Morgan slowly opened the door. The French officer helped Morgan to his feet. Morgan felt the world swirling around him and his knees buckled, causing him to fall to the ground.

In the distance, he heard a shout and the slam of a car door. Then a strangely familiar voice said to the French officer, "I know this man."

Morgan looked up and saw John Davis, the American

contractor he had met on the roof of the Intercontinental. John's face was one of astonishment as he pushed his way towards Morgan. He knelt beside him.

"Morgan, right?" said John. "What the hell happened?"

"Kidnapped. Need a doctor."

John's eyes went wide, then he said to the French officer, "This man is a U.S. citizen. We need get him to the U.S. Embassy."

The French officer looked at Morgan, then said something to the Afghan. The Afghan shook his head and raised his voice, waving his arms in the international symbol for 'no way'.

In a hurry, John reached down and tried to help Morgan to his feet. "We better leave while these guys are still impressed by the French."

"I can't stand."

John kneeled down and wrapped Morgan into a bear hug, then with tremendous strength, lifted him into a fireman's carry. "Jesus, Morgan, you're gonna' make me play hero, huh?"

The Afghans were shouting, but the French officer was standing between John and the Afghans, covering them as they moved towards a French armored vehicle.

Another French soldier opened the back door of the armored vehicle and John laid Morgan inside.

John and the French officer climbed into the vehicle. LeGrange then said something stern to the driver, who spun the vehicle around and raced the armored vehicle in the direction that Morgan had come.

John leaned over Morgan with a first-aid kit and said, "Tell me where you're hit."

Morgan felt himself slipping into unconsciousness. He looked at John and said, "Victoria Solano. U.S. State Department employee. Held hostage south of Jalalabad. Needs help."

John listened, then grabbed a pen. Morgan saw him scribbling the note on the back of a gauze packet.

Then darkness swooped in on Morgan.

IV

Chapter Sixty-Four

Darkness had descended on Vitters' village. Despite the late hour, Victoria was awake in the silence of her hut. Two older female villagers were snoring in the next room.

The immense weight of her new reality was sitting on her. Victoria had heard of how prisoners discussed the hopelessness, lack of control and desperation that can take hold during confinement. She felt all of those emotions as her mind drifted relentlessly to the pain of what would become of her life if she should ever make it back to the real world. She lamented how she should be counting down the days and minutes to her next assignment in the State Department or getting ready for a date: not wondering if she would live to see tomorrow in a hut in the middle of the Afghan desert.

With no other choice, she had continued to help with the medical requests of her captors. On a daily basis, she had traveled by car with one or more of Vitters' men to separate villages, where she had provided care and attention to people associated with Vitters' network.

While on the second of these visits, she had found a large splinter of wood that ended with a long, sharp end in an outhouse. She had hidden it in her clothes and then, upon returning to the village, placed it under her bed of straw, thinking it might provide a useful tool in her next escape attempt.

As the day had worn on, though, the thought of how easily she had been recaptured entered her mind. Worse, she knew she had gotten off easy. She realized with pain that the idea of using a sharp stick to stab her way out of the clutches of a group of well-trained Green Berets and their paid guards was as foolish an exercise in human hope as she could participate in.

She pulled the sharpened shard of wood from the straw below her. She gripped it with both hands and snapped it in half. The pieces made a slight clunking sound as they scattered to the side of the room where she threw them.

Somewhere in the distance, she heard a dog bark. It was a strange, angry series of barks that she had not heard before from outside the village. Within moments, added to the sound of the dog was the distinct sound of boots on the gravel outside. People were moving.

Then she heard a sound that lightened her heart in a way she had not experienced in nearly a week. The sound of a helicopter's blades beating the night air. It was distant, but distinct. She knew from experience that only Western forces within Afghanistan would be flying in the darkness, a skill that required the latest in technology and experience.

She sat up, feeling a rush of hope. Maybe Morgan had escaped. Maybe it was a rescue crew come to find her.

For a moment, the beat of the rotors in the night air continued. Then, with deflating predictability, the sound began to fade into the night.

Victoria lay awake for a long time, hoping for the sounds of a conflict that would signal a rescue attempt. Nothing came, though. Only the endless silence that accompanied the pure night that so many Americans who rotated through the country called 'Boogey Dark'.

For some reason she could not explain, hope did not fade from her this time.

Chapter Sixty-Five

Ramstein Airbase, Germany

Morgan knew he was in a dream.

He was watching something die. For a moment, he thought it was an animal. Then he thought it was a person. Then he wasn't even sure that anything was dead. He tried to walk away, but every direction he turned, he saw only endless trails. Something told him they all led to danger. He had to leave.

A part of Morgan's brain was waking and the dream began to end with that same premonition with which all dreams conclude. He felt the strange panic and the growing wave of consciousness. His eyes fluttered open. A soft moan came through dry lips.

The room was bright. He felt stiffness throughout his body.

He tried to move his extremities and felt a dull throb in his left leg, as well as tightness in his shoulder and right thigh.

He fixed his gaze on the room again and saw that he was in a hospital. His was the only bed in the room. He sensed that it was an American military hospital, because in the distance he could smell bacon: an odor unique to what most Americans would call the civilized world.

Morgan inched his way into a sitting position and looked at the side table. On it was a pitcher of water and nothing else.

Morgan reached out and slowly poured a glass of water. The motion felt surreal, as if his hands belonged to another person. He tried to let his brain piece together what was happening.

He could remember his escape from the Taliban. He could remember driving himself in the SUV. He remembered being at a checkpoint. That someone familiar had come to his aid: but, nothing more.

He finished the water, then found the call button, which was mounted to a thick wire and hanging on the edge of his hospital bed.

A few seconds later, the door opened and a short woman with light-brown hair entered, wearing U.S. Air Force insignia. A warm sensation of safety washed over Morgan.

"Good Morning, Sergeant Huntley," said the nurse. "I'm Sergeant Andrews."

"You have no idea how happy I am to see you."

"How are you feeling?"

"I don't know. How long have I been here?"

"Two days. You were flown in from Afghanistan with severe blood loss. Total time from your injuries, according to your chart, has been about 72 hours, give or take a few."

Morgan nodded. "Was I the only one brought in?"

"You were brought here with several other soldiers requiring medical attention, but I can't disclose that information to you."

Sgt. Andrews felt Morgan's pulse and took some notes.

"How bad was I?" asked Morgan.

"I've seen worse. We calculated that you lost almost half of your normal blood volume by the time you arrived at the first medical unit."

"Where was that?"

The woman looked at the chart, then said, "Looks like you were brought to a Forward Base south of Kabul and then you were transported via helicopter from there to Bagram."

Morgan nodded, then said, "Wait. How did you know my name and rank? I was carrying no ID."

The nurse smiled and was about to say something when a voice came from the doorway, "That's because I was looking for you, too."

Through the door came a woman who Morgan vaguely recognized. She was African-American, in good physical shape and was wearing the unit badge for Army CID.

"Mind if I have a word with him alone?" asked Special Agent LeShaunda Collins.

Sgt. Andrews walked from the room. LeShaunda closed the

door. She then extended her hand in greeting.

"Special Agent Huntley, I'm damn glad to see you alive. I am Special Agent ..."

"LeShaunda Collins," Morgan said. "What the hell are you doing here?"

"Colonel Kzaltry."

"What about him?"

"Just about the time you went missing, someone tried to kill him."

"Shit. Did he survive?"

"Yes, and I was assigned to his case. Turned out he had a hell of a story to tell. About you being caught up in a shitstorm out there in Kabul. By the time I started trying to hunt you down, GenetiGreen had reported you as missing."

"Glad someone did."

"Kzaltry and I were able to convince the Pentagon that too many people knew about your disappearance to leave you out to dry."

"How did that go over?"

"Not well, but we'll get to that in a moment. I put word out across all the services in Afghanistan that you might be in trouble and to provide aid if you turned up. Once you arrived at that Forward Base, a chain of events was set in motion that allowed me to have you secured here at Ramstein. And for me to get a free flight to Germany."

Morgan looked at LeShaunda Collins for a long while, trying to decide if she was being straight with him. Finally, he asked, "Where is Kzaltry?"

"He's safe. Still in the hospital, actually. We can cover his story later. I want to debrief you first."

"No. There is a State Department employee abducted at the same time as me. We were separated before I could escape. We need to get assistance to her immediately."

LeShaunda looked at Morgan with raised eyebrows. "It

sounds like we do. In order to do that, though, I'm going to need you to bring me up to speed. I need to know what I'm dealing with. I promise I won't waste your time. Give me an hour: then we'll get moving on outstanding issues."

"How do I know you're not working with or for Thompson and the other bastards at CID?"

LeShaunda smiled. "Because," she said, "I've had Franklin arrested. He hired two former MPs to put that hit on Kzaltry."

"How did you piece that together?"

"Thompson. I think he was feeling real bad when he realized how this was shaping up. Really, I think he wanted to make sure his own ass was covered when he started thinking that he might get charged with being an accessory to the attempt on Kzaltry's life. He knew Franklin was still close with a couple MPs who had been doing Franklin's dirty work. Turned out Franklin paid these two morons to target Kzaltry. They were more than willing to roll Franklin to save themselves. From there, to make a long story short, it all fell into place."

Morgan sat up in the hospital bed and stared at Collins for a long moment to ascertain whether she was joking. Finally, he said, "Look, I want to trust you and give you everything I know. But, the last time I did that, I ended up sold-off to the Taliban. You're going to have to give me something legit."

Special Agent Collins gave Morgan a disgruntled look, then pulled a smartphone from her pocket. She scrolled through the phone's functions, then held it up for Morgan to see.

On the phone was a copy of Franklin's arrest photo.

Morgan's face broke into a smile. "I always wondered if he would smile or not for a mug shot."

Chapter Sixty-Six

Morgan gave a full account of events to LeShaunda Collins, starting with the assignment of the case by Franklin through his escape from the Taliban. Collins took copious notes. They did not finish in an hour, but Morgan knew this debriefing was possibly the most important of his life.

When Morgan was done, LeShaunda reviewed her notes in silence. Finally, she said, "That fits with the background I've accumulated on this case."

"Good. Now tell me about Franklin's arrest."

"Once Kzaltry brought me up to speed on his side of things, I leaned on Thompson. When I told him about Kzaltry's story, he got nervous. He told me about Franklin's MP friends. In fact, he told me that Franklin had used them before Kzaltry."

"Did Franklin have them do the break-in at CID Forensics in the Wooster case?"

"Thompson hinted at that. The two men confirmed it. We arrested Franklin on that, Kzaltry AND accessory to murder for Jason Milner."

"Did you have a smoking gun on the accessory charges against Franklin?"

"Remember Kzaltry mentioning something about the German government notifying Franklin's office of their suspicions of a drug cartel in Afghanistan? Franklin tried to deny ever receiving it, but we found a copy on his hard drive in an encrypted file. The picture that entire story paints and what's happened to Kzaltry are all pretty bad for Franklin."

"Sure. And you've got motive on Kzaltry and the CID break-in. But what about Jason's death and the rest of this? Surely Franklin didn't want me dead so bad that he needed the CIA to get involved or to kill my friend."

"You learn funny things talking to wives and lovers," said Collins, a smile crossing her face. "Franklin had a little piece of action on the side. She defended him when I put her under questioning. His wife, though? When she found out that Franklin was having an affair, she turned on him."

"You sure play mean, Agent Collins."

"It's the only way to play. According to his wife, Franklin wanted to embarrass the Provost Marshal of the Army with this whole thing. Make it look like the Provost Marshal's lack of oversight allowed this mess to escalate in the deaths of two soldiers and two CID agents. That would have opened the door for Franklin to get a big promotion to Provost Marshal."

Morgan thought it all over for a moment in silence, then fixed LeShaunda with a hard stare. "You going to see it through to a Court-Martial?"

"And go down in flames like you? I've got more sense than that. I've agreed to play dealer-broker."

"I'm not sure I like the sound of that."

"The Army's position is that they want to sweep this all under the rug. I don't know if you've heard, but McChrystal resigned after getting caught by *Rolling Stone* criticizing the President."

"Holy shit. Are you kidding?"

"I wish I was. The Army is up to its elbows in embarrassment right now. They need this thing to go away quickly and quietly. They're going to give Franklin an Honorable Discharge in exchange for his silence. Thompson will be gently eased out to pasture. Kzaltry has agreed to keep his mouth shut in exchange for a command post in DIA. And your safe passage back, of course."

Morgan shook his head and smiled. "Great. Now I owe Kzaltry." He then looked back at Collins. "What's being offered to keep me quiet, though?"

"Well, the Army is willing to see that you go straight to Warrant Officer School and get a billet anywhere you pick, just so long as you sign an NDA. Or you can have an Honorable, if that's what you want instead. There's one more thing, though."

"What's that?"

"They want to flatten Vitters' camp. Him and his men. For that, they need you to provide the location."

Morgan shook his head. "My friend, the State Department employee, she's a captive there."

"We were afraid of that. Word came out from State around the time of your disappearance that a Victoria Solano had gone missing. Is that who we're talking about?"

"That's right. She was abducted and taken to the camp."

"The Army might just consider her collateral damage, Morgan."

"Then I don't talk."

"Don't be a fool, Morgan. Given enough time, the Army can figure out Vitters' location on their own. Don't pass up a deal when you can get it."

Morgan laughed and reached for his glass of water. "I'm going to guess that the Army told you that time is short and that getting me to talk is critical. Word will reach Vitters eventually that I escaped. He'll assume that the Army will lean on me for information. Based on that, he'll shift locations as soon as he learns of my escape. If the Army has any chance of actually getting him before he moves, it's if I tell them where to look. Right now."

Collins smiled and bowed her head, then looked back up at Morgan. "Okay. You're right. Will you talk or not?"

"I'm not helping unless there's a plan to get Victoria Solano out of there."

"I understand what you're saying, but the Army doesn't want more people with knowledge of the situation. A rescue raid would mean bringing our Special Forces and their commanders into the loop to make plans to kill their own brothers in arms, retired or otherwise. That ain't going to fly with anybody up or down the line. Or worse, to go beg the Navy for help, which isn't going to happen. There would be bodies, questions, briefings, press, families ..."

Morgan held up his hand. "Whose side are you on here?"

"I'm just saying, Morgan, the Army doesn't have an option to get Victoria Solano out of there that they're willing to take. They're going to level that village, with or without your help."

Morgan laid in bed, silent.

Collins stood to leave. She grabbed her notebook and said, "Thanks for the debriefing."

As Collins reached for the door, Morgan said, "You still playing deal-broker?"

Collins waited in the doorway and gave a slight nod.

Morgan pushed himself up and said, "Will you take an offer back to the Army for me?"

"Sure. What is it?"

Chapter Sixty-Seven

Somewhere south of Jalalabad, Afghanistan

Morgan held the wheel of an up-armored Chevy Suburban as he traversed a well-worn dirt track southward. A GPS system on the dash flashed a steady, red arrow towards the geo-coordinates he had entered before exiting the main highway from Jalalabad.

He was, according to the GPS, about fifteen minutes from reaching Vitters' village. Waiting on the highway behind Morgan was a convoy of American HUMVEEs. These were under the command of a team of Green Berets from the Army's 1st Special Forces Division, who had been assigned by the Army as Morgan's escort.

Their orders, however, were only to bring Morgan as far as this dirt track and then to give Morgan one hour to himself. Beyond this information, the Green Beret's briefing had covered nothing more. If Morgan returned with an American identified as Victoria Solano, the Green Berets were to provide escort for both of them directly to Bagram Air Base. From there, Morgan and Victoria would be immediately flown back to the U.S. for debriefing.

If Morgan returned with anyone else, though, that person would be considered a hostile and treated accordingly.

Ahead in the distance, Morgan could see Vitters' *Arbakai* manning the first checkpoint, still far outside of the village. As he approached, he could see one of the *Arbakai* speaking into a small handset radio. Morgan slowed and then stopped for the men. With their rifles raised, the guards approached the vehicle cautiously.

"What do you want?" the man at the driver's side window asked with surprisingly good English.

"I am here to see Vitters."

"I do not know who you are talking about. Turn around."

"I'm not turning around. Tell Vitters that Morgan Huntley is here to see him."

"I told you to turn around."

"You'll have to shoot me before I turn around."

The *Arbakai* considered Morgan with a mix of confusion and amusement. He stepped back and spoke into the radio just out of Morgan's earshot.

Morgan did his best to look calm as the other *Arbakai* kept his eyes locked on him, despite the fact that his heart was racing.

"Drive to the next checkpoint."

Morgan nodded, half-saluted the men and drove forward slowly.

As he passed over a crest, Morgan could see the huts and poppy fields were just another minute ahead. The checkpoint that the guard had referred to was at the edge of the village. Already, he could see Vitters walking to the checkpoint at a brisk pace, a U.S. M4 carbine in his hands.

As Morgan pulled to a stop at the checkpoint, he noticed that Griggs was twenty yards to the left, kneeling behind a wall. He had a man-portable anti-vehicle rocket known as a M47 'Dragon' pointed at Morgan's SUV. They made eye-contact, so Morgan nodded at Griggs and gave him a grin.

Vitters had his carbine aimed at Morgan's windshield. "Turn off the car and step out."

Morgan followed the instructions and stepped out of the Suburban. He then turned around with his hands in the air in an attempt to show that he was unarmed and unwired.

Vitters took several steps towards Morgan, his rifle still trained on him.

"I see Griggs has got a nice little toy," said Morgan. "Can I assume that Freer or Farrat has also got a sniper rifle trained on me?"

"Are you alone?"

Morgan said, "I asked first."

Vitters looked like he could spit blood, his face slowly growing red with fury.

"Freer has got a direct line of fire on you, yes, so don't try any shit, Huntley. Now, tell me: are you alone?"

"I think you know the answer to that. How would I have gotten my hands on such a nice, American vehicle if I didn't have a little help?"

"Ground troops? Air support?"

"Air support only. The Army wants to keep its hands clean."

For a moment, it looked as if Vitters didn't believe Morgan. Then Vitters biceps bulged in anger. "Fucking hell, Morgan."

Vitters looked towards Griggs to see if he could hear their conversation. Then he said to Morgan in a more quiet voice, "You somehow escape from the Taliban and you go rushing back to the Army? After everyone in the whole chain of command above you tried to screw you over or worse? Morgan, they're not going to let you out of here alive. Please don't tell me you came for the girl."

"Yes, for the girl."

Vitters laughed and shook his head. "No way, man. If it's going down like this, she is going to hell with me."

"I've got a deal, Captain. You could, too, if you're smart."

"Oh, please, tell me about this deal."

"In exchange for helping the Army figure out where to place a few missiles, I got one chance to come ask you to hand over Victoria. If I'm not back with her shortly, I'm getting blasted along with you and everyone in the camp. I'm either dead or walking out of here with Victoria."

"I don't care about that deal, Morgan. You got a deal for me? I'm not handing over a sweet bargaining chip like your girlfriend for nothing."

"Your deal is less optimistic, though it is fair. I convinced the Army that you wouldn't want your villagers going up in a cloud of dust. I sold them on the idea that you would be willing to give them a mobile target outside of the village to hit. In exchange for that, the Army is willing to tell your family that you re-enlisted and were killed in action. Same for everyone on your team. Otherwise, they're just going to vaporize you and be done with the whole thing."

Vitters body was shaking with anger. He raised the carbine to the level of his eye and took aim at Morgan's face. "I think I'll feel better about the whole thing if I just pop you now."

Morgan didn't move, instead keeping his gaze fixed on Vitters.

Vitters, still aiming, said, "These are the people that we were supposed to be saving when they sent us here, Morgan. If you do this, you'll be sending them back to the Stone Age."

"Your villagers will also get a payoff. They'll get a huge contract from the DEA to sell opium to Europe for five years, automatically renewable if certain output goals are met. I've seen the paperwork. It's a great deal."

Vitters grew visibly angry. "We came here for a purpose. Me and my men have fulfilled that mission," he spat.

"Why any of us came here is for the historians. Good intentions or not, you crossed a line you never should have crossed. You knew this day could come. It's here. Don't take everyone with you."

Vitters snapped the rifle down, away from Morgan and clenched it in a death grip. "I gave the Army everything they asked and then some. This is my time."

"We volunteered for it. Like it or not, we made a choice."

Vitters shook his head. "We made a choice without being shown the fine print. We fight for a country that doesn't give a shit who we kill or where, so long as they don't have to do it. If we are lucky enough to make it back, we're handed a register at McDonald's. No, Morgan. We didn't make a choice. We were sold a load of shit."

"It doesn't change this situation."

Vitters held a hand to his temple, then smiled. "I see. You're pissed about being sold off to the Taliban."

"Among other things."

"If I tell you that I'm sorry, can you get me out of this? One soldier to another?"

"I'm done making deals. What's on the table is all you get."

Vitters looked back at Griggs, then back at Morgan.

Morgan said, "Time's running out on all of us. Don't let your villagers die like this. They don't deserve it."

"I don't deserve it."

"Maybe, but you know your villagers don't deserve it. Especially if you believe that your mission was to help them. Neither does Victoria. What good does letting everyone die achieve? Come on, Vitters. You're not that guy."

"Don't try to play psychologist, Huntley. It doesn't suit you."

Morgan stood there, waiting.

Vitters said, "How about I kill you and let her go in return?"

"If they see me go down, they'll assume the deal is off and blow the whole place."

"I'll put her in the SUV and send her away first."

"She won't know where to go."

"Written directions are quite effective."

Morgan shrugged and said, "Fine. You've got me there."

Vitters nodded. He pressed on an earpiece and said, "Farrat. Bring the girl to Checkpoint Echo."

Morgan leaned on the SUV and waited.

Vitters glared at Morgan, his face contorted in thought. "How did you get away from the Taliban?"

"Beat one of them with a rock as he took a dump. Shot the others. Ran like hell."

Vitters laughed a big, whooping laugh. "You shitting me?"

Morgan shook his head.

"Ain't that something?" Vitters looked on at Morgan with what appeared to be pride.

The two men stood there, staring at each other, waiting for

Victoria. Morgan thought he saw Vitters' eyes drifting off into thought, like he had seen so many times before in their conversations in Kabul.

Farrat appeared from around the corner of the outer wall of the village with Victoria in his grasp. She was wearing the clothing of an Afghan village woman. Her hands were tied in front of her.

As she took in the scene before her, her mouth fell open when she saw Morgan.

"Morgan!"

Morgan nodded at her. Vitters held up his hand for Farrat to stop out of earshot. He stared at Morgan. "Your plan. How was it supposed to go down?"

Morgan glanced up and then said, "Well, I'm sure by now the air surveillance has identified you and your men. They want all four of you in one, maybe two cars. Otherwise, they'll flatten the whole place to be sure they got everyone."

Vitters nodded.

"Would my men know what's coming?"

"Up to you."

"This isn't fair to them."

"About as a fair deal as they'll get. Plus, it's fair to the villagers. Fair to your families."

"How do I know the Army will tell their families such a nice story?"

"You don't. Just have to take it on institutional faith. Then again, the Army doesn't like dealing with families who want answers. I would wager on them telling a lie long before I would bet on the truth."

Vitters shook his head. He stood there for a long time, his eyes locked on Morgan. Then he then waved for Farrat to bring Victoria forward.

As Farrat came near, Vitters said, "Put Sergeant Solano in the vehicle."

"What the hell is this, John?"

"Put her in the car," ordered Vitters.

Vitters and Farrat stared at each other, then Farrat shoved Victoria towards the driver-side door.

"No," said Vitters. "Passenger side."

Farrat brought her around the front hood and then opened the passenger door for her. She climbed in and Farrat slammed it shut. He then walked back towards Vitters' side.

"What are you waiting for?" asked Vitters, looking at Morgan.

Morgan gave Vitters a subtle nod. He then walked back towards the SUV and opened the driver door.

As he started the engine and pulled away, Vitters said into his earpiece, "Meet me at the car in two minutes."

Farrat followed slowly after Vitters, looking back towards Morgan's departing SUV.

* * *

Victoria knew she was staring, but couldn't help herself. She felt as if she was having a very surreal dream from which she would wake at any moment.

Her hand reached into her tunic and felt the sharp splinter of wood, which she had carried with her all day. She pricked her finger on it and felt the sharp pain shoot through her brain. Apparently, this was not a dream.

Morgan was driving the SUV at breakneck speed down a dirt trail away from the camp. Victoria wanted to urge him to go even faster, but was afraid to speak, lest it destroy some spell that was allowing this to occur. Questions were flooding through her brain.

Finally, Morgan looked at her and their eyes met for a brief second, then he looked back at the trail ahead as they raced past the last checkpoint outside of Vitters' village.

"How?" was all she could get her lips to ask.

"I'll explain once we're safe."

"Are we not?"

"I don't know. There's a pair of Predator drones overhead. The Army is supposed to smoke Vitters and his men. You never quite know what the Army plans to do, though."

Victoria nodded and looked ahead.

Chapter Sixty-Eight

Las Vegas, NV

In a secure, heavily air conditioned room just outside of Las Vegas, Nevada, a row of Air Force officers wearing flight suits sat before a bank of computers. On the monitors were images of black-and-white landscapes: the video feeds from drone aircraft positioned throughout the world.

Captain Victor Bellasario had manned his station for four hours, watching a black-and-white thermal image of Eastern Afghanistan. Behind him, hooked to the audio feed were his commander, Lt. Col. Sam Jarett, and a brigadier general from the Army named Loden. While it wasn't unusual for top Air Force brass to coordinate a mission directly from the operations room, it was odd for an Army general to be this close to the action.

Bellasario's thoughts, though, had drifted from the oddities of his guests to the images on his screen about thirty minutes prior, when an armored Suburban had entered his Area of Operations over a village suspected of harboring terrorists. According to Bellasario's briefing from Loden and Jarett, the man in the SUV was to meet with four men, who would then presumably enter their vehicle and depart: at which time, the four men were to be eliminated in a surgical strike.

If, however, the targets did not enter a vehicle as expected, Bellasario had already been approved to open fire on any huts or other structures that the men took refuge within: collateral damage or not.

To this point, the situation had progressed slowly. The man who had arrived to the village in an SUV had spoken with one of the terrorists far longer than anyone had expected. During that time, Loden had positively identified three of the men as confirmed targets of the strike. They had watched as a woman was brought from the village and shoved into the SUV. The driver of the SUV had driven off quickly, presumably aware that something was about to happen.

Bellasario had thought all of this was a bit odd, but as the three men had departed towards the center of the village, a fourth man had appeared from a nearby field, carrying a large sniper rifle, on a course to rendezvous with the other men. Using the advanced optics on the Predator drone that Bellasario was piloting, they had zoomed-in on the man's face, which General Loden was now carefully inspecting.

"That's our fourth," said General Loden. He looked at Lt. Col. Jarett with a smile and said, "Wherever those four men go in the next five minutes, do not lose track of them."

Lt. Col. Jarett nodded and said through the headset to Bellasario, "Captain, prepare for 'go-no-go' code."

"Roger."

They watched as the four men got into an SUV parked at the back of the village. The SUV's engine started. The vehicle then rolled out of the village, heading south, further into the mountains.

General Loden said, "Don't lose them."

"Yes, sir." Bellasario tried to swallow his annoyance with the comment, since it would be nearly impossible to lose the SUV in broad daylight as it roared through the Afghan desert.

Three minutes later, the SUV was well outside the village and in open terrain.

Lt. Col. Jarett said, "Clear for weapons hot. Engage targets."

"Roger. Weapons hot, clear to engage."

The Predator drone that Lt. Bellasario piloted carried a pair of Hellfire Anti-Tank Guided Missiles. Designed originally during the Cold War to destroy Soviet tanks, they packed enough wallop to punch through several inches of high-grade steel. The missile's reputation for high reliability had made them useful in targeted strikes during the War on Terror, even if they were utterly overpowered against the thinly skinned pick-up trucks and SUVs that they encountered these days.

Chapter Sixty-Nine

South of Jalalabad, Afghanistan

Vitters drove the SUV hard, heading down a lone track into the mountain range south of the village.

Griggs was riding shotgun, his Dragon Anti-Vehicle launcher between his legs. Farrat and Freer were in the back seat, their own weapons with them.

"Captain? I think we deserve a SITREP," said Griggs.

Vitters looked at Griggs. "Our base of operations has been compromised."

"By Morgan Huntley? How did the Army find him?"

"He escaped."

The blood was draining from Griggs' face as he contemplated the situation. "We should have given the girl to the Taliban instead."

"What does the Army know?" snapped Freer.

"I told you, we're compromised. We're evacuating to our defensive position in the mountains. From there, we'll regroup."

Farrat leaned forward. "How much time do we have, Vitters?"

Vitters said nothing.

"John?"

Vitters still said nothing. The tension in the SUV grew as the men realized just what Vitters' silence meant.

Griggs slammed his fist on the side of the door. "Damnit, I told you we should have killed that fucking CID agent."

"It's going to be okay, Griggs. We're going to make it."

* * *

Morgan pushed the accelerator hard, watching the clock and hoping to make it back to the convoy in time.

Just then, in his rearview mirror, he saw a ball of flame in the distance. Morgan slammed on the brakes.

Victoria looked at him and asked, "What is it?"

"Get out."

Morgan stepped out of the SUV. Victoria did the same and they met at the rear.

In the distance, they could see a cloud of smoke rising into the air.

"What's happening?" asked Victoria.

Before Morgan could explain, a streak of fire raced straight across the blue sky at high altitude. A moment later, it took a sharp angle downward and plunged towards the earth, seemingly a fiery lance from Zeus himself.

It exploded just beyond the horizon in a brief plume of flame, which then disappeared almost as quickly. Moments later, a muffled *crump* resonated across the landscape.

Victoria looked at Morgan and asked, "Was that what I think it was?"

Morgan nodded. "The Army's idea of a clean resolution."

Victoria looked back at the smoke in the distance and said, "Get me out of here."

She headed back towards the SUV.

Morgan watched a moment longer, then followed after her.

As he got into the driver's seat, Morgan looked at Victoria. She was staring at him.

He reached over to hug her and, to his surprise, she met him halfway. They held each other tight and Morgan could feel Victoria's tears on his shoulder.

"I'm sorry," Morgan said. "I'm …"

"It's okay," she said. "Just get me home."

Chapter Seventy

Maryland

A steady, autumn wind was swirling and leaves were falling in rapid succession outside of Morgan's parents' kitchen window. In the background, Morgan could hear the last quarter of the late-afternoon NFL game coming to an end on the television in the living room. He sat on a stool at the kitchen island his parents had installed two years ago, watching as his mother frosted a batch of Halloween-themed cookies.

They had sat in silence for a long time as Morgan slowly drank a beer. He sensed there was something she wanted to talk about. Finally she said, "Morgan. I've been thinking a lot about something."

"What's that, Mom?"

"I saw you in the hallway this morning as you were crossing back from the bathroom to your room. I saw something on your shoulder that made me very upset."

Morgan took a drink from his beer. "No work questions, please."

Shelly put down the frosting knife and looked at Morgan with the eyes of punitive grip that only a mother could summon. "You disappeared for two months. Do you know how worried we were? How many voice messages did I leave you?"

"I've apologized. It was work related."

"That's not the point. For the last nine years, I've been worried sick about you. Day in and day out, there's a small part of me that can't sleep at night. I went along with the Army thing, because it made your dad proud. I thought when you joined this CID unit, the worst of my fears were over. Then I see a nasty scar on your back …"

"I have a tough job."

"I want to know how long you're going to keep this job."

Morgan took a swig of his beer. "I don't know right now."

Shelly took Morgan's hands. "You know your career choice takes something out of me. I know that's why Laura left. I don't know if any woman can handle this kind of stress. Think about that, will you?"

Morgan nodded. "Thanks, Mom. I'll keep it in mind."

Shelly returned to frosting the cookies. "Speaking of women, are you seeing anyone special these days?"

Morgan grabbed a freshly frosted cookie and shrugged. "I've been talking with Victoria Solano."

Morgan's mother dropped the frosting knife and looked at him. "Laura's friend?" Then she smiled conspiratorially. "Well, I guess that's alright. Does Laura know?"

"Yeah, she does."

"Is she okay with it?"

"I don't really care."

"Is Victoria worried about what Laura thinks?"

"Neither of us is worried about it."

"Well, you might want to bring it up. These things are important. You don't want to offend someone."

"We don't care what she thinks."

Shelly grimaced with displeasure. "Where does Victoria live these days? I thought she was working with the State Department."

"She does. She's been reassigned to D.C."

In the background, Morgan could hear the game ending and his dad called out, "*60 Minutes* is starting."

Morgan looked at his mother questioningly.

"It's his favorite show of the week now. Why don't you bring him a beer and watch it with him. He won't say it, but he was worried about you."

"Sure."

Morgan grabbed two beers and walked into the living room. He handed one to Daniel Huntley and they toasted each other.

Daniel took a long drink and then sighed. He said, "Good to have you around."

"Thanks, Dad."

The familiar intro to *60 Minutes* started and they watched the feature stories get introduced by Scott Pelly. One of them was on joblessness among Americans under 30.

"Everybody wants a handout," said Daniel Huntley.

"Who doesn't?" asked Morgan.

Morgan's dad turned and said, "If you ask me, your generation has it too easy. The generation, what do they call them? Millennials?"

"How is that?"

"Your generation has been given everything. You've been asked to sacrifice very little for what you have."

Morgan looked at the television screen. A segment on joblessness among young Americans was beginning with an interview of a seemingly befuddled college graduate who couldn't find work.

Morgan looked back to his dad, who was patiently awaiting a response.

"Sure, Dad. I guess we do have it pretty easy."

From the Author

Thank you for purchasing *Invisible Wounds*. My sincere hope is that you derived as much entertainment from reading this book as I enjoyed in creating it.

If you have a few moments, please feel free to add your review of the book at your favorite online site for feedback (Amazon, Apple iTunes Store, GoodReads, etc.).

Also, if you would like to connect with other books that I have coming in the near future, please visit my website for news on upcoming works, recent blog posts and to sign up for my newsletter: http://www.dustinbeutin.com

Sincerely,

Dustin Beutin

About the Author

Dustin Beutin is a native of Chicago and a fan of murky conspiracy theories. It was during his undergraduate work at Purdue University that his love of the written word took root in the fertile ground of studies in global politics and world history. Following service with Teach for America as an elementary-school teacher in Chicago, Dustin chased his creative dreams to the MFA program in Screenwriting at USC's acclaimed School of Cinematic Arts.

Lured into remaining in Southern California by his lovely wife, he now lives at the beach, far from the snow shovels of the Windy City. Among a series of critical and scholarly recognitions for his portfolio of full-length screenplays, Dustin has been recognized by the Academy of Motion Pictures' Nicholl Fellowships in Screenwriting for his works *Bataan* and *Washington Fog*. Intrigued by the freedom of the fiction novel format, *Invisible Wounds* is Dustin's first novel.

Glossary of Terms

Bagram Air Base: U.S. Air Force base located North East of Kabul, Afghanistan.

Camp Eggerts: U.S. Army base attached to the U.S. Embassy in Kabul, Afghanistan.

Capt.: Abbreviation for U.S. Army rank of Captain.

Chief: Abbreviation for U.S. Army rank of Chief Warrant Officer.

CIA: Central Intelligence Agency, a bureau of the U.S. Federal Government responsible for intelligence on matters outside the United States.

CID: Acronym for the U.S. Army's Criminal Investigation Command, responsible for investigating major crimes that occur within the Army, involving Army personnel, or Army interests.

Col.: Abbreviation for U.S. Army rank of Colonel.

Darweh: Village in central-east Afghanistan

DEA: Acronym for the U.S. Drug Enforcement Agency, responsible for investigation and control of drugs deemed to be illegal for sale in the United States.

DIA: Acronym for Defense Intelligence Agency, a bureau of the Federal Government that reports to all major branches of the U.S. military and provides intelligence specifically to the services.

DOD: Acronym for the Department of Defense, a civilian agency of the U.S. federal government that is led by the Secretary of Defense.

FBI: Acronym for the Federal Bureau of Investigation, a U.S. agency reporting to the Federal Government that investigates major crimes.

GECO: Acronym for Gustav Genschow, & Company, an ammunition manufacturer based in Germany.

Gen.: Abbreviation for the U.S. Army rank of General.

Herat: City in Afghanistan.

Intel: Short for Intelligence, usually in reference to military intelligence.

ISAF: Acronym for the International Security Assistance Force, a joint mission of NATO in Afghanistan.

Jalalabad: City in eastern Afghanistan.

Kabul: Capital of Afghanistan.

KAIA: Kabul International Airport. Also used to refer to the military base at Kabul International.

Lt.: Abbreviation for the U.S. Army rank of Lieutenant.

Lt. Col.: Abbreviation for the U.S. Army rank of Lieutenant Colonel.

Maj.: Abbreviation for the U.S. Army rank of Major.

Massoud Square: Location in downtown Kabul, Afghanistan.

Mazar-E Sharif: City in Afghanistan, location of a U.S. Consulate.

MP: Acronym for Military Police, operating similar in scope to local police officers.

NATO: Acronym for North Atlantic Treaty Organization, a defense alliance formed by numerous countries in Europe, plus Canada and the United States.

Ramstein: Location of a U.S. airbase in Germany.

Sgt.: Abbreviation for Non-Commissioned ranks of Sergeant within the U.S. Army.

State: Short for the U.S. State Department, the bureau responsible for embassies and diplomacy on behalf of the United States.

At Roundfire we publish great stories. We lean towards the spiritual and thought-provoking. But whether it's literary or popular, a gentle tale or a pulsating thriller, the connecting theme in all Roundfire fiction titles is that once you pick them up you won't want to put them down.